BEND THE PUCKING RULES

USA TODAY BESTSELLING AUTHOR
RACHEL LEIGH

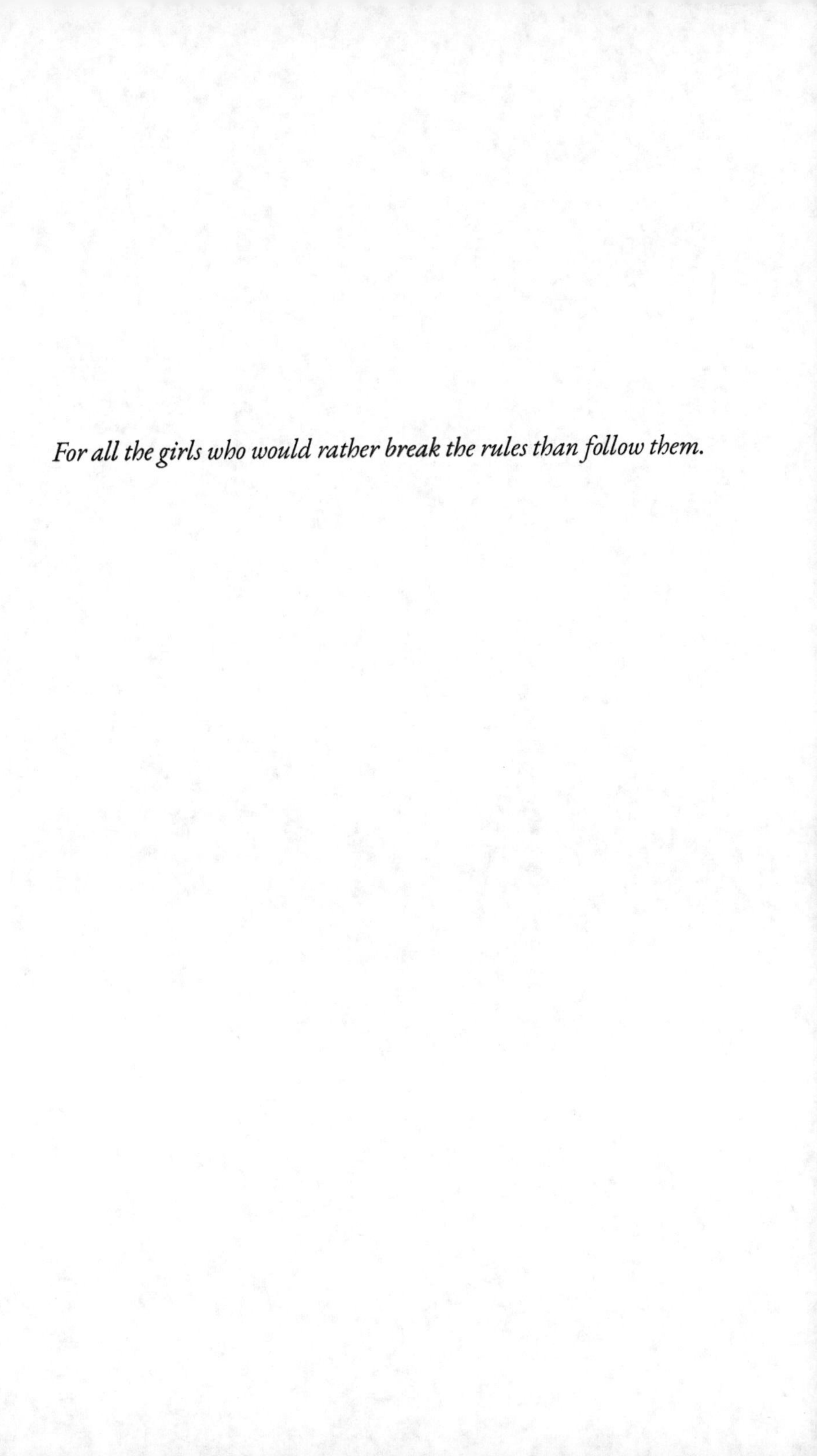

For all the girls who would rather break the rules than follow them.

Dear Reader

BLURB

Bend The Pucking Rules is the second book in the sexy and suspenseful Ice Lords Series. An Enemies to Lovers, Why-Choose, College Hockey Romance.

I know too much and now, I'm paying the price.
One secret shattered my world.
Three boys wrecked my life.
And one of them just might own my heart—if only he could remember.
As Callan fights to piece together the memories we shared and the time we lost, I'm caught in the crossfire of rival teams, bitter betrayals, and players who would love nothing more than to watch me fall.
Someone is out there.
Whispering. Watching. Waiting.
And if I want to survive, I'll have to trust the very people who broke me.
Aidric. Sebastian.
Maybe even Callan
Sebastian says he hates me.
But hate doesn't burn this hot.
I see it in his eyes. I feel it every time he looks at me.
I'm just not sure if his fire is meant to save me, or burn me.
When Callan finally remembers, will it be enough to put us back together?
Or will the bond I'm building with his best friend tear us all apart?
They say you can't have the best of both worlds.
But I'm beginning to realize, the three of us were never meant to live by the rules.

PLAYLIST
CLICK HERE TO LISTEN
https://spoti.fi/3ERtOMG
Forget Me by Lewis Capaldi
How Did You Love by Shinedown
Surrender by Natalie Taylor
Empty by Letdown
Get You The Moon by Kina
The Archer by Taylor Swift
Inside Us All by Creed
Perfectly Broken by Banners
I Lost Myself by Munn
Skin and Bones by David Kushner
I'm Sick of Trying by Vaboh
Pray by Jessie Murph
Paralyzed by NF
Heathens by Twenty One Pilots
If You Want Love by NF
Half A Man by Dean Lewis
Liability by Lorde
I'm Not The Only One by Sam Smith
Hold Me While You Wait by Lewis Capaldi
Warriors by Imagine Dragons
Haunted by Beyonce
Glory And Gore by Lorde
Unsteady by X Ambassadors
Watch Your Back by Sam Smith

CHECK OUT THE: PINTEREST BOARD
https://pin.it/4bpWuRRmO

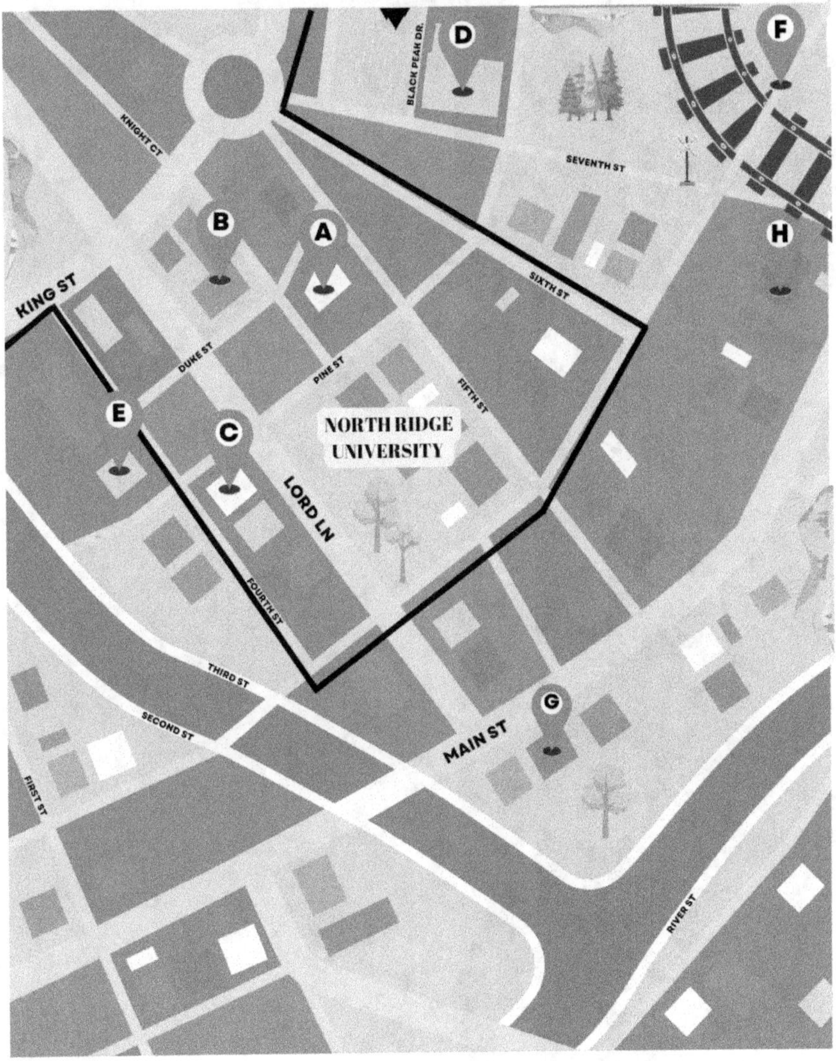

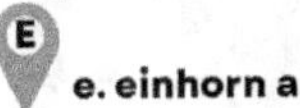

A library

B fifth street student center

C athletic center

D hockey house

E e. einhorn arena

F rosewood-u campus

G hospital

H faraway archery range

PROLOGUE
15 YEARS OLD

THE LIGHTS IN THE RINK GO OFF ONE BY ONE, BUT I stay behind, still in my pads, skates unlaced and ankles sore. I'm not practicing anymore; I'm killing time. Stretching the hours between this place and the hell waiting at home.

Coach left twenty minutes ago and the janitor passed through once. I think he saw me, but he didn't say a word. He knows.

I'm not the kid people ask questions about; I'm the one they pity in silence.

The cold air clings to me, but I welcome it. At least it's clean and honest, unlike the stench of cheap whiskey and bad decisions that clings to the walls of my father's trailer.

"You planning to sleep here or what?"

I glance up and see Aidric leaning against the side of the rink, helmet tucked under one arm, smirking like he can see straight through me.

I roll my eyes. "Didn't think anyone was left."

"Didn't think you'd still be here." He drops his gear onto the bench and shrugs. "Or maybe I did."

I don't respond. Aidric's one of those guys who doesn't ask permission to speak, he just does. He's a year older, already tall and cocky, and skating like he was born to do it. He's a good friend, though. At least, he tries to be.

He sits down and glances at me sideways. "You ever heard of the Ice Lords?"

I frown. "The team?"

"Not the hockey team." He chuckles. "Ya know how my brother's a senior at North Ridge University?" he asks, like he wants me to reassure him of the fact.

"Yeah," I grumble.

"Well, a couple nights ago, I heard him talking on the phone. Said something about a secret society and initiation."

I blink. "The hell are you talking about?"

Aidric leans in slightly. "There's this group, not just athletes, but a legacy. These guys have real power. They call themselves the Ice Lords. And if you're in, you're *in*. They handle everything from winning games, getting good grades, making money, and even securing cover-ups for any stupid shit they do."

Shaking my head, I try not to think about how much something like that could change the course of my life. If there's anything I've learned from my shitty life, it's that having hope is dangerous.

"Sounds like bullshit."

"Sounds like opportunity," Aidric counters.

"Why are you telling me this?" I throw up my hands, confused and refusing to let that little glimmer of hope cling to me. I don't want it.

Aidric shrugs. "Because I trust you, and because you don't scare easily. It's still a few years away, but if we play our cards right, maybe we can get in."

That would be a fucking dream, but I don't tell him that because dreams aren't attainable for people like me.

When I don't say anything, he stands and grabs his helmet again. "Anyway. Figured you'd want to know in case you're tired of being a punching bag."

Swallowing thickly, I watch as he walks off without another

word. The thought of something bigger and better could be just the thing I need right now because everything outside of this rink feels pointless. It's another reason I stay late, watching the ice and just breathing it in. This isn't just the only place I can find peace, but it's also the only place that reminds me what it is to truly live.

The janitor eventually clears his throat, keys jingling in his hand, and I stand, grabbing my bag and getting to my feet. The walk home isn't far, and as soon as I get to the door, I already know what's awaiting me on the other side.

Sure enough, the air already reeks of liquor and cigarette smoke. The door barely opens before I hear my father's voice, slurred and sharp.

"You think you're better than me?" he snaps, appearing in the hallway, shirt half-buttoned, eyes wild. "You think that fucking jersey gives you value?"

I keep my head down, grip tight around the strap of my backpack. I try to ignore him and push my way to my room, but he grabs me as I pass, his hand unrelenting around my arm.

"Get off me!" I try to pull away, but he only holds tighter, nails digging into my flesh. "Let go!"

It was the wrong move because his slap comes fast. The back of his hand cracks across my cheek, jerking my head sideways. My cheek explodes with heat, and I taste copper.

My father is a good six inches taller than me and has way more muscle. His body is tight with rage, the usual anger somehow even more potent tonight.

When he steps in, breath thick with whiskey, I know it's only going to get worse from here.

"You're nothing, boy," he hisses. "You think some school, some scholarship, and some rink is going to rewrite who you are?"

I stare at the floor, quiet and unblinking, face burning as I try to do the one thing the rink taught me to do—survive. This is his game. He always wants a reaction, wants to feel bigger than me, stronger than the bottle he never puts down.

When I don't play along, he presses his finger into my chest.

Right over the jersey, right over the number that gives me more purpose than he ever could.

"You'll never be more than my fuck-up son."

He grabs his drink from the table beside us and throws his empty glass against the wall, causing it to shatter on impact.

I don't flinch—not anymore. His punishing grip finally loosens as he no doubt goes to search for another cup, or hell, he might just drink from the bottle at this point. Either way, I refuse to stick around and find out.

I hear him finally calm down on the other side of my door. He's probably face down on the couch sleeping it off. Not wanting to risk a run in with him again, I forgo any thought of dinner as I toss my bag in the corner, reminding myself to steal some change from around the house to wash my hockey gear with later.

My heart is still beating rapidly and the idea of falling asleep early isn't appealing, so I pace my floor, trying not to let my father get to me. Once I've exhausted myself and it's past midnight, I sit on the floor in the dark.

For a moment, I almost let my father's words take root in me, almost allow them to drag me under to that dark place that takes days or even weeks to crawl out of. It's hard not to when that's all I've been told for years now, that I'll always be less than enough.

Then I remember what Aidric said earlier about the Ice Lords —the power and the loyalty. That's when that stupid feeling I try so hard to keep buried pops into my head, and a dangerous plan begins to form.

Hope is what has me standing, walking over to my bag to get out my phone and begin my research. If this secret society exists, I'm going to find it, then I'll make sure they invite me in if it's the last thing I do.

My father's words play on repeat in my head, but as I dig deeper to find what's hidden behind secret firewalls, his insults begin to fall away.

And for the first time in my life, I think maybe I could be something more. Maybe, just maybe, I could be an Ice Lord.

CHAPTER ONE

SEBASTIAN

Callan's blood is still under my fingernails.

I scrub my hands raw in the hospital sink, but it won't come off. Not the blood, and certainly not the memory of him twisted in that wreck, half-conscious and calling out for Avery.

Aidric leans against the tiled wall, arms crossed, jaw ticking. "How the fuck did this happen?"

"She called me," I mutter, eyes down as I watch the blood run down the drain. "She was screaming so loud I could barely make out what she was saying."

I'm not sure I'll ever forget the sound of her screams.

We got to the scene of the accident before the fire fighters even cut him out. I can still hear the metal shrieking as the jaws of life peeled open the driver's side door. Avery was barefoot, fighting to get past the barricade.

She was the first one on the scene, and she dialed 911 on the way. We pulled up as she was grabbing a fire extinguisher from her car to try and keep the flames away from Callan. Once they died down, she tried to climb through the window to him, screaming for him to stay awake. His eyes stayed on her the whole time, and when we were forced back by the emergency crew, Avery nearly lost her mind.

Aidric had to hold her back while the paramedics swarmed Callan. Once he was on the stretcher, we were able to see him before he was loaded into the ambulance. I remember grabbing his bloody hand, promising him he'd pull through this. And he will.

But the wreckage doesn't chill me nearly as much as the figure I saw running into the trees, away from the scene as soon as we pulled up. He was wearing one of our black ceremonial cloaks with gold stitching at the collar, along with one of our masks. Not the knockoff ones or a Halloween costume—it was one of ours because they have a special crest stamped into the side of them.

In my gut, I know the masked figure had something to do with it all. I didn't even notice the fucker until Avery threw the fire extinguisher into the tree line, not wanting to let it near the flames or hot surfaces. Even in an emergency, she seemed to be thinking straight. Despite all of her screaming, she was the only one of us who was actually prepared for the scene.

Before we got into our car, I told the cops to check the brake lines. Avery said Callan was on his way to her because someone broke into her dorm and left a cryptic note with a bloody arrow. She said he couldn't stop, that he was slamming the brakes and nothing happened. It wasn't hard to do the math and I have an inkling that the masked asshole in the woods is who we'll be searching for.

I figured the cops would brush me off and chalk it up to paranoia or assume that Callan was driving impaired, but I brought it to Mr. Cromwell anyway. Callan's dad has some pull here and there was a quick report sent his way just minutes after Callan arrived at the hospital. Sure enough, the brake line was cut.

I haven't told Aidric about the masked figure yet. I'm not sure why. Maybe it's because part of me is still hoping it wasn't one of us—an Ice Lord. Even if, in my gut, I know better.

Aidric sent one of the newest recruits to Avery's dorm to clean up the mess. They were told to bring anything that looked out of place straight to The Chamber. When we found blood on the arrow shaft, we immediately had one of our insiders run it through the system. Now we wait.

This wasn't just sabotage; it was a message from one of our own, or someone pretending to be. That's the thought that has been plaguing me, wondering if we really have a traitor in our midst and who would be after Callan specifically.

My skin is red when Aidric shuts off the water and places a hand over mine, a clear warning in his gaze that I need to stop. Even I know I'm spiraling, but there's nothing I can do about it right now.

There was so much fucking blood.

"Let's go," Aidric says, and I follow him to our best friend's side, the one who has been with us since the moment he stepped into the world of the Ice Lords. He isn't just a friend to us; he's a brother, which is why this is all the more excruciating.

Time passes as we just stare at him, waiting for a change. It's been hours and he hasn't even moved. Avery sits in the chair beside him, her hand in his and her eyes bloodshot from how closely she's been watching him.

I stare at Callan in disbelief, wondering when everything got so fucked up.

His face is almost unrecognizable beneath the bruising, burns, and bandaged jaw.

Aidric stands, taking Avery by the shoulder even as she scowls.

"You can give me that face all you want, Little Devil, but you need to get something to eat or at least drink."

I'm shocked by his tenderness with her, but I'm even more shocked when she slowly stands, her legs wobbling slightly as she obeys him. He doesn't let her get far before he puts a hand on her back and helps her along.

Aidric isn't one to touch girls like that, not gently. But after he saw what she did for our boy, I think we are both looking at her a little differently—at least, for now.

I take the seat beside Callan, my legs tired, like they've been carrying someone else's weight.

"You look like shit," I mutter under my breath.

He doesn't respond, obviously, but I keep talking because the silence is too damn loud.

"Callan," I say softly. "If there's any part of you still in there, wake the fuck up. We need you. I need you."

I chuckle. "Look at me getting all mushy and shit. You see what the hell you've done?"

I bite the inside of my cheek and drop my head. "You always knew when something was coming," I whisper. "Even before the rest of us saw it. So what the hell, man? Why didn't you see this?"

I lift my eyes to the bandage stretched across his chest, hiding the bruises along his ribs. Thankfully, he was seat belted in. That's probably the only reason he's still breathing.

Fuck. That mask won't stop replaying in my head.

I lean in, voice dipping low. "One of them was there, Callan. One of us. Wearing the cloak and the mask. I don't know if it was real, or some twisted replica, but they were there."

My fists clench at my sides. Guilt rises like bile in my throat. "I should've told Aidric and Avery, but I didn't because I don't know who the hell to trust anymore."

My eyes lock on his. Still closed and still too quiet. "I know it's not Aidric," I mutter. "But it could be someone else, someone close. Someone we've looked in the eye." I exhale, slow and sharp. "But I also know it's not her." I say the words like a line drawn in blood. "It's not the girl you fell for—the one you'd set the world on fire for. Avery's hands are clean."

My jaw tightens. "But someone's aren't. And we're running out of time to find out who the hell it is before someone else gets hurt."

CHAPTER TWO

AVERY

ONE MINUTE CALLAN'S VOICE IS CRACKLING THROUGH the phone telling me to stay where I am, and the next it's the sound of tires screeching, metal folding, and my world tipping sideways.

I don't remember how I got there, just the taste of panic and my foot pressing the pedal to the floor. I vaguely remember calling someone, but when I saw Callan's car in flames, I knew I had to act.

Screams tore from my lips that didn't sound like my own as I fought the fire with the small extinguisher in my trunk.

His car was upside down, steam pouring from the hood, flames lapping the edges of the grass. His name tore from my throat as I ran barefoot across shattered glass, my lungs ripping open with each breath.

I tried so hard to crawl into the car with him. If he was going to die there, then I wanted to burn with him. But then I was pulled back, kicking violently.

Aidric held me in a way I wasn't used to, not demanding or rude, but like a security blanket. Sebastian stood by my side as I took Callan's hand one last time before they rushed him to the hospital. They both saw me cry, felt me break irrevocably, and they never left me.

Instead, we drove in silence all the way to the hospital and at one point someone gave me shoes and a hoodie.

It's now been two days.

I sit beside Callan's bed, counting the rise and fall of his chest like it's the only thing keeping the earth on its axis.

They said it was a miracle he survived, but I'm not sure that's true. Miracles are just another lie the world tells to make the living feel less guilty. Someone did this to Callan. I feel it in my soul. This wasn't a miracle, and it sure as hell isn't a coincidence.

The IV clicks with a steady drip, syncing with the slow beep of the heart monitor. I press my forehead to the back of his hand, my tears soaking into the bandages.

Lacing my fingers through his, I stare down at the wreck of him. His face is a brutal canvas of bruises, his eyes swollen shut, lashes stuck together like broken threads. A wicked gash runs from his jaw to the corner of his mouth, stitched tight where a shard of glass was pulled free. Both arms are mummified in thick gauze, hiding the burns seared into his skin.

They were more superficial, but still need to be wrapped to prevent infection for now. The doctor told me if I hadn't had that fire extinguisher then he would likely need full body skin grafts. Someone else said that Callan was lucky I was there for him, but they clearly know nothing.

Someone is after me, and because of that, they went after him too.

Sebastian says he's still breathing and that's all that matters. Even broken, he's still fighting. Yet, I can't help but feel like I didn't do enough, that nothing ever would have been enough.

I swallow hard as I try not to replay the scene over and over in my head. Inhaling a shaky breath, I grit my teeth and force myself into the present. I can't break now, not while Callan still hasn't woken up.

"Aidric's right," Sebastian says, voice quieter than usual. "You should get some rest."

"Not yet," I whisper. "They're going to try and wake him today. I'm not leaving until he opens his eyes."

Aidric steps forward, eyeing me like I might break if he looks too hard. The sharp edges are still there, but the fire behind them has diminished. For the first time, I think he's actually worried.

"Then what?" he asks, voice rough. "You think if you're here when he wakes up, it'll fix this? You think staying is going to undo what happened?"

I clench my fists, the burns on my own hands wrapped up. It hurts like hell, but that's why I do it. I deserve the pain. It's centering and also reminds me that I'm stronger than any of them give me credit for. And I will not be talked down to like this. I won't allow Aidric to make what Callan and I have into a small fleeting thing.

"What the hell am I supposed to do?" I shout, turning on them. "I kept your damn secrets and I played by your twisted rules! I did exactly what the three of you asked of me, and look where that got us."

Gesturing around the room, I pin them both with a glare. "I tried it your way and look what happened. You can't even promise one of your own people safety."

Aidric scrubs a hand down his face, jaw clenched. "You should've burned the damn box when we told you to."

"I didn't tell anyone," I fire back, shaking my head as more tears try to fall. "Shove your accusations up your ass. You're just pissed because your star player's out for the season."

Aidric's eyes flicker. "You think this is about hockey?" His voice is tight. "Callan's not a fucking game piece, Avery. He is my god damned brother."

I scoff at him, exhausted and trembling from lack of food and sleep. "Then maybe you should've protected him better."

That hits harder than I expected, or wanted. Aidric's face falls in a way I didn't know was possible for a statue like him, and I almost take it back. But then that sorrow he let shine briefly turns into rage, and I ready myself for a fight.

Sebastian steps in, calm but cold. "Enough. Not here. We need to be quiet or they'll kick us out."

I let out a bitter cackle. "Oh, you want me quiet now? So you two can go back to running this sick little society without anyone questioning it?"

"Don't twist this, Avery," Sebastian says, tone low. "We're trying to hold it together."

"Yeah?" I can't help the humorless laugh that escapes me. "How's that working out for you? Callan's in a hospital bed because you all wanted to play king. You wanted power, made deals and played your stupid little games. And guess what? You got what you wanted. But Callan, your *brother*," I say using air quotes, "is the one who paid the price."

I glance between the two of them, standing on shaky legs with the weight of it all. "Who's next? You? Aidric? Or are you both too arrogant to think this can't touch you?"

Aidric exhales sharply and shakes his head, like I'm not worth the fight right now.

I laugh again, a dry, cracked sound. "Fuck you both. Get out and leave me alone so I can clean up the mess you made."

Neither of them moves at first, but I hold my ground. When Sebastian meets my gaze, I know I've won this round. For a flicker of a second, there's something almost like regret in his eyes.

"We're not your enemies, Avery," he says softly. "Not today."

But I turn my back before I can believe that—before I can *want* to believe it.

The door creaks open and Mr. Cromwell steps inside wearing a tailored black suit and polished shoes, his cologne cutting through the sterile scent of antiseptic.

His eyes flick from Aidric to Sebastian, then finally land on me. There's something almost gentle there.

"Avery," he says softly. "You're still here."

I nod, swallowing past the lump in my throat. Every time I see one of Callan's family members, guilt claws a little deeper.

They don't know.

They don't know Callan is lying in that bed because of me. Because of a single call I can't take back.

Aidric and Sebastian slip out, but Aidric's gaze brushes over me like a curse before he disappears.

Mr. Cromwell picks up the paper bag holding my lunch, the scent of stale fries leaking from the seams. "Have you eaten?"

I shake my head. "Not yet."

I don't tell him that the last time I ate was before Callan's car flipped into a twisted wreck.

"I've arranged for a surgeon to fly in from New York," he says. "The best for Callan."

"I'm just glad he's alive," I whisper, the words nearly breaking me in two.

When he first arrived, they couldn't figure out why he wasn't waking up. It wasn't until yesterday they found a small brain bleed that caused pressure to build in his head, rendering him unconscious.

A surgeon here created a small hole in his skull to prevent further buildup of fluid and pressure, but with him still not awake, his father left early to make some calls and to get an hour of sleep. The rest of the family has trickled in and out, but I think Brogan must have told them about us in some way or another because no one questioned me staying by his side.

A nurse comes in the room, updating Callan's father and saying they sent his records to the surgeon coming today. After looking over his bandages and checking his fluids, the nurse makes her way out and I'm left staring at all the white sterile gauze that covers Callan's body.

Even when his body heals, the scars will stay. He'll always know it was my call that did this to him. I just hope he doesn't spend a lifetime blaming me.

As for his future in hockey, he'll fight like hell to get back in the game. I know him. Hockey is stitched into his soul.

"I didn't realize you and my son were so close," Mr. Cromwell says.

"Me either," I murmur, voice cracking. "It just...happened."

He rests a warm, heavy hand on my shoulder. "He's lucky to have you, Avery. Brogan too."

A beat of silence passes before he clears his throat. "I just don't understand who would do this to my boy."

"He doesn't deserve any of this," I say, my voice trembling.

"If you hear anything, bring it to me first. I don't trust the cops in this town."

I nod, standing to go to the bathroom so I can splash a little water on my face.

If only he knew there's someone out there who knows the truth, and if I don't find them soon, I'm terrified Callan won't be the last to fall.

A year ago I thought of myself as the quiet girl, the one who sat in the background and didn't make too much noise. But I have a feeling I'm no longer the person who was afraid to chase after what she wanted while fighting to keep it.

This time I won't be sitting by and following orders. In fact, I think it's about time I pull out my tactical bow with the hundred yard scope.

Whoever messed with Callan is about to find out something very important about me. I never miss.

CHAPTER THREE

AVERY

"AVERY." BROGAN'S VOICE FLOATS TOWARD ME, muffled and distant. "Avery, honey. Wake up."

The light of the hospital room stings my eyes, and I blink rapidly, finding Brogan standing over me, her smile lopsided with worry.

Panic flares hot and fast as I throw the scratchy blanket off me and shoot upright. "What happened?"

"It's okay, babe," she says quickly, her voice smoothing over my panic. "The ventilator's out. They've been tapering the sedative and he's starting to wake up."

I don't wait for her to say anything more. Stumbling off the loveseat, my heart hammering in my chest, I rush to Callan's bedside. He lies motionless, face still battered and pale, but he looks lighter somehow.

"How long was I out?" I ask, not tearing my gaze from him.

"Since I got here. Three hours." Brogan gives a soft shrug. "You needed it, Ave. I just didn't want you to be pissed if he woke up and you were sleeping."

"Thank you," I whisper. "I'm glad you woke me."

I wrap my hand around Callan's, squeezing gently. "I'm here, Callan. I'm not going anywhere."

Suddenly, his eyelids twitch, fluttering like wings. Then they fall closed again.

"The doctors said it might take a while," Brogan says, her voice steady and reassuring.

I nod, heart in my throat. I can wait. I'll wait forever if I have to. He's alive and that's all that matters.

I sit down in the chair beside him, and I watch. I count every flutter of his lashes, every twitch of his fingers.

Brogan leaves for cheer practice after squeezing my shoulder and promising to come back. I barely even register the door closing behind her.

Hours drag by, heavy and slow. Dinner carts rattle down the hall. My stomach growls, but I ignore it. Nothing matters except him.

"Please come back to us, Callan," I whisper.

Just then, he moves. Part of me wonders if he heard me, if he knows I'm here and woke up to see my face.

His lashes lift and this time, his eyes stay open.

My heart jumps. "Hey." I lean over him, smiling so hard my face aches. "How was your nap?"

I can't seem to find any other words as I stare into his green eyes. He's awake, he's alive, and he's mine.

Callan groans, muscles straining as he tries to push himself up. I try to stop him, but before I can, his arm gives out and he slumps back with a hiss of pain.

"Easy," I whisper, barely grazing his shoulder with my fingertips, terrified I'll hurt him more.

He settles, his stare pinning me to the spot. His brow furrows. "Where am I?" The words are rough, dragging like gravel out of his throat. He tries to clear it and I reach for the water on the table, fresh from when dinner trays came around.

Hesitantly, he sits forward, taking a small sip, but it's clear he is still confused. "Where am I, Avery?"

I brush my fingers across his cheek, pretending my heart isn't splitting seeing him this way.

"You're in the hospital. You...there was an accident."

Confusion clouds his features. He tries to sit up again, craning his neck to scan the room before settling back against the pillows. It's clear he's agitated as he tries to look anywhere but at me.

"Where's Brogan?" he croaks.

"She had to go to practice, but she'll be back," I say, pointing my thumb toward the door.

His frown deepens. "Cheer practice?"

I nod, feeling the tension coil tighter in the room.

"That doesn't make sense. Her season hasn't started."

His words are more of a murmur to himself, not said to anyone in particular.

"Callan, it's the middle of November. Of course the season has started."

He stares at me in shock, shaking his head slowly. His eyes blink heavily and for a brief moment I wonder if they might stay closed for a while, letting him drift back off to sleep and recover a little bit more, maybe get his bearings.

"Avery, I'm not dumb. This is still the beginning of my season. We haven't even played our first game yet."

I try to think of how to tell him what all has happened in the past few months, but my words fail me. He must see something on my face because his twists in a scowl.

Suddenly, he yanks at the IV in his arm.

"Callan, stop. Please, don't do that." I reach for his hand, trying to make sure he doesn't rip it from his arm completely.

He slaps my touch away like it burns. "Don't touch me."

The venom in his words hurts more than I could have imagined and I have to fight with myself not to snap at him. We're past that; we have figured our shit out. Recoiling from him, I blink fast, trying with all of my might to keep the tears away.

"It's okay," I say quickly, trying to mask the sting. "You're confused. You've been through a lot, baby."

His eyes darken as he grabs my wrist and twists. "Don't call me that. Why are you even here, Avery?"

It feels like he's ripped my heart out and thrown it against the wall.

Don't take it personally, Avery. He's confused and hurting. He doesn't mean it.

I force a breath and quietly reach for the call button on the bed remote, pressing it without him noticing and keeping eye contact the entire time. He doesn't look away, just breathes heavily with so much hate in his gaze my stomach twists.

"You've been heavily sedated," I tell him. "It's normal to feel disoriented. But you're safe now."

He growls, his grip turning punishing, and the bandages on my arm dig into the burns there. They are no doubt bleeding, but I latch onto the pain and use it to keep pushing forward.

"You need to tell me what the fuck is going on, Avery. Right now. Why am I here? Why are you here?"

My throat dries up. The doctors said not to overwhelm him. But looking at him now—desperate and furious—the truth is the only thing left.

"You were in a car accident," I say softly. "You were coming to help me."

"No." He shakes his head violently, the heart monitor spiking from agitation. "No, that's bullshit. Why the hell would I be coming to you?" His eyes narrow. "I can't fucking stand you, Avery."

The words slice me open. Tears blur my vision and before I can stop them, they fall silent and steady down my cheeks.

I nod numbly before yanking my wrist free. A nurse rushes in, alarmed. She barks something down the hall and ushers me out, but I move on autopilot, the world around me spinning so fast I don't know which way is up.

My actions got him hurt. I'm the reason he is here. He hates me. He doesn't remember.

That's the only thing going through my head as I move down the hall and out the doors. My body doesn't feel like my own when I get outside. I just keep walking until I can't anymore. The lack of food and sleep hits me all at once. Collapsing against a tree, I pull out my phone and do the only thing I can think of.

CHAPTER FOUR

SEBASTIAN

"What the hell, Avery. Calm down, you're not making any goddamn sense."

Her sobs crackle through the speaker, so sharp I yank the phone away from my ear.

"They said he has some memory loss," she finally chokes out. "They said it's not uncommon, that he might get it back slowly but..." She trails off, strangled by another broken cry.

"But he doesn't remember you?" I ask, softer this time. The fight's bled out of her voice and, damn it, something about it digs under my skin. "Avery, he's alive. That's what matters right now. He'll remember eventually."

"You weren't there," she snaps, voice splintering. "You don't understand, Sebastian. You didn't see how he looked at me. I don't know how much time he's lost and that scares me."

The line goes dead and I lower the phone. A strange feeling stirs in my chest and for a second I think maybe I should go find her and see if she's okay. But that would be crazy because I'm the last person she needs.

"He's awake." My voice is distant, thinking about what Avery said. Callan can't remember and that isn't just inconvenient for her, but dangerous too.

Aidric looks up from the edge of his bed. "'Bout damn time. I had no doubt our boy would come back. What the hell was she screaming about?"

"She's spiraling," I say, slipping my phone in my pocket. "Apparently he doesn't remember her and she's wrecked over it." I sigh. "Can't say I blame her."

Aidric straightens his spine. "Memory loss?"

I nod. "Standard trauma shit. He'll get it back eventually."

"This isn't good, Seb. We're gonna need eyes on him at all times."

My brows pinch. "Why?"

"If he starts to remember shit from that night, what do you think is going to happen? He could panic, or worse, he could start talking, thinking it's correlated to his accident."

"Oh, shit," I breathe, getting to my feet.

"And if the wrong person hears him..."

He doesn't finish. He doesn't need to.

"Fuck." I run a hand down my face. "Klein was already sniffing around the hospital yesterday. It's only a matter of time before he questions Callan about the accident. If he slips up and says the wrong thing—If he remembers Evan before he remembers the cleanup..."

"He could crack," Aidric says flatly. "And if he does, it won't just be him on the line, it's all of us. Every Lord tied to that night, even Avery."

"I mean, let's be real. It's not our fault," I say. "It's not like we pushed Evan off that cliff."

"No," Aidric agrees. "But we covered up a crime. The cops don't care that we didn't push him. But they will care if they know we left him there to die."

"We all know that asshole detective doesn't give a shit about what happened to Evan, he just wants to catch us holding the shovel so he can pin something on the Ice Lords."

Aidric rubs his eyes, getting to his feet as he stretches his arms above his head. "We need to get to the hospital. See what we're working with."

There's a heavy silence before I mutter, "Practice?"

"I'll text Coach. He owes me."

"And Avery?" My voice is soft for some reason, as if it's taboo to ask about her. But after how much she's been involved in our lives lately, the secrets she knows bits and pieces of, I feel like we need to have eyes on her too.

"Let her have her little meltdown. We just need to make sure she doesn't crack under the pressure of all of this. The last thing we need is either of them talking."

I tilt my head. "She's in deeper than she realizes."

"She hardly knows the surface of the secrets we hold and that alone could cost her, her life," he says. "And if whoever's fucking with her is using her to get to us, it won't be her paying the price, it'll be us."

"Then we get ahead of it." I square my shoulders. "We find out who's behind this and remind them who the fuck they're dealing with. No one touches our house, and no one touches her."

Aidric smirks. "Careful. You're starting to sound possessive."

I shake my head. "She keeps pushing back at us and next time I'll do more than shove my cock down her throat to shut her up. I'll fuck some sense into her. Hard. That's not possession, Aidric, it's ownership. We *own* her."

Aidric barks a laugh. "She could probably use a good fuck after how hysterical she sounded. Maybe you'll find her reset button."

I can't help but chuckle as we make our way to the car. "She's got a dark side hiding in there," I mutter. "I think she just needs someone to drag it out."

We leave the house in a hurry, knowing time is of the essence.

It's a ten-minute drive to the hospital, but the second we step into Callan's room, I know we're not getting him alone. His family is taking up the space. There's Brogan, the twins—Rome and Wilder—his dad, even his youngest sister, Lake, along with his stepmother.

But it's Callan sitting up that catches me. He's got a grape popsicle in his hand and a lazy half-smile stretched across his bruised mouth. I can't remember ever seeing him so relaxed and carefree.

For a second, I wonder if he'll even recognize us, but when he lifts his popsicle like he's toasting us, I know. The breath of relief I have over that is intense. Missing a few months of memory usually comes back within a week or so after an accident, but when people lose entire years, that doesn't always return.

"What's up, boys?" he calls, voice rough but bright.

"How ya feeling?" I ask, hanging back as his family circles him. His stepmother runs a hand through his hair that looks freshly washed, the blood staining it from earlier gone as she combs it back away from his face.

He shrugs, that smile never leaving his face. "Like I got hit by a truck, then blown the fuck up. Other than that, pretty damn good."

I snort. "At least your sense of humor survived."

"Gotta laugh through the bullshit," Callan says with a chuckle. "My memory's fuzzy, but it'll come back."

"That's a shame," Aidric says. "How far back we talking?"

I elbow him hard enough that he stumbles. Now's not the time to dig. The last thing we need is to trigger repressed memories that make him confused in front of his family. It'll cause too many questions.

Callan frowns, thinking. "Feels like pre-season. Month, month and a half maybe. I remember getting to campus and the party where we..." He pauses then throws a wink our way, clearly referring to the night we triple teamed two puck bunnies. "Anyway, everything after that is gone."

My stomach sinks.

That's everything—everything with Evan, everything with

Avery. We sure as fuck can't have him remembering shit at the wrong time.

Aidric and I exchange a look. We don't even need words to know this is bad, like really fucking bad.

At least our boy is benched for the season. He's safer here, surrounded by people who think he's still the same golden boy. Seeing the team or the guys could trigger memory flashes and we need to keep that contained as much as possible.

At least remembers what being an Ice Lord is, even if he might not recall some of the depraved shit that came after.

Speak of the devil, the door swings open and Avery steps inside, her smile strained at best. The second she sees us, it collapses altogether.

Brogan moves fast, slipping an arm around her waist. "Hey, babe," she says low, herding Avery back toward the hall. "Let's talk outside."

Aidric jerks his chin at me and I follow them, curiosity sharpening my every step.

"What's up?" Avery asks, wide-eyed, glancing back at the door. Just before it shuts, I can see Callan's face pinched with confusion and anger. Shit, he really doesn't remember their little make-up sex sessions.

Brogan hesitates before grabbing Avery's hands. "We think...we think it's best if you don't visit for a while. Callan's confused, Ave. Waking up to you alone in his hospital room...he didn't understand why you were there. It sort of freaked him out. He won't let any of us talk about you and gets angry anytime we bring up your name."

Avery recoils, her hands falling from Brogan's as I approach. A single tear cuts a path down her cheek. And damn if there isn't a twisted part of me that wants to lick it off her skin. I bet she tastes like pain and defiance. Like something forbidden.

"I get it," she says thickly. "Makes sense. Doesn't make it hurt less, though."

Brogan pulls her into a hug. "He'll remember. And when he does, you two can pick up where you left off."

Avery tries to swallow, and I can see this getting worse if Brogan continues talking. "I really do care about him, Brogan. More than I ever wanted to."

For some reason, that punches harder than I expected. For fuck's sake. They had, what, one date and a fuck and now it's some kind of epic love story.

"For the love of God," I mutter, reaching Avery's side as I roll my eyes.

"Kick rocks, Sebastian," Brogan fires back.

"Better yet," Avery sneers. "Eat shit."

God, I fucking love her mouth. Does she have any idea how much I want to fuck it every time she talks back to me like this?

"I'll gladly do both," I drawl. "Once I figure out what the hell's going on here."

"Go away," Avery snaps. "We're having a private conversation. Not everything revolves around you and your selfish bullshit."

I step closer, lowering my voice to a deadly calm. "Selfish? You're the one trying to force something with a guy who doesn't even remember a time where he didn't despise the ground you walked on. Sounds like you're the one who needs to leave."

The look of raw, brutal pain on her face does something unexpected to me and I don't like it. I hate that I recognize it, hate that it feels too familiar, like a wound I thought scarred over years ago getting sliced back open right before my eyes.

I turn my head away before I do something stupid like apologize, or worse, grab her face and kiss her until she forgets how sad she is.

"Just ignore him," Brogan says, hugging Avery tighter. "I think Callan just needs a little space. You're doing the right thing."

Avery wipes her cheeks and straightens, spine stiffening. "Okay," she whispers. "I'll give him space. Besides..." She spins toward me, a wicked glint in her eye. "I have other things to take care of."

Yeah, I know exactly what she means. The box, the notes, the bloody warning no one can explain.

Brogan promises to grab pizza and hang out at their dorm later, and Avery agrees. Then she walks away with her head bowed like she's carrying the weight of the world.

I don't think, I just move.

"Tell Aidric I'll catch up later," I toss over my shoulder at Brogan.

She narrows her eyes. "Stay away from her, Sebastian."

I flash my teeth at her in a grin and saunter off because there's no fucking way I'm staying away.

Not now. Not when she's walking like she has a plan. If Avery thinks she is going to run off and do something reckless without me, then she's sorely mistaken. If my little lamb wants to run into fire, you best believe her wolf is going to be at her back, hunting her the entire time.

What's that saying again? Oh right. When the lamb walks into the fire, it's because its flames are safer than the wolf.

CHAPTER FIVE

AVERY

No anger, or armor—just exhaustion. I'm empty, and he knows it. All I had to eat was a granola bar today and my hands are still trembling.

"Can't do that," Sebastian says, grinning like the fucking devil. "You said it yourself, we've got things to do."

"I said *I* have things to do," I snap, barely glancing at him. "There was no *we* mentioned."

"That's the part you keep forgetting," he says. "There's no you versus us anymore. We're in this together whether you like it or not, Little Lamb."

Without warning, he slings an arm around my neck, pulling me against him like we're old buddies instead of enemies barely tolerating each other.

My stomach knots instantly, instinct screaming at me to pull away, but I know better. Showing weakness around Sebastian is like bleeding in shark-infested waters. If I move away, he'll only find a way to be closer.

"We sent the blood sample off," he says casually, like we're discussing the weather. "The one on the arrow shaft. Should have something back soon. A name, maybe. A warning. If we're lucky, maybe a body."

I shake his arm off and grind my teeth. God, I hate needing them to help me figure this shitshow out. And I hate it even more that part of me knows they're my best chance of making it out of this situation with all my body parts intact.

"Whatever," I grumble, punching the elevator button. "Just keep your bullshit accusations to yourself."

The elevator doors slide open and I step inside without looking back, praying he'll stay put, but his footsteps are right behind mine.

"Is there something else you need?" I snap.

"Not really." He smiles wide. "But I'm not letting you out of my sight. I'm coming with you."

"Coming with me where?"

"Wherever you're going," he says easily, like it's already decided.

I sigh, turning as the doors close. "Fine. I'm going to the woods where I buried the box."

Sebastian's brows lift, mildly impressed. "That so?"

"Someone's gotta do the dirty work," I say with a shrug. "Maybe I'll find something that'll give us a clue as to what's going on. Or I'll find some evidence that will help me bury you and Aidric."

He chuckles under his breath. "That's cute."

In an instant, he reaches over and slams his finger to the emergency stop button. The elevator jolts to a halt, and I stumble, catching myself on the railing.

"What the fuck, Sebastian?"

He moves fast. One hand fists the back of my hair, the other wraps around my waist, yanking me against the hard line of his body.

I feel every inch of him—the heat, the tension—and worse, the hunger. One minute he was grinning and laughing to himself, the next I feel like I just got caught by a special kind of hunter.

Not one who searches for food to live, but one that kills for sport and smiles when they do it.

"Let's get one thing straight, Little Lamb," he murmurs. "You don't get to disappear. Not tonight. Not until we know what's coming."

I swallow hard but keep my gaze level. "I'm not yours to track."

He barks a laugh in my face, startling me. "You are *ours*, have been since the minute you overheard something you shouldn't have. The sooner you accept that, the easier this gets."

His hand slides higher along my ribs, stopping just shy of my breast, his thumb skimming beneath it as goosebumps erupt across my flesh.

"I'll find something I can bury you with, you won't own me forever." The confidence in my voice is lacking, even to me, but I hold his gaze, defiant until my last breath if that's what it takes.

"You can dig all you want," he whispers. "But when you come up empty, you'll be on your knees. You'll swallow your apology, and my cock, like the good little lamb you are."

My heart pounds so hard it rattles my ribs, but I don't let him see my fear. Instead, a slow smirk curves my lips. "Deal," I whisper.

He freezes. "You're out of your mind," he says, almost disbelieving.

"You heard me," I purr. "If I don't find anything incriminating on you and Aidric, I'll drop to my knees and give you your apology." My hand reaches out, cupping his balls before I squeeze just tight enough to be a warning. "But when I'm right, you walk away. You leave Callan and me the hell alone."

He laughs, dark and broken, like the sound scraped up from some place deep inside him. "You really think Callan will choose you over the brotherhood?"

"I don't care what you think, *Sebastian*," I snap. "I believe in him and the future we wanted to build together."

His smile twists. "Such a shame he doesn't remember those perfect little plans."

I yank my arm free and shove past him, voice raw. "I truly fucking hate you, Sebastian."

His hand brushes my wrist and his voice drops. "You keep saying that." He turns me so that I have no choice but to face him as his finger brushes over my cheek. "I just don't believe that you mean it."

The air between us crackles like a live wire. I lean into his touch and I swear, for a moment, he softens between us. But I'm not the lamb he thinks I am, and I think I need to remind him of that.

I slam my knee up, hard, catching him off guard and right between the legs.

He stumbles back with a vicious grunt, pain flashing across his face. But even now, he's smiling.

He's so freaking unhinged.

Before I can blink, he's crowding me again, backing me against the elevator wall.

One of his hands grabs mine and forces it down until I feel him. My mouth falls open on a gasp and the pleasure he gains from that alone is written into every one of his features.

The hard, brutal evidence of just how much he likes this war we're waging is just under my palm.

"You feel that?" he snarls, voice dripping with disgust and hunger. "That's what your hatred does to me."

I yank my hand away like it burns, punching the button to restart the elevator, and it jerks back into motion.

"Good," I toss over my shoulder as the doors open again. "I hope I just gifted you the most agonizing case of blue balls in the history of mankind."

Sebastian stays frozen for a beat, then, like a storm breaking, he laughs like the maniac he is. "God, you're fun when you're feral," he says under his breath, stepping out of the elevator after me.

"Don't follow me," I stammer, almost tripping over my own two feet.

He tilts his head, amused. "You really think I'm the kind of guy who listens?"

"I think you're the kind of guy who pushes people until they snap. And one day, someone's gonna snap on you."

He grins. "Promises, promises."

I turn sharply and stalk down the hallway but I feel him trailing behind me. He's not too close, but he's close enough.

Once I'm through the hospital's automatic doors, the chill of night air feels like a smack to the face, the spot where my tears fell drawing my attention back to what happened in the hallway.

"Wait up."

But I don't stop. "Sebastian, go back inside," I shout over my shoulder. "I'm not in the mood."

"Yeah, well, I need a ride."

I spin around to find him jogging to catch up, hands in his pockets like he didn't just pin me against an elevator wall and threaten me ten seconds ago.

"You need what?" My eyes nearly bug out of my head at him. There is no way he's getting into my car with me.

"I came with Aidric and he's staying with Callan. I'm not Ubering to the middle of the woods."

I shake my head, pulling out my keys. "Not my problem."

"Technically, you're heading there anyway."

"*Technically*, I'd rather set myself on fire than be trapped in a car with you for ten minutes."

He smirks. "Romantic. Do I make you that hot?"

I glare at him. "You are not getting in my car, Sebastian."

But he's already moving, brushing past me like the conversation's over. "Shotgun," he calls as he yanks open the passenger side door and slides in like the seat was made just for him.

I stand there for a second, torn between leaving him and blowing up my own car out of spite. If I let him win, then he'll just keep pushing. But if I walk away now, the walk to the woods would be a nightmare and there is nothing stopping him from following me.

With a sharp, furious exhale, I shove down my pride, choke back the urge to strangle him with the seat belt, and slide into the car.

"I swear to God," I mutter, gripping the wheel until my knuckles turn white. "You so much as breathe wrong and I'm pushing you out the door and into oncoming traffic."

"You'd miss me," he says, his hand sliding over to squeeze my thigh. His touch sends an unwanted jolt through me. When he looks my way, I'm certain he felt it too.

I turn my body toward him and flutter my lashes. "Maybe I would," I say, running a finger over his hand. "Or maybe..." I grab his finger and pull it back as I twist his wrist. His body curls inward with a grunt, pinned and at my mercy. "Maybe I'd aim for you."

He laughs, head pinning against the seat as I throw his hand back at him. "You're cute when you're all homicidal."

Ignoring him, I reverse out of the parking space and take a sharp turn onto the road without another word.

For a few minutes, we drive in silence, the tension louder than either of us.

"You handled things better than I expected back there."

I don't look at him. "Back where?"

"The hospital. Seeing Callan like that."

My hands tighten on the wheel. "Don't."

"Fine," he says casually before his gaze flicks to me. "You don't actually think Aidric and I are behind any of this, do you? You have to know we'd never hurt Callan like that."

"I think you're exactly the kind of person who likes to play God with other people's lives and I firmly believe none of this would have happened if you didn't pull Callan into your bullshit," I say point-blank. "So yeah. You're on my list."

He lets that sink in. "And yet here we are, driving through the dark together."

I slam the brakes harder than necessary at a stop sign. "Do you want me to kick your ass out of this car?"

He doesn't flinch, just tips his head toward me with that maddening glint in his eyes. "Not until we're in the woods, Little Lamb."

I slam my foot on the gas and peel off down the road. He doesn't say another word. I think he knows better at this point.

CHAPTER SIX

SEBASTIAN

SHE DOESN'T SPEAK FOR THE REST OF THE DRIVE, BUT her silence is loud. It's in the way her fingers twitch on the steering wheel, the way her jaw clenches like she's barely holding herself together.

When the car rolls to a stop near the trailhead, she kills the engine. "Let's get this over with."

"Look at us being a team now," I say, voice smooth. "You and me, partners in petty revenge."

She glares at me so I open the door and step out into the cold. "Come on. Let's go digging."

I watch her leave the car, my infatuation with her growing to new heights. I have no idea why I keep pestering her like I do, no one usually holds my interest for more than fifteen minutes. But there's something about the way she blows me off or bites back. I like it. I want to play with her more and see just how much of a fight she'll put up when I shove her over the edge.

I get out of the car, noticing the woods are quiet and covered in fog. Trees loom over us and it's pretty fucking eerie. Avery leads the way, her flashlight cutting through the darkness.

I trail a few feet behind, hands in my pockets, watching her move and keeping an eye out for anything suspicious. "So," I say, voice low and even. "You bring all your dates out here, or am I just special?"

"Shut up, Sebastian."

I smirk, wanting to see if I can make her smile just a little bit. "I'm just saying...woods, dead of night, you and me."

She glances over her shoulder, eyes gleaming in the light of the moon. "If this is your idea of foreplay, you're worse than I thought."

"You think this is foreplay?" I drawl, grin widening. "Baby, we haven't even started."

She huffs and picks up her pace before suddenly stopping with a gasp. Her breath fogs the air and I rush to her side. Her hand trembles, the flashlight she was holding falls, landing on the post hammered into the ground with a red ribbon tied to it. A note hangs there, fluttering lightly in the wind.

"Someone is always watching"

Avery shakes off the shock quickly, not touching anything and I feel oddly proud of her for that. I pull a black glove out of my pocket along with a plastic baggie because you can never be too prepared. Being an Ice Lord has taught me to never underestimate the people around me.

"This is it," she whispers, looking down at the ground and ignoring me as I seal the note. With her heel to her toes, she starts counting her steps. Once she's there, she drops to her knees and starts ripping into the soil like she's angry with it.

I lean back against the nearest tree, arms crossed, watching her dig like she's trying to claw down to hell itself.

The red ribbon flutters weakly from the post, and my gut twists. Something feels off, like we're being watched even now.

Fuck! Why didn't I think of this sooner?

I pull out my phone, thumb hovering over the screen. I tap into the locked folder, the one we all agreed we'd never need.

The video loads and I press play, watching the grainy, shaky footage. Avery is alone, crying and digging with the box sitting beside her.

"What the hell are you doing?" Avery demands. Her face is red, fingers covered in dirt as she stares at me.

Ignoring her, I keep watching, making sure I have something definitive before I bring it to her attention. She was so fucking pissed about this video and showing her without reason would just send her on another rampage.

Suddenly, something flickers on the far left of the screen.

I rewind and pause, then zoom in.

There, on the video from weeks ago, is a figure standing just inside the trees, watching Avery while wearing a white hockey mask and a black cloak.

My stomach drops.

The faint sound of her sobs from the video bleed into the air again, just loud enough for her to hear.

She stops digging and her head snaps toward me.

"Come here," I say, sharper than I mean to. "Now."

She wipes the back of her arm across her face and stalks over, breath shaky. "If this is about that stupid—"

"It's the video," I cut in. "The one from the night you buried the box. I was watching it and there's something you need to see."

She freezes, the fight draining from her expression before she gets closer.

Her lips part. "Show me."

I turn the screen her way, then, without warning, she snatches the phone out of my hand. Her muddy fingers smudge across the screen as she grips it tightly, eyes glued to the footage.

"I saw something on there proving you weren't alone that night."

"No shit I wasn't alone." She gestures to the phone. "Your minions were out here recording me."

"I'm not talking about one of us. At least, I don't think it is. I was the one recording you; we haven't gotten the others involved."

I reach for her, steadying her hand so the phone doesn't slip, then rewind and pause, zooming in on the masked figure. "Look."

Her breath shudders and she shoves the phone back into my chest. "Who the hell is that?"

She grabs my jacket, fisting the fabric. "They were there, Sebastian. Watching me—they were fucking *watching me.* You were here and didn't notice anything?"

Air scrapes into her lungs as she looks around in a panic, twisting and turning as she slowly begins to hyperventilate.

"They could be here right now. With the fog. Oh God."

She grabs for me again, pressing her body to mine before her head snaps back to her car. "I need to get my bow. I need...I..."

Avery's hand goes to her chest and I take her by the shoulders, forcing her eyes to meet mine.

"Avery, breathe."

She shakes her head, frantic. "Why didn't I see them? Why didn't I feel it? I was so fucking..." Her voice cracks. "I was so fucking stupid."

"Stop," I snap, grabbing her tighter. "Don't do that."

"Don't do *what?*" she snarls. "Lose it? Because that's all I've got left, Sebastian."

Her hand flies out as she takes a step back. "I'm caught up in this web of lies and crime when all I wanted was to become a psychologist and help other people not to feel like they were drowning in their lives."

Her muddy hands run through her hair, dirtying it in a way that has her looking equal parts unhinged and savage. And for some unknown fucking reason, my dick twitches in my pants at the sight.

"I was so stupid to get involved in any of this, stupid enough not to be paying attention to my surroundings when I was burying evidence."

I step toward her and she tries to move back, but I catch her in my grip, pinching her chin in my fingers. "You're not stupid.

Whoever that was, they wanted to send a message and they just did."

Her chest heaves, ragged and uneven. She tries to close her eyes, but I pinch her harder. "Look at me," I say quietly.

She hesitates, but when she obeys, her eyes are shining, cheeks streaked with dirt and tears.

"You're not alone in this," I say softly. "Not anymore."

She swallows hard. For a moment, something flickers behind her eyes—fear, grief, sadness. Then, as fast as it came, it's gone and replaced with steel.

"Good," she whispers. "Because next time they're watching, I want them to see me coming."

Ripping herself from my grip, she turns into the night, cups her hands around her mouth and shouts. "You hear me, asshole? I'm onto you. If you weren't such a chicken shit, you'd show your face. Come and get me!"

A slow, feral grin tugs at my mouth. *Damn, this girl is such a badass.*

"There's my little lamb."

She doesn't glare this time; she just exhales sharply and turns back toward the shallow hole.

"We finish this," she says, voice flat. "Then we find out who the fuck is hunting us."

Avery drops back to her knees without a word, hands diving into the soil again.

I watch her for a beat, then I crouch beside her and dig in too, yanking away roots and damp dirt.

She doesn't stop me, which means she might finally realize she can't do this alone. And for once, I'm not about to rub that in. Normally, I'd throw it in her face and twist the knife just to watch her scowl and fire back. But not this time. Because something about the way she's been crumbling makes me want to steady her. I want her to rely on us—rely on me.

Not because I think she's weak, but because I know how strong she's been trying to be. She carries everything like it's hers alone to fix. And maybe that used to be true, but not anymore.

And if I'm being honest with myself for once, part of me needs her to need me because somewhere along the line, she stopped being just another complication.

The air's colder down here in the valley, and my gut tightens with every inch we uncover. Then my fingers hit something hard. I brush the dirt away, revealing a hockey puck. It's cracked and painted black and red, but that's not what sends my heart into my throat. Avery turns the flashlight on it, showing Callan's number painted on the surface—#11.

Avery's hand flies to her mouth, a ragged sound breaking loose. "No. No..."

I pick the puck up and slide it into my pocket. Underneath it is a folded, soaked note. I peel it open, mud smearing the edges and read the words out loud, "Who's next?"

Avery staggers back like she's been shot. "Oh my God. Oh my fucking God—"

I grab her wrist before she falls. "Hey. Look at me."

She shakes her head, panic rising fast. "They know. They know we're digging. They know we're here. They know—"

"Avery." I grip her shoulders. "Stop."

Her whole body shakes.

I pull her closer, arms locking around her before she can fight me. She stiffens, but only for a second before she crumbles against me.

I lower my head beside hers. "There's something you need to know."

She tenses. "What?"

"I saw them," I say quietly. "At the crash. The same cloak and mask. It was running into the woods when we pulled up."

Her breath catches, and she jerks back just enough to meet my eyes. "And you didn't fucking say anything?" Her voice cracks, raw with betrayal.

"I was trying to get answers first," I grit out. "I didn't want to blow smoke without proof. I didn't want to make it worse. We didn't even know about your room at that point."

"No," she hisses. "You didn't want to admit it might be one of your precious Ice Lords."

I don't say anything because she's not wrong.

Her chest rises and falls like she can't get enough air. "You let me think I was crazy. You let me think I was losing it."

"I didn't know who to trust," I grind out. "I still don't."

I stand up and take a step toward her without thinking. "Avery—"

"Don't," she spits. "Don't touch me. Don't lie to me. And don't stand there acting like you're any different than whoever was in that fucking mask."

I should back off and let her have space. But something about her defiance, even now, makes my blood burn with fury all over again.

"You think I liked keeping this from you?" I say low, snaring her wrist in my hand. "You think I like seeing you fall apart?"

For a second, we just stand there breathing hard, body to body, our breaths fogging the air between us.

Her pulse thrums under my grip, and my fingers tighten when she tries to pull away.

She stares up at me, anger and pain flickering in her eyes. "You just want to control me. You and Aidric both."

Her breath saws in and out, but her eyes burn. Without thinking or caring, I pull her in and crush my mouth to hers.

She gasps, fisting my jacket as her anger, hatred, and pain spill into my mouth. She pushes me away, then pulls me right back in.

This kiss is brutal and messy, our teeth clash, tongues tangling as if they're at war with one another. She tastes like earth and something sweet and fuck if it doesn't undo me.

Her hands drag down my back as I shove her against the nearest tree, pinning her there.

She moans, a broken sound she tries to swallow down but I hear it and I feel it.

I break away, panting. "You hate me," I rasp.

Her eyes flash. "More than anything."

I slam my mouth to hers again, this time harder and deeper.

Her body arches into mine, and she bites my bottom lip in defiance so I return the favor. She gasps as the taste of copper seeps onto our tongues.

"That all you've got?" she breathes, voice wrecked.

I grin darkly. "You want more?" I grind against her, my hard cock pressing against her stomach, mouth dragging down her neck, tasting sweat and sin and everything we've both tried to bury.

Then, in a swift motion, I scoop my arm under her ass and lift. Her legs wrap around my waist, her spine crushing against the tree.

She clings to me, her breath catching, nails digging into my shoulders through the fabric of my shirt.

"You gonna beg for it?" I whisper, my voice rough with need. "Or do I have to drag it out of you?"

Her answer is a defiant roll of her hips and a moan that slips past her lips, taunting me.

One hand slides down between us, my fingers slipping under the waistband of her leggings. She's hot and soaked, and I press two fingers into her like I've got something to prove.

She gasps, head tipping back as her thighs clench around me.

"God, Sebastian."

"Say my name again," I growl, curling my fingers just enough to make her cry out. "Say it like you mean it."

"Sebastian," she whimpers.

"Louder," I demand, dragging my mouth along her jaw. "Let the fucking trees hear it."

She moans again, voice shattered and trembling. "Sebastian!"

That sound wrecks me.

I pump my fingers harder, deeper, grinding the ball of my palm against her clit. She shudders, head snapping forward as she buries her face in my shoulders, biting down on the fabric to muffle the screams tearing out of her throat.

"You sure are wet for someone you hate so much," I murmur against her skin. "What does that make you, Little Lamb?"

She trembles, lips parted like she wants to spit something back but all that escapes is a broken sob as her body locks up.

"Say it," I demand. "Say what it makes you."

"A whore," she whimpers. "It makes me a whore."

"Damn straight it does. My little lamb is a dirty little whore."

My words nail into her, right along with my fingers, and she seems to get off on them because she rides my palm harder, grinding deep as if I can dig out the side of her begging to be set free.

Her tight cunt clenches around my fingers. Her hips buck, breath ragged, fingers tangled in my hair. Every little sound only pulls me further under her spell.

I wanna bend her over right now, shove those leggings down, and bury myself so deep she forgets anyone else has ever touched her. I want her begging me to stop while also begging me not to.

But I don't move yet because I need to feel her fall apart and break in my hand first.

Her walls clench tighter and she cries out as she soaks my fingers.

Her ragged breaths slow and I press my forehead to hers, slick with sweat. "You still hate me?" I murmur.

She nods slowly, dazed. "So much."

"Good." I drop her down like she's nothing. "Hate me harder because I hate you more."

I plan to ruin my little lamb for anyone else, even the one she wants...Callan.

My best fucking friend.

Fuck. What did I just do?

How did I momentarily forget about him? Like he doesn't even exist and he's not lying in a hospital bed with memory loss.

A pang of guilt hits me right in the chest. My need for control, and lack thereof, took the lead and I royally fucked up.

Suddenly, a sharp crack comes from the woods and we both freeze.

Avery pants, eyes dazed as she adjusts her pants that are now drenched in proof of her arousal. "What the hell was that?"

"I think someone's out there," I whisper, pulling her body close to mine. I wrap my arm around her waist, holding her firmly. "We need to get outta here."

But before I can move, she shoves past me.

"Avery!" I whisper growl.

She storms toward the tree line, hands clenched into fists. "Come on out!" she screams into the dark. "You want to stalk me and threaten me, then come out and fucking face me. Be a man, if that's even what you are. I think you're just a fucking coward."

She spins in a slow circle, chest heaving. "I'm not scared of you! You hear me? I'm not fucking scared of you!"

But her hands are trembling, voice fraying at the edges.

I grab her arm and pull her back. "That's enough."

"No!" she shouts, trying to break free. "I'm done hiding. Whoever the fuck they are, they don't get to win!"

"Not like this." I tighten my grip. "You're playing right into their hands. You don't have a weapon; neither of us do. What do we do if they come at us with a knife, or worse, a gun."

She fights me for another beat then crumples against my chest, breath shaking. "I hate this. I hate not knowing who it is. I hate not knowing who I can trust."

I rest my chin lightly against her hair. "They'll be back," I tell her. "And next time, we'll be prepared."

She nods, the movement bringing me a little comfort after the way she just stormed out here and screamed that she was ready to lay her life on the line for the truth. And that's the thing, right then I realized I don't want her to die for our secrets. I want to keep her as mine.

Shaking off the insane thought, I lead her by my side and I

don't let go of her until we're at her car. "I'm driving," I tell her. "You're too worked up right now."

She doesn't fight me, just slips into the passenger seat and lets me close the door. I watch as she folds her knees to her chest, defeat and worry settling into her bones. How she can go from someone scared to a fighter in seconds baffles me. I think it's one of the reasons I can't bring myself to look away from her.

I never know what Avery is going to do next, and that equal parts thrills me and terrifies me.

Chapter Seven

AVERY

If there was one word for what I'm feeling right now, it would be regret.

Why the hell did I kiss him, let alone let him put his fingers in me? Granted, I wasn't in my right mind. I was frantic, panicked, angry, and feeling every damn emotion on the spectrum. But to let him finger me?

And worse, he enjoyed it. Probably more than I did. I felt it in every move, every pull of his mouth, every sharp press of his fingers. He liked having me pinned there, knowing I'd given in.

God. I can't stand Sebastian. He's cold, ruthless, and arrogant. He's everything I despise in a human being.

Now I hate myself almost as much as I hate him.

I dig my nails into my palms until the sting forces my breath to steady. No. I won't let him get under my skin. But the truth is, he's already in there, buried like a splinter I can't dig out. Has been ever since he pushed his cock between my lips on that damn altar.

The drive back is a blur. I stare out the window, refusing to look at him, refusing to speak.

Sebastian doesn't push. He doesn't smirk or taunt, and

somehow that's worse. Because it means he's probably thinking about it too.

The second he pulls up outside my dorm, I unbuckle and fling myself out the door.

"Avery," he says, voice quieter than I expected.

"We don't need to talk about it," I snap. "Any of it. Ever."

A grin tugs at the corner of his mouth. "I was just gonna say I'll call an Uber to get me home."

"Oh." I gulp, cheeks flushed. "Well, thanks for getting me back here."

"Don't mention it. I mean, after all..." His grin sharpens. "I sort of owe you one for that kiss. Not to mention, what followed."

I reach across the center console and punch him square in the shoulder. "Don't be a fucking asshole, Sebastian."

He laughs. Should've known he'd be an ass about this. For a second I thought maybe regret hit him as hard as it did me. But no, he was just biding his time to throw it in my face.

In one swift motion, I yank my keys out of the ignition and slide back out of the passenger side door.

My heart hammers loud enough to drown out my thoughts as I bolt up the stairs. I don't stop until I'm locked in my room, back pressed against the door.

"You're the one who's an asshole," I whisper to myself. "An absolute asshole."

But no matter how many times I say it—no matter how many times I try to convince myself it meant nothing—I can still feel his mouth on mine and his warm hand down my pants.

He broke apart our kiss to remind me that everything fueling that moment was hate, and that's what I hold onto. Not the way he kissed my neck as if I was his goddess to worship, not how he breathed me in as if I were the only oxygen left on earth. Just the hate—searing, passionate, once in a lifetime hate.

Brogan walks through the door, pizza box balanced on one arm, and a six pack of spiked seltzer clutched in the other.

"Movie night," she says brightly, but as her eyes sweep over me, her smile fades. "You okay?"

I force the best fake smile I can manage. "Yeah, just tired."

She tilts her head. "You sure?"

I shake my head fast. "I'm fine. It's just...it's been a day."

Brogan steps inside, kicks off her shoes and sets the pizza and seltzer on the desk.

"I figured we could use a break," she says, flipping open the box. "And I've got good news, sort of."

"News?" Piquing my interest, I give her my full attention. With any luck, Callan's memory has returned.

"Yup," she quips. "If things stay stable, they might move Callan out of the ICU in a couple days."

My breath catches. "That's amazing, Brogan."

While I'm happy Callan is showing improvement, I can't help but dwell on the fact that he still can't remember what we shared. I wonder if he ever will.

"Yeah," she beams. "They're already talking about rehab once he's healed enough." She grabs a slice of pizza and sinks into the bed. "It won't be easy, but it's progress."

I nod, throat too tight to speak. Callan is making progress and here I am letting his best friend get me off in the middle of the goddamn woods.

I sit beside her with a slice in my hand and I force myself to take a bite I can't even taste.

Brogan presses play on *How to Lose a Guy in 10 Days.* It's the same movie we always watch, and we laugh our asses off every single time.

For a while, I pretend I'm watching. I pretend everything is normal and I'm not drowning in guilt. But halfway through, my phone buzzes on the nightstand. I glance over and my eyes widen when I see it's an unknown number.

Frowning, I pick it up.

Unknown: Nice performance tonight in the
woods.

The pizza slips from my fingers, hitting the box with a dull thud.

Brogan looks over. "What is it?"

I snap my phone facedown. "Nothing." I clear my throat. "Just a spam call."

But my heart is racing because someone was there *again*, and this time, they wanted me to know.

Fortunately, Brogan doesn't press me about the text. I think she's learning when to back off and I'm grateful for that. The last thing I want to do is explain what's really been going on in my life.

We continue to watch the movie—sort of. Brogan laughs at all our favorite scenes, then throws popcorn at me when I don't react.

I try. I try so fucking hard. But all I can hear is that message buzzing through my brain:

Nice performance tonight in the woods.

They saw me. They saw Sebastian. They saw *everything*.

Another text comes through, and this time I hold my breath as I pick up my phone. Brogan doesn't seem to notice, so I turn it over slowly, stealing a glance at the screen. That's when I see the picture that was sent—Me, pinned against that tree with my legs wrapped around Sebastian. No message, just a picture that speaks a thousand words.

My heart drops deep into the pit of my stomach as I stare at the image. It's grainy, but unmistakable. My fingers curling around his hair, his mouth devouring mine like it was owed to him. It's too hard to see what's going on between us, but this is enough to destroy everything I've built with Callan.

My throat burns as I slam the screen face-down on the comforter like that'll somehow erase the image from existence.

Brogan stirs beside me, murmurs something under her breath,

then settles again with a sigh. I stay still, barely breathing, heart pounding against my ribs.

I press the heels of my hands to my eyes and try not to unravel.

What the hell does this person want? A chase? Revenge? To hurt us all one by one?

He already got to Callan—sweet, stupid, brave Callan. He's lying in a hospital bed, broken and bruised, and I'm here fucking around with his best friend like my world hasn't already fallen apart.

A sob punches out of me before I can stop it.

I slide off the bed quietly, my fingers trembling as I pick up my phone again.

I cross the room and my reflection catches in the mirror, flushed and ruined. I don't even recognize myself.

"What are you doing?" Brogan asks, her eyes barely open. She looks as exhausted as I feel.

"Just need to use the bathroom. Be right back."

Stepping into my slippers, I pull open our dorm room door and exit with my shoulders slumped, defeat feeling too heavy to carry.

Once the door is closed behind me, I look at the picture on my phone one more time, just to be sure. Just to burn it into my memory so I never forget how far I've slipped.

My thumb hovers over the message, and for a second, I consider replying, but I don't even know what I'd say. Maybe something along the lines of: *Fuck you! Come out and face me already!*

None of it matters because whoever is doing this, they don't want a conversation; they want control. And right now, they've got it.

They didn't just get inside my head this time. They sank into my guilt and that's where the real damage starts.

I stand in the hall for a few minutes, just staring at my phone, debating texting Sebastian so he knows what's going on. But I decide against that because I don't even want to discuss the kiss, let alone the fact that someone other than us knows it happened.

Swiping away the remnants of any tears on my cheeks, I push the door back open slowly, fully expecting Brogan to realize something is wrong. She always knows.

But when I close the door and step farther into the room, I see she's asleep on my bed. Curled on her side, nostrils flaring slightly with each breath.

With the pizza box still open and the seltzers she brought untouched, I go to her empty bed and slip beneath the covers, tugging the blanket up to my chin.

The movie is still playing, but I don't even watch it; I just stare through it, trying not to think about the kiss, or the photo, or the fact that someone's out there pulling strings and watching me fall apart.

With any luck, sleep will drag me under before I completely fall apart.

Chapter Eight

SEBASTIAN

I LACE MY SKATES TIGHTER THAN USUAL, LIKE MAYBE cutting off the blood flow will distract me from the chaos in my head. But all it does is piss me off more.

"Move your ass, Banks," Coach barks, blowing the whistle as we fly into another drill. I push off the line, blades cutting into the ice, but my head's not in it. It's still in the woods—with her.

Avery fucking Castle. God, I hate her. I hate the way she talks back. I hate the way she gets under my skin. I hate the way her mouth tastes like sin and salvation and some version of heaven I shouldn't be allowed near.

But that kiss? *Goddamn.*

That kiss damn near brought me to my knees. I might have dipped my fingers in her and relished in the way my name sounded on her lips, but it didn't touch the way her lips felt against mine. That kiss did more damage than anything else because it wasn't just heat, it was something deeper. It was a line we should have never crossed but barreled straight through.

"Keep your goddamn stick on the ice!" Coach snaps.

I slam the puck off the boards harder than necessary, skating wide and fast before swinging around and slicing down center ice.

My lungs burn and my thighs scream, but it's not enough to clear her from my head.

Not the sound she exhaled into my mouth or the way her walls clenched around my fingers like she wanted to push me away and pull me closer. And definitely not the look in her eyes when she came.

That wasn't fear or hate—that was desire.

"Sebastian!" Coach shouts. "Focus or get the fuck off my ice."

I pivot fast, grinding to a stop near the bench, and shoot him a glare. "Got it."

But I don't have it because everything is upside down. Callan is still in the hospital. Klein is sniffing around like a bloodhound with something to prove. And now I've got the girl I loathe imprinted on my goddamn lips.

The puck drops again and I throw myself into the play, jostling shoulders and slashing angles, pretending every player in front of me is a ghost I need to bury. Because if I slow down, even for a second, I know she'll crawl back in. Her wild eyes and open mouth saying she hates me while pulling me closer.

By the time practice ends, my legs are burning and my jaw aches from gritting through every drill. Back in the locker room, the guys are high on adrenaline, talking about last week's win.

Slade yanks off his jersey and flings it across the bench. "Tell me y'all saw that last-minute rebound. Almost as good as the one in last week's game. I should've gotten a fucking medal for that shit."

"You tripped over your own stick during the game," Aidric says, towel slung around his neck. "Puck just happened to bounce your way."

"Still scored, didn't I?" Slade grins wide.

"We won because of Callan's setup," Noah cuts in from the corner.

Slade goes quiet for a beat. "Yeah," he says, rubbing the back of his neck. "Dude always knew how to line it up."

Everyone falls silent. The laughter stops and the clatter fades.

Because Callan's not here, and there's a good chance he won't be for a while.

"Coach says he might be out for the season," Slade finally says.

Aidric doesn't look up from the bench across from me. "He's not out; he's benched. Big difference."

"Dude's in a hospital bed, man." Noah sighs. "He can't even remember our last game."

"He's not out," Aidric repeats, jaw tightening. "He's coming back."

I yank off my pads and toss my jersey into the laundry bin, sinking onto the bench beside Aidric.

Noah grins from across the room, shifting the subject. "Did you all see that brunette at the gym yesterday? Tight ass, dark hair." He whistles low. "Thought I was gonna pull a muscle just watching her stretch."

A few of the guys snicker.

"She looked kinda like Avery," Noah continues, grinning wider. "Bet she'd be a good time."

Something sharp snaps through my chest, and my hands curl into fists before I can stop them.

"She's not your type," I mutter, reaching for my water bottle.

"Avery?" Noah raises a brow. "Says who? My type is all women."

"Yeah, Avery. She's a fucking headache," I snap, louder than I mean to. "Girl thinks she's smarter than everyone else, always running her mouth like she's got something worth saying."

Aidric glances at me, sharp-eyed.

Noah just grins. "Headaches can be fun. You just need the right kind of medicine." He cups his balls and gives them a little shake, drawing a round of laughter from everyone except Aidric and me.

My jaw tightens. "If you're desperate enough to put your dick in a pussy that's already been claimed by our boy, be my guest."

Even if I did stick my tongue in a mouth that's already been claimed.

That kiss was so much deeper than anything else we did. It was twisted and raw and I felt it. Felt it more than I've ever felt anything in my life.

Fuck.

Noah just laughs, slapping a hand on my shoulder like I didn't just damn near bite his head off. "Relax, Banks. Didn't know you were so invested."

"I'm not," I spit out too quickly. But all I hear is the echo of Avery's breath against my mouth and the low, broken way she said my name when I pinned her to that tree.

Yeah. I'm not fucking invested.

Aidric watches me from the corner of his eye, his mouth twitching like he knows something I don't.

"So," he finally says when it's just the two of us. He leans forward, elbows on his knees. "You gonna keep pretending she doesn't get under your skin, or should I start placing bets?"

I don't answer because no matter what I say, it won't change the fact that he's right. She does get under my skin and I have no idea what the hell I'm going to do about it.

I finish getting dressed in silence while the rest of the room breaks into more shit talk about girls, game stats, and where they're going tonight.

"Hey," Aidric calls, catching my eye before I reach the door. "We're hitting The Effing Bar for a drink. Darts, pizza—something low-key tonight."

I shake my head, slinging the strap of my bag over my shoulder. "I'm out. Heading to the gym."

Aidric raises a brow. "You never go to the gym after practice."

He's right, I don't. But lately I've been doing a lot of shit I don't usually do.

"Need to clear my head," I tell him.

He studies me for a beat, then nods slowly. "Right. Let me know if you want backup for whatever shit you're spiraling about."

"I'm good."

But we both know that's a lie.

Fortunately, the gym is empty, so I don't have to engage in small talk with the regulars. Unfortunately, that also means I'm stuck in my own fucking head again.

I pop in my ear buds and crank up the volume to "Empty" by Letdown.

I start with the bag, hitting until my knuckles go raw under the wrap, and it's still not enough. I lean over the bar of the weight bench, breath heaving.

She's still there.

And worst of fucking all, he is, too.

What a perfect chaos cocktail—my old man who broke me and the girl who eventually will, both stuck in my damn head at the same time. Fuck them. They don't matter, but the fact that I'm still thinking about them pisses me off even more.

I load the bar with more weight than usual and drop onto the bench, my adrenaline already pushing into my bloodstream.

My chest rises and falls as I wrap my hands around the bar. Then I push.

One rep. Two. Three.

The strain feels good, like it was earned. Even if every press is an exorcism of her.

Not just her, but also the mask in the woods, the crash, the flash of fear in Avery's eyes last night, seconds before she kissed me like she wanted to cut her own heart out.

I keep going until my arms shake and my shoulders burn. Then I drop the bar back onto the rack with a heavy clang and sit up, drenched in sweat.

I drag my forearm across my brow, wipe my hands on my shorts, and lean forward, elbows braced on my knees.

Without any thought behind it, I grab my phone, unlock it, and type out a message.

> Me: Feel like playing detective tonight?

Three dots appear, then vanish before reappearing,

> Little Lamb: On my way to visit my mom.
> Won't be back until late.

I stare at the screen for a second too long. *Of course she is.* Of course she's doing something pure like she's not tangled up in everything dark I touch.

I toss my phone into my bag and head for the showers. Might as well go to the bar and drink myself into oblivion. Nothing else seems to be working.

I walk into the shower room and barely miss bumping shoulders with a guy going out. Seems he was the last one in here so I've got the place to myself.

Dropping my bag down on the bench, I turn the handle to full heat before stepping out of my shorts and getting under it.

With one hand braced against the wall, an image of her flashes in my mind. Not a recent one—it's her dancing in The Lord's Lair a couple weeks ago.

The way her hips swayed to the beat, head dropped back without a care in the world. She knew we were watching. She knew I was watching. And fuck if I didn't notice her.

My free hand trails down, finding my erection as I fight to quiet her voice in my head. The way she gasped and the way her lips tasted like fury and surrender.

She hates herself for what we did, I know she does, and I'm both satisfied and broken over that.

I work myself with short, sharp strokes that match every unspoken thought in my head. Her mouth, her fingers tangled in my hair, the way she bit my bottom lip like she was trying to hurt me, or mark me.

Her voice plays on a loop, telling me not to touch her. But I did it anyways and she fucking loved it—until she finished and came back to her senses.

I groan, biting down on the inside of my cheek as I pump faster. The tension coils deep in my gut. My hips move on instinct, chasing it—chasing her. The memory of her pinned under me against that tree. That filthy, desperate kiss.

I imagine her on her knees, lips swollen, eyes wide.

"Fuck, Avery!" I pant as my orgasm slams into me. I gasp as I come, fists clenched, forehead pressed to the tile and her name snared behind my teeth.

Guilt gnaws at my insides for getting off while thinking about my boy's girl, for touching her, and worse, for wanting to do it again.

Both hands hit the tiled wall and I drop my head down with my eyes closed and my mind tortured.

I'm going to wreck you, Avery Castle. But I can't do that when you're hiding from me.

She said she was busy tonight, as if that means anything. Like she gets to call the shots now. Since when?

I slam the shower handle off, steam curling around me as water slides down my skin. But it's not the heat making my pulse pound—it's the thought of her. Of what she's doing, and who she's with. Is she thinking about me? Is she still pissed?

It's maddening.

This ache isn't just desire—it's something worse. A need to see her, to feel her, to be near enough to shatter that carefully constructed wall she's hiding behind. Maybe if I just catch a glimpse of her face, the tension in my chest will ease.

A slow smile tugs at my mouth as I grab a towel and wipe my face.

I'm done waiting.

I'm coming for you, Little Lamb.

CHAPTER NINE

AVERY

My mom's room hasn't changed. It never does. Same twin bed tucked into the corner with pictures of her old life taped to the corkboard I hung up months ago. At first, I used thumbtacks, but the nurses made me take them down. They said they were too sharp for someone in her condition.

Someone in her condition. Like that makes it easier to swallow. Like it's not code for a woman whose mind is fractured and sees shadows where there are none and reacts to threats that aren't real.

She doesn't look at me when I walk in, doesn't even flinch. She just sits by the window, tracing invisible patterns into the armrest.

"I brought you flowers," I say, holding them out to her. "Sunflowers. Your favorite."

My throat tightens as I cross the room slowly and set the flowers on her dresser. I shove them into a rinsed-out milk jug that I cut the top off because they don't allow glass vases here. It's the only thing heavy enough not to tip over. It's not glamorous by any means, but it does the trick.

"They had fresher ones," I say softly. "But I picked these because I thought you'd want the brightest ones."

She doesn't respond, so I sink into the chair across from her, resting my elbows on my knees, watching the way her gaze skips past me. There's a split second where I think she might say something. Her hand stills and her lips part. I find myself holding my breath, but then she blinks hard and turns her head away. Just like that, I vanish from her world again.

I push myself up from the chair and move to the window, pressing a hand to the sill as I stare out at the garden below. The sun is beginning to set, casting long shadows across the lawn.

At one of the small round tables, a man and woman sit together. She's in a wheelchair; he's beside her, dealing out cards. They laugh at something and smile, the kind of smile that feels like muscle memory.

I think back to playing *Uno* with my mom and dad and how effortless our happiness was.

I blink away the memory. There's a chance my mom will never be able to play again. I'm not sure her mind will ever be settled enough to focus on something as simple as a card game.

When I turn around, I see that she's watching me now. But it's not the way a mother should watch her child. Her gaze is locked on mine, her body rigid in the chair. It's a look I've seen before, like something inside her mind is trying to place me and coming up with something dangerous instead.

Her fingers dig into the arms of the chair, knuckles white with tension. And just like that, I know we're about to spiral again.

"Why are you here?" she rasps.

"I came to see you, Mom," I say gently. "I brought you flowers." I look at them, hoping she'll follow my gaze and relax.

"You shouldn't be here." Her eyes narrow. "You're not supposed to be here."

"It's okay, Mom." I inch closer. "It's just me, Avery."

"No." She jerks back. "No, you're not. You're her." Her voice rises with a mix of fear and fury. "You're evil!"

My stomach drops. "Mom, it's me," I whisper, reaching for her hand. "I swear, it's just me, your daughter..."

"Don't touch me!" she screams, and before I can pull back, her hand flies out.

Fingernails dig into my skin, raking down the side of my neck.

I stumble back with a gasp, hand flying to my stinging wound. When I pull my hand away, I see blood.

The tears come fast and unwanted. Because it's not the scratch that hurts, it's the look in her eyes, like I'm a threat she'd rather see gone.

I back away, trembling. "It's okay," I murmur, more to myself than her. "She doesn't know. It's not her fault. It's *not* her fault."

It still hurts like hell though.

I move to the corner of the room, my throat tight, body shaking. Suddenly, the door comes open, and I expect to see a nurse, but it's Sebastian.

He steps in like he's a wanted guest, a lopsided grin on his face and a bag of candy in his hand. "I brought sour patch kids."

I blink at him, stunned. "What the hell are you doing here, Sebastian?"

He lifts the bag slightly, as if that answers everything. "Your mom mentioned they were her favorite. Figured I'd come bearing gifts."

I just stare at him, heart still thudding, hand clutching my neck. Of all people to walk in right now, it had to be him.

He glances past me toward my mom, then back again. "You okay?"

I swallow hard, head shaking slowly as the memory of the last time he was here runs through my mind. I saw him in the garden with my mom, a smirk on his face and calculation behind his eyes. But today, that edge seems to be dulled. There's something gentler and quieter in his gaze, and I hate that it throws me off.

"You need to leave," I snap as I cross the room toward him. My hands press flat against his chest, shoving him toward the door before it can close behind him.

He can't be here. Not when she's unraveling and I'm barely

holding the pieces together. The last thing I need is Sebastian Banks witnessing this broken part of me, offering that cool, clinical judgment of his. Dismantling my already-crumbling world with a single look.

His gaze moves to my neck then my hand and he puts up resistance. "What happened to you? Are you okay?" The look of real concern on his face takes me by surprise.

"Get out," I say again, quieter this time. "Please."

Before I can force him through the doorway, my mom's voice cuts through the tension behind me.

"Sebastian?" she says calmly, almost childlike.

I stop, and so does Sebastian. Glancing over my shoulder, I find her standing now, more composed than she was minutes ago, confusion softening her features. Her eyes flicker from me to him, then down to the candy in his hand.

"Sour patch kids," she says, her voice tinged with delight. "You remembered."

It's not the fact that he remembered that rattles me; it's that *she* did.

My mom doesn't even remember me, her own daughter, most days, but she remembers him? His name and his face—a single conversation with a stranger about her favorite candy, one that I didn't even know took place?

To my utter disbelief, she moves toward him slowly and wraps her arms around him in a tight embrace. He stiffens for a moment, blinking down at her as if he's unsure how to react. Then he returns the hug, one hand setting awkwardly on her back.

"I knew you were sweet the first time I met you," she says against his chest.

My throat locks. I can't move—can't breathe.

She pulls back, beaming up at him like he's her favorite person in the world. "Thank you for the candy. You always know how to cheer me up."

Sebastian's eyes flick to mine, uncertain now, like he's not sure what the hell just happened either.

I don't know what to do with the way this encounter rearranges everything I thought I knew.

My chest cracks wide open, tears springing to my eyes. My feelings are all over the place. On one hand, I'm relieved, grateful even, that she remembers something real. That there's still a piece of her somewhere beneath all the frayed parts.

That relief curdles when I feel the sting on my neck and see the blood on my hand. My own mother looks me in the face and calls me evil. Yet, here she is, trusting Sebastian without fear, while her arms are wrapped around him and a smile is plastered on her face.

Then there's Sebastian, being careful and gentle...*and kind.* I've never seen him like this, and I don't know what to make of it.

I watch as Sebastian leads her to her chair in front of the window, giving her the candy as she sits. I stand by idly, staring as she rips into the bag immediately, fingers shaking with excitement as she pulls out a handful of sour patch kids. I don't know if she's even allowed to have candy right now, but I don't stop her. How could I? This kind of happiness is a rarity. She's smiling—*really smiling.* And even if it is Sebastian who gave her that joy, I can't bring myself to be bitter.

Before I realize it, Sebastian is beside me watching her too.

"She told you her favorite candy?" I whisper, not taking my eyes off her.

He nods once.

"And you remembered?"

He glances at me, eyebrows raised. "I remember more than you think."

That shouldn't affect me, but it does. It lands somewhere deep and lodges itself in my chest.

We stay like that for a while, just standing in the stillness of a room that, for once, doesn't feel like a war zone. My mom eventually dozes off, candy lying in her lap, sugar coating her lips and her head tilted gently to the side. She looks peaceful, like the storm inside her has quieted for now.

I stare at her, my throat tightening. "One day, that could be me," I whisper. "I could end up like her. Gone, but still breathing."

Sebastian shifts beside me. I feel the warmth of his hand hover near my back, close enough to notice, far enough not to cross a line. "That's not your fate," he murmurs. "You're not her."

"You don't know that," I say. "It could be in my blood, just waiting. And if that's how I go out, I hope someone pulls me back from the edge sometimes. Someone who doesn't give up like my dad did."

I pause before saying, "He stopped visiting last year. Said it was too hard. Then I found out he's dating some airhead named Dina who's half his age and has an eleven-year-old daughter."

Sebastian's brow lifts. "Damn. That's cold."

"I'm supposed to go home for Thanksgiving and pretend everything is fine," I say bitterly. "Pretend *I'm* fine."

"Don't," he says immediately. "You don't owe him anything. Your mental health comes first, Avery."

I glance at him, surprised that he actually called me by my name.

"I'm not going home either," he says after a beat.

I tilt my head. "Why not?"

His jaw tightens and his face shuts down like someone flipped a switch. "No reason."

Bullshit. But I let it go for now.

"Okay," I say quietly. "Sounds like we're both skipping Thanksgiving this year."

His eyes meet mine, and for the first time all day, I don't feel completely alone.

The moment lingers too long, and when his eyes drag down to my lips, I remember what we did in those woods last night.

Guilt creeps back in like an unwanted visitor, but one that

needs to be there because it stops me from doing something stupid again.

I think of the text I got. The picture that shows proof of my weakness and betrayal. It feels like a bullet to the heart. My breath catches in my throat and suddenly the room feels smaller.

What did I do? And worse, what the hell am I still doing? Looking at him like that? Feeling at peace in his presence? This isn't okay. None of it is okay.

I take a quick step back. "I have to go."

Sebastian straightens. "What? Go where?"

"I forgot I have to get up early tomorrow to shoot before class." The words tumble out like a scramble of excuses. "Archery competitions coming up. I need to train."

Sebastian's brow lifts, reading between the lines but choosing not to call me out. "Alright. I should get going anyway. The guys wanted to grab a drink, but I bailed. Probably should make an appearance for a beer or two."

I blink. *He bailed on them to come here?*

That doesn't track, not for Sebastian Banks. I swallow the lump in my throat. "Why'd you come here, Sebastian?"

He smirks lazily. "To bring your mom candy."

I shake my head. "No. Why'd you *really* come?"

His bravado falters for a second. "To keep an eye on you," he says finally. "Someone out there wants to hurt us and like it or not, Little Lamb, you're tangled in that mess now. Can't be too careful."

I laugh. "I think I'm safe here."

His gaze flicks to my neck and the angry scratch. "You sure about that?"

My spine stiffens. "My mom didn't mean to...she would never hurt me."

It's a lie but one I won't unpack for him.

He slips his hands into his pockets, shoulders hitching up. "Honestly? I don't know why I do half the shit I do. Impulse control isn't exactly my strong suit."

"You thought it'd be a fun chance to antagonize me than hang with your boys?".

"Not completely." A faint grin tugs at the corner of his mouth. "Though I won't pretend it's not a perk."

I roll my eyes and start toward the door.

"I just wanted to make sure you were safe," he adds.

I pause. "Since when do you care?"

His expression darkens a shade. "Since you stole our secrets," he says quietly. "And now that you know them, protecting you protects us."

My jaw tightens, but I don't respond because saying I don't want their protection won't change anything. I just want this nightmare to end. I want justice and the truth, and I want it before any of us are too far gone to save.

Sebastian follows me as I approach a nurse, letting her know my mom fell asleep in her chair.

Then, even with my heavy sighs and eyerolls, he keeps following me. "I don't need an escort, you know," I mumble as we push through the front doors and step outside. The air is cooler now, sending a shiver down my back. "I'm perfectly capable of walking to my car without being babysat."

"Not taking chances," Sebastian replies smoothly, hands still buried in his pants pockets. "Could be a stalker out there waiting to attack you."

I shoot him a glare. "Could be someone out there waiting to attack you."

"True. But you've got a track record of getting yourself into trouble."

"I also have a track record of surviving it," I counter.

He glances at me but doesn't say anything because he knows it's the truth.

We reach my car, and he stops a few feet away while I pull the door open. "I'm good," I say softly, not looking at him.

"Didn't say you weren't."

A beat of silence stretches between us then I gulp, knowing I'll probably regret what I'm about to say.

"Thanks," I mutter, just loud enough to be heard. "For showing up and...for not making things worse. I guess."

He smirks. "It's a rare skill. Not ruining things."

"You should use it more often."

He chuckles under his breath and steps back as I climb into the driver's seat. The door closes with a soft thud, shutting out the world. I just sit for a moment, fingers resting on the steering wheel, heart still tangled in knots I don't know how to undo.

When I lean back against the seat, exhaling slowly, for some fucked-up reason, I smile.

It's soft and fleeting, but it's there. And the second I feel it, I hate it. I hate how easy it is to forget how complicated all of this is when Sebastian's around.

I still haven't told him about the photo that was texted to me, and as more time passes, I know I should. It still haunts me—still makes me question all my morals and how I can give in to temptation so damn easily. It's not like that with just anyone, though. I would never kiss a random hot guy in the middle of the woods.

It's Sebastian. He gets under my skin in ways I can't explain. Those eyes that look like they're staring straight into my soul, his goofy-ass smile, and that cocksure attitude. Not to mention his perfectly sculpted body and dimples for days. He's like a fucking drug.

I guess I just keep hoping that if I ignore the text and the photo long enough, it'll stop meaning something. Like maybe no one will ever know. But I know that's bullshit. This person sent it with an agenda, and it's only a matter of time before they share it with someone else.

I need to tell Sebastian. And I will—eventually.

CHAPTER TEN

AVERY

THE ARROW SLICES THROUGH THE AIR, LANDING IN THE center of the target with a satisfying hit.

I lower the bow slowly, exhale, and shake out my arms. My muscles ache from repetition, but I welcome the burn.

The range is nearly empty this morning with just a few early risers, but something feels off. I look around, hoping to shake the uneasy feeling inside me. That feeling like someone is watching. Lately, it's always there and I fucking hate it.

When I don't see anything out of the ordinary, I nock another arrow and pull the string taut against my cheek. But before I release, a shiver runs down my spine.

I drop the bow to my side and do one more sweep of the range, still seeing nothing. It's just paranoia and it's completely normal given my situation.

I shake out my arms again and force my gaze back to the next arrow, but my fingers fumble at the nock. Sweat prickles along my spine as the wind kicks up, rustling the leaves near the tree line.

Totally normal—totally harmless. *So why does it sound like footsteps?*

I swallow hard and scan the woods again, but it's empty, just like every time before.

Jesus, Avery. Get a grip.

But I can't, because what if it's not nothing? What if it's me? What if I'm spiraling? Like her.

I press my fingers to my temple, hard, willing the intrusive thoughts to fade. *You're not your mom. You're not hallucinating.*

But she didn't think she was either. She doesn't realize what she hears and sees isn't real.

One day she was fine, and the next she wasn't.

My stomach flips. I bend down like I'm adjusting my stance, just to breathe. Just to remind myself the ground is still solid.

But whispers creep in my mind.

What if none of this is real?

What if I've made it all up? What if this isn't some game or warning or threat? What if this is the start of my own collapse?

My chest feels heavy, like the trees are closing in and suffocating me. I drop my bow to the ground and grab my phone out of my bag, hands shaking so hard I nearly drop it twice. The screen blurs, tears I didn't even know I was crying making it hard to see. I don't even hesitate when I tap Sebastian's name.

It rings once before he picks up.

"Sebastian," I gasp the second he answers. "I...I didn't know who else to call."

There's a pause, like I caught him off guard. "Avery?"

"I'm at practice. At the range," I say, breaths coming fast and shallow. "I know you probably think I'm insane, but I think I might be going crazy. I feel like someone's watching me again, and I keep hearing things that don't exist and I can't...I can't breathe."

Another beat of silence.

"I just needed to talk to someone who actually knows what's been going on," I whisper, voice breaking. "Because I can't talk to anyone else about masked stalkers and notes buried in the woods. You're the only person who knows this world."

He exhales slowly, voice softer than I've ever heard it. "I'm coming."

"You don't have to—"

"I'm already on my way. Just stay put."

The line goes dead, and I just stand there, clutching the phone to my chest like it's the only thing tethering me to reality. Like Sebastian fucking Banks is the only one who can pull me back and that thought terrifies me almost as much as everything else.

I'm not sure when he gets here. One second I'm curled on the ground, knees tucked to my chest, the next I feel his hand on my back.

"Hey," he says softly. "You're safe. I'm here."

I lift my head and see him crouched beside me, dressed in a cut-off sleeveless shirt and black gym shorts, sweat glistening along his temple and down his throat like he came straight from the gym. The look in his eyes surprises me. He's not smirking, or taunting, he's just watching me with genuine concern.

"There was someone out there," I tell him, voice cracked and breathless. "At least, I think someone was. I was practicing, and suddenly I had this sick feeling, like something was off. Like there were eyes on me from the woods."

He doesn't say anything at first, just looks past me, scanning the woods. "There's no one there now," he says finally.

That's what breaks me.

"I know," I whisper. "That's what scares me the most. I couldn't see them."

I look at him, and it all rushes in—the guilt, the fear, the exhaustion. The pressure I've been keeping bottled under my skin like a bomb.

"What if I'm making this up?" My voice shakes. "What if I'm turning into her? What if I'm already halfway gone and I don't even know it?"

"You're not your mom," he says quietly. "You're not losing it."

"You don't know that," I say, wiping the tears from my cheeks. "It could be buried in my blood, waiting to pull me under like it did her."

Sebastian's jaw ticks, but his voice stays calm. "You're not making this up. Someone *is* out there. We've seen the signs. Me, you, Aidric, even Callan. You're not alone in this. I saw the masked man, we have a video of him. He *is* real."

My throat tightens, and before I even realize what I'm doing, I'm collapsing into the sweat-slick warmth of his chest. He freezes, but then his arms are wrapping around me, holding me tight.

I don't mean to and I don't know why I stay, but right now, it feels safe and I don't want to let that go.

After a moment, Sebastian's voice cuts through the silence. "We're putting together a benefit at the rink next weekend. A masked skating event in Callan's honor."

I pull back slightly, wiping my face. "A masked event?"

"Yeah. A public fundraiser with some local press. Coach is on board and the whole team's in."

"I want to help," I say instantly, something like purpose flaring through the numbness.

He nods. "We could use it."

I manage a weak smile. "That's really nice of you guys. I'm sure it'll mean a lot to Callan."

His eyes hold mine for a second longer than necessary, like he's trying to read between the lines of what I'm really saying.

A few minutes pass in silence before I finally pull myself together. My limbs ache, and my skin feels tight from crying, but I stand, a little steadier than before.

Sebastian straightens his back and watches me like if he blinks too long, I'll shatter.

I swipe under my eyes and look out at the range, where my arrows are still sticking in the target. "I should probably drop out of the competition," I tell him. "With everything going on...it's too much. I can't focus."

Sebastian steps closer. "No, you shouldn't."

I glance at him, brows furrowed.

"Compete," he says firmly. "Compete and win. That's what Callan would want."

Just like that, everything stills. The air, the sounds, even my heartbeat.

Callan. His name alone sends an ache through my chest.

"I'm sorry," I say suddenly, voice cracking.

Sebastian straightens, confused. "For what?"

I swallow hard. "For the woods and what happened between us."

He stares at me, jaw clenched, but he says nothing.

"Callan is a good guy," I continue, lip quivering. "He doesn't deserve that kind of betrayal. And when he remembers, because he will, I'm going to tell him everything. I have to."

Sebastian looks away, draws his fingers across his mouth, slow and tense. "That's your call."

"If I don't tell him, someone else will."

Hesitantly, I reach into my pocket and unlock my phone, pulling up the text, along with the image. My thumb hovers for half a second before I turn the screen toward him.

I wasn't going to mention it, but it feels like the right thing to do. As much as part of me can't stand Sebastian, he deserves to know. Besides, that part of me is shrinking the more and more I see him. The more he's there for me, the less I want to fight him.

His eyes darken and he takes the phone, his fist tightening until I hear the faintest crack of his knuckles.

"Motherfucker," he growls, barely audible.

I watch him pace a slow circle, thumb against his temple. "I'm going to find whoever did this," he says, jaw tight. "And I'm going to break them in half for the hell they're putting us through."

He turns back to me, his expression calmer but still carved from steel. "I've gotta get back to campus. I cut out of my kinesiology class early and can't miss my next class. Professor's a real dick and already hates me."

He pauses, gaze searching. "Let me drive you home. Leave your car and I'll bring it by later."

"I'm fine," I say, even though my pulse still hasn't settled. "Really."

He hesitates, like he doesn't quite believe me. "You sure?"

"I'm sure," I tell him.

He lingers for another moment, then nods once. "I'm only a call away if you need anything."

"Thank you," I tell him sincerely, before throwing in a little bit of our typical banter. "Just so we're clear, I still hate you."

His mouth curls up in a grin. "Hate you more, Little Lamb."

I watch as he walks away, feeling a smile of my own creep up.

After dropping my gear off in the clubhouse locker, I head toward the parking lot alone, my boots crunching the gravel. I reach my car and dig for my keys then pause when I see drops of red on the ground.

My pulse stutters and against better judgment, I follow them, each step heavier than the last. When I reach the trees and the drops end, I spot something lying on top of a pile of brush.

My stomach sinks. *No!*

I crouch, my hands trembling, and carefully pick up the picture of my mom and me. The one that was in my music box, the same box I buried and someone dug up and left on my bed.

My fingers curl around the edges of the picture as if I can will it to make sense. But nothing about this does.

I stand tall, still gripping the photo as I force myself to look around the area, scanning the shadows, daring them to move.

This time, I want to see someone. I want them to step out so I can scream in their face, or better yet, drive my car right over them.

"You're a coward!" I shout, voice ripping through the trees. "You hear me? A fucking coward!"

The echo dies and leaves rustle, then from the edge of the lot, a figure steps into view. I spin, blood pumping hot, until I see who it is.

"Benson," I gasp, clutching my chest. "It's just you."

He steps into view from the gravel path, hands tucked into the front of his hoodie, a gentle smile tugging at his mouth. "Easy, slayer," he says. "It's just me."

I force a breath out, pulse still wild. "Sorry," I say quickly, shoving the photo into the side pocket of my bag before he can notice. "Just...some asshole driving too fast down the road."

He lifts a brow but doesn't push. "Sounded like you were ready to wage war."

I fake a half-laugh. "Yeah, well it's been a long week."

"Yeah," he pauses, features softening as he steps closer. "I heard about Callan. I'm really sorry. That's rough. If you need anything at all, just say the word."

"Thanks, Benson. That means a lot."

"Of course," he says. "Just make sure you're taking care of yourself too, alright?"

I shrug. "I'm trying."

He gives me a small smile, then steps back. "Alright. I'll let you get out of here. I need to head out and sharpen my skills before the big competition this weekend."

I force a smile and offer a slight wave. The last thing on my mind right now is the competition, when it should be the only thing on my mind. A few weeks ago, I was revved up for this, ready to go and take first place. Now, I don't even care. I just want Callan to be better and for everything else to even itself out.

Benson heads back through the parking lot, stopping for a moment as he shoots a glance over his shoulder. "And Avery?"

"Yeah?"

"If it ever feels like too much, don't try to carry it alone."

His words linger long after he disappears. I exhale slowly, glancing back toward the woods one more time. No one is there, but there's this quiet ache of unease inside me I can't seem to shake.

CHAPTER ELEVEN

SEBASTIAN

THE KITCHEN SMELLS LIKE STALE BEER, BURNT PIZZA, and muscle salve. Aidric's parked on the counter, nursing a protein shake like it's whiskey while I slap turkey and cheese between two slices of bread, trying to pretend I'm not thinking about her.

Spoiler alert: I'm always thinking about her.

"You ever wonder how we haven't all died of food poisoning living here?" I mutter, holding up a heel of bread dotted in green mold.

"Nope," Aidric deadpans, grabbing it from my hand. "We're tough as hell. Tainted food can't touch us."

He balls the slice into a dense lump and shoves it into his mouth with a grin.

I recoil. "You're fucking disgusting."

He chews exaggeratedly. "Little penicillin never hurt anybody."

"Maybe it'll kill whatever STDs you picked up from that skank you raw-dogged two nights ago."

"In that case," he says, digging through the bag for another moldy piece, "maybe you should have some, too. Never know what you or Callan might've caught from our little whore, Avery."

My grip tightens around the countertop. "I didn't fuck her," I bite out. "And for the record..."

I stop talking. The words are in the back of my throat, but I force them down. If I say anything more, he'll clock it for what it is. Not just defense, but possession and interest. She's Callan's girl. Maybe not officially—maybe not even now. But she was.

"Whatever you say." Aidric smirks, tossing the bread bag on the counter. "But I know that look. You're already in deeper than you should be."

I toss the bag of old bread into the trash with more force than necessary. "Drop it."

His grin widens, but for once, he lets it go.

I exhale sharply, grab a knife, and start cutting the sandwich. My appetite's shot, but I need something to do with my hands before I punch a hole in the wall just thinking about her.

"She's unraveling," I say quietly. Aidric doesn't answer right away. He just watches me, waiting for me to elaborate. "I think she should stay here."

He barks a low laugh. "You want Avery Castle living under our roof?"

"She's not safe," I tell him. "Someone's fucking with her—with all of us—and she's one bad night away from shattering."

Aidric's brow lifts, skeptical. "And you think bunking her here's gonna fix that?"

"She offered to help with the masked event," I say, leveling him with a look. "This gives her a reason to be here and it gives us a way to keep eyes on her without her feeling like a prisoner."

"So let me get this straight," he says slowly. "Your plan is to bring the most unpredictable girl in the county into our house of secrets, hand her a job tied directly to Callan, and pretend like she's not a fuse standing right next to a match that's already lit."

I glare at him. "It's not about pretending, it's about surviving. She's involved whether we like it or not. At least this way, we can monitor her."

Aidric's jaw ticks, but eventually he nods. "Fine. Just don't come crying to me when your little lamb bites the hand that feeds her."

"She's not biting anyone," I mutter under my breath.

Aidric hops off the counter and tosses the other slice of moldy bread in the trash. "You're sure this has nothing to do with the fact that you've got a raging hard-on for the girl you were supposed to break?"

I glare at him. "This has everything to do with the fact that someone is two steps ahead of us. Someone who isn't just watching her, but getting in her head. That video, the texts, her music box, the photo of her and me in the woods. How the fuck does someone even get their hands on that shit?"

"Photo of you two?" Aidric cuts in, brow arching. "What photo?"

Fuck. I said too much. Got carried away and let it slip. I scrub a hand over the back of my neck. "It was nothing. Just a shot of us in the woods."

His eyes narrow. "You sure about that?"

"Goddamn it." I blow out a breath. "Fine. We kissed in the woods. Someone was watching and sent proof."

Aidric whistles low. "Since when do you just kiss girls?"

I scowl. "It was just a kiss."

He claps a hand to my shoulder. "Uh huh. Just a kiss with the girl Callan was falling for. Sounds real simple."

"I didn't plan it," I grit out. "It happened but it was just a fucking kiss that meant nothing."

I almost tell him the rest, but I won't go there. He's already having a fucking field day.

"Meant nothing to who? You? Or her?"

"Both of us," I snap. "Now fucking drop it. It's no big deal."

Aidric lifts a brow, unimpressed. "Crossing that line is bad enough, but crossing it with feelings? That's a fucking landmine, man."

"There are no feelings," I shoot back defensively.

"If you say so." He leans against the fridge, arms folded. "You sure she didn't kiss you with an agenda? You ever stop to think she might be playing you and Callan?"

"She's not." I hesitate. "She called me today while she was at archery practice. She thought she was losing her mind. When I got there, she was curled up on the damn ground, Aidric. Shaking and crying. You know Avery, she doesn't cry unless she's angry."

His expression shifts slightly, still skeptical, but not dismissive.

"She's spiraling," I continue. "And yeah, maybe she pisses me off from time to time, but if she goes down, we go down with her. She knows too much, and she...she matters."

"Matters," Aidric repeats, voice flat.

I glance away, guilt chewing a hole through my ribs. "Callan would've protected her."

He walks to the sink and stares out the window. "If she stays here, she follows the rules. She doesn't go snooping through our private shit, doesn't start shit with the guys, and she sure as fuck doesn't get a key."

"She won't need one," I say. "She won't be here long enough to need it."

Aidric sighs. "Jesus Christ. The next time we bring a girl into this house, can we make sure it's one who doesn't want to burn it down?"

"No promises."

He shakes his head but nods once. "Whatever. But if she steps out of line again I'm not pulling any punches, Seb."

I smirk. "When have you ever?"

He laughs, tossing a casual wave over his shoulder before disappearing out of the kitchen, leaving the mess he made for the housekeeper to deal with tomorrow.

I stand at the counter in silence, eating the rest of my sandwich wondering how the hell I'm going to convince Avery to stay with us until this shitstorm blows over. There's no way she'll agree. But if worse comes to worst, I won't give her a choice.

My little lamb is going to come play in the wolves den whether she wants to or not.

Chapter Twelve

AVERY

It's been three days since Sebastian and I found the threat in the woods. Three days of unanswered questions and trying to pretend like things are fine.

I haven't told Brogan about what happened between Sebastian and me. Haven't told her about the texts, or the photo I found of my mom and me either. I haven't told anyone anything outside of Sebastian, and every time I close my eyes, I replay it all in my head. But every morning, when that heavy sense of dread makes me question even getting out of bed, I remind myself I have archery practice, classes, and a thousand other reasons to keep moving, so I do.

Pulling open the door to my room, I'm halted when I find Sebastian and Aidric both standing there like a goddamn SWAT team.

Aidric's arms are crossed, jaw locked. Sebastian has that lazy grin that means he's about to do something I'll hate. I don't even have time to mentally prepare myself for their bullshit, so when Sebastian speaks, it's like a cold bucket of water being dumped over my head.

"Morning, Little Lamb," Sebastian says innocently when he's anything but. "Going somewhere?"

"Class," I say flatly, shoving my bag strap higher on my shoulder. "Get out of my way."

"Yeah, see, that's not gonna happen," Aidric mutters, reaching past me to push the door open wider.

Before I can even process it, he's inside my room, touching my shit.

"Excuse me?" I snap, spinning around after him. "What the hell do you think you're doing?"

"Packing," Aidric says, already grabbing my duffel bag off the floor and opening drawers.

I lunge after him. "Put my stuff down!"

"Can't do that," Aidric says, shrugging me off like my grip means nothing to him. "You're coming to stay with us for a while."

"The hell I am!"

Sebastian leans in the doorway, arms braced wide like a wall. "It's not up for debate."

"Oh, it's not?" I hiss. "You don't get to decide where I live, Sebastian."

"Actually," he begins, "we do. Because whoever's playing this game with us is watching you. They're targeting you and it's only gonna get worse. You're not safe here. Not to mention, you put Brogan in danger by being here too. What if this person comes in here to hurt you and they get her instead?"

I pause for a moment, not having thought of it that way. I figured that having a roommate would keep me safer, give this stalker a reason not to get too close. But the arrow in my bed should have proven to me otherwise.

Aidric tosses a stack of folded clothes onto my bed. "You're moving into the house. End of story."

I tear my bag off my shoulder and toss it down as I attempt to put my clothes back in my drawer to no avail. Aidric just yanks them right back out.

As much as they have a point, I'm not someone who handles big changes well, hence why I struggle so much with everything falling apart around me. While I want to keep my best friend safe, I also don't want to be any closer to these guys than I have to be.

"You two are unbelievable." My breaths are heavy as I run around after Aidric, trying to grab things before he can. But he just takes them from my grasp like I'm a toddler.

"Maybe," Sebastian says, following me around my room, "but we're also right."

"No," I say, pointing a shaking finger at him. "You don't get to bulldoze my life just because you suddenly decided I'm worth protecting."

"You've been worth protecting since the second shit got dangerous," Sebastian fires back, taking me by surprise.

"Do you think it's normal for our society to allow anyone to know their secrets? Do you think we're trying to get you to fall in line for funsies?" He's nearly yelling now, more worked up than I've ever seen him.

"I think you like control and you saw the perfect opportunity to exercise it over me."

Sebastian throws his head back, laughing like that's the funniest thing he's heard all year.

"Avery, every inch of you screams defiance. Why would we seek to hold someone under our thumb that we know will fight us every step of the way?"

I cross my arms over my chest. "Because you like a challenge."

He shakes his head, blowing out a long breath. "Think what you want, but Callan will be pissed if we don't keep you safe and he suddenly remembers your little relationship."

I scoff. "So this is about Callan now?"

"Whether you like it or not, you're in this with us. And if you keep trying to handle it alone, it's going to eat you alive."

Aidric looks at me from where he's zipping my bag. "Unless you want to end up like your mom."

My blood turns to ice and I turn to look at Sebastian.

Sebastian's jaw ticks. "Too far."

My heart sinks to my stomach. "You told him?"

"He already knew. Found out when I did."

Aidric doesn't flinch. "But am I wrong?"

Did Sebastian tell him about my fears of turning out like my mom? About my dad walking out on her? Or that he's playing house with some woman barely out of college while my mom withers away in a care facility?

The thought makes my stomach twist.

I scowl, turning away because if I look at him another second, I might actually scream. Just when I thought things were smoothing out and maybe I could catch a damn break, they pull this shit.

And the worst part is, I know staying with them makes sense.

Brogan spends more time at Hayes' place than our dorm, and I do let my thoughts spiral when I'm alone. I've felt the slow slip into obsession, the hunger for answers I can't find. Just last night, I sat on my bed making a list of all the evidence we've found.

I know I'll be safer there, but I'll be damned if I admit it out loud.

I glower at both of them. "You know this is kidnapping, right?"

Sebastian shrugs. "Let's just call it protective custody."

Sebastian must read the war on my face because his voice shifts, softer now. "Hey," he says, but I don't look at him. "You wanted to help with the masked event, right? This'll give you a chance to plan, prep, and work out the details. We could use your brain on this."

My eyes flick to him, hesitant. "So now I'm a charity case with a clipboard?"

He smirks faintly. "Nah. You're our chaotic little event coordinator."

I roll my eyes, but a stupid part of me relaxes a little. It's not much, but it'll be a distraction and a reason to stay that people will believe.

My retort to his comment dies in my throat when my phone buzzes in my bag. I hurry to it, pulling it out of the side pocket.

Brogan's name flashes across the screen and I swipe open the message.

> B: Callan's been moved out of the ICU. No change with his memory yet, but thought you'd want to know.

I stare at the message, reading it twice like the words might change. He's still the same, but he's out of the ICU and that has to count for something, right?

Sebastian must see the shift in my mood. "What is it?"

My mouth goes dry. "It's Brogan. They moved Callan out of the ICU."

Aidric halts mid-pack of my shit, his sharp gaze on me.

Sebastian's jaw flexes, his mouth parting slightly. "Did she say anything else? Like if he's remembering?"

I shake my head. "Still nothing. But this is good. It means he's stronger, which also means it's only a matter of time before he remembers." I stuff my phone back in my bag and sling it over my shoulder. "I have to go there."

Sebastian steps toward me. "Avery, don't. Just wait. Give him time. You showing up there might confuse the hell out of him all over again. Or worse, it could bring up memories he isn't ready to face, not of you, but everything else."

"I don't care." My voice cracks. "I need to see him."

"Avery—"

"Don't," I cut him off. "I'm not asking for permission."

Aidric snorts, shoving a hoodie into the half-packed duffle bag he tossed on my bed. "Told you she'd bolt the second you tried to lock her down."

"I'm not bolting," I snap. "I'm going to check on someone I care about. Unlike the rest of you, I don't treat people like pawns."

Sebastian steps into my path, jaw tight. "I'm just trying to protect you."

"Well stop." I push past him and yank the door open. "Because I'm not the one who needs protecting right now."

And just like that, I run. But it's not how Aidric said, I'm not fleeing from Sebastian; I'm going to Callan, the one who calms the storm of emotions in my chest, even if he can't remember. We had a plan before all of this; we were figuring it out. If he can just remember, then maybe I can have him back and the safety that comes with knowing we have each other's back.

People say I'm the one that saved him in the car accident, but what they don't know is that Callan saved me all those years ago before I broke his break his heart.

His room is quiet when I step inside. A dim light spills from a lamp in the corner and the rhythmic beeping of machines has been replaced by the steady sound of his breathing.

It's a beautiful sound, him breathing on his own.

He's all alone, asleep, so I quietly close the door behind me and watch him for a moment.

The difference in the way he looks is mind-blowing. The color has returned to his skin. His lips aren't blue anymore, and there's less tension around his eyes. He's not hooked up to a tangle of wires and tubes, just a simple IV and a heart monitor.

God, he looks so much better.

I inch closer, each step stealing a little bit of the air from my lungs. I sit beside him, carefully, afraid to wake him, but also desperate to at the same time.

Callan's mind may not remember what we had, but maybe his body will.

I reach out and brush a knuckle along his jaw, His skin is soft and warm. I lean in, heart pounding and press a soft kiss to his lips without expectation because I need to feel him this way; I need one last kiss if this is all I'll ever get of him.

His eyes flutter open mid-kiss, flicking from me to the ceiling to the machines and back to me again.

"Avery?"

My breath catches. "Hey," I whisper. "You're okay."

His brow furrows. "Why...what are you doing?"

"Shh," I whisper, cupping his cheeks in my hands as I press my mouth to his again, this time, I feel him kiss me back and I'm not sure if he wants to, or if it's just a reaction.

For the first time in a while, I feel alive again. Tension crackles between us, electricity that he's sure not to miss. He has to feel it, too. He just has to.

My tongue tries to slither between his lips, but he resists and I pull back, knowing I went too far.

"What the fuck, Avery?" Callan gnashes. "Why'd you do that?'

I gulp, feeling the pang of remorse in my chest. "I...I'm sorry." Tears prick the corners of my eyes. "I just thought maybe, it might help you remember."

His eyebrows cave, confusion etched in his features. "Remember what exactly?"

My shoulders lift, heart heavy. "Us."

The door bursts open before he can respond.

"Avery!" Brogan's voice is sharp, slicing through the moment like a scalpel. "What the hell are you doing here?"

She storms in and grabs my arm, pulling me out into the hallway before I can even explain.

"You can't just come here, we've talked about this," she snaps, keeping her voice low but fierce. "What were you thinking?"

"I...he's not unconscious. He's awake now and isn't it best to try and jog his memories instead of helping him repress them?"

She shakes her head, concern for her brother clear on her face. But I'm worried too, and I can't even fucking see him. "You being here will just confuse him more. Or worse, piss him off."

I swallow hard, shame crawling up my throat. "I'm sorry, B. I just don't know what to do anymore."

Brogan folds her arms, pinning me with a look. "Seems you've been keeping yourself pretty busy. What's this I hear about you and Sebastian getting close?"

I blink. "What?"

"Don't play dumb. People have seen you together. Heard you've been hanging out."

I hesitate. "It's not like that."

"Then what is it like?" she asks, eyes narrowing. "Because Callan's in there with a shattered memory, and if you're out here getting cozy with his best friend..."

For the first time since I met Brogan, I look at her differently. She never accused me of lying before, and her brother might be hurting and in a hospital bed, but her acting like this toward me is too far.

"We're not getting cozy! And me going to stay with them for a little while has nothing to do with me trying to be closer to him."

Damnit. Why did I just say that?

"That's not what I meant," I spit, hoping I can save what I just said.

Brogan throws her arms out wide, pinning me with a death glare. "Are you fucking serious, Ave? You're planning on staying with them?"

"Just for a little while. It's not that big of a deal."

"It's a huge deal! Why on God's green earth would you ever want to stay at that testosterone-infused house with those guys?" Brogan turns her back, pressing her fists to her temples with a frustrated breath. "Jesus Christ."

"I'm not doing anything reckless," I add quickly. "They're putting together some kind of masked skating event for Callan and I offered to help organize it."

Brogan slowly turns back to face me, one brow lifting. "So you're staying at the hockey house to help them plan a party?"

"It's not a party," I say. "It's for Callan and honestly, I just...I don't want to be alone right now. You're always gone and I'm happy you found someone to share your life with, but I just lost my person and I'm falling apart not being able to even see him. Being alone in that dorm room is killing me, B. I feel like I spiral ten times a day and I need something to do, something to focus on."

The words slip out before I can stop them. The last thing I want to do is make her feel any guilt for me going to stay with them. But obviously I can't tell her I'm being forced.

Her face softens. "Avery..."

"I'm not okay, B. I know I haven't said that out loud, but I'm not. And staying over there will make me feel like I'm doing something. Like I'm not just sitting around waiting for him to forget me completely. I'm not getting close with Sebastian; he just talks to me when the panic hits and for some reason it helps."

Her jaw clenches like she wants to argue, but something in her eyes shifts. "You should've just told me that."

I sigh, rubbing my eyes with my fingers, probably smearing my mascara. "I didn't want to drag you into more chaos. You're always at Hayes' anyway and I didn't want to make you feel like you had to stay behind for me. You're happy with him and I want you to keep being happy."

She steps closer, pulling me into a hug. "You're an idiot," she mutters into my hair. "A selfless idiot, but still an idiot."

I let out a shaky laugh. "Guilty."

Brogan pulls back just enough to look me in the eye. "Fine. Stay there. But if those assholes so much as breathe sideways, you call me. Got it?"

"I promise."

"And we're still doing pizza and movie nights. I don't care how busy they keep you."

I nod quickly. "Wouldn't miss it."

She studies me for another beat. "How long?"

"Not long. Hopefully just until the event is over. I'll be out before Callan's home, I swear."

Brogan nods, but I see the wariness still behind her eyes. "Alright. But if this gets messy, I'm dragging you out by your hair."

I chuckle. "Deal."

Little does she know it's already a mess. But I will rise. This stalker didn't just mess with me, they messed with someone I care about. And that means war.

Chapter Thirteen

CALLAN

Brogan walks in, arms crossed and worry etched into every line of her face.

"Hey, Cal," she says as the door clicks behind her. "How're you feeling?"

I shift upright, muscles aching, but not nearly as much as my mind. "Better," I mutter. "Stronger, I guess."

She walks closer, settling into the chair beside my bed. "That's good. Everyone's been asking about you."

I nod absently, gaze drifting toward the closed door. "Why does she keep coming here?"

Her expression falters for just a second. "I..I don't know."

"She kissed me," I say, still trying to piece it together. "Out of nowhere. I didn't know what the hell was happening."

I pause, waiting for her to say something—anything.

"But I felt something," I continue. "It wasn't just confusion. It was like...I don't know. Like something snapped awake inside me. When I blinked, I saw her. Not here in this room but at one of my games. She was in the stands, watching me, and I think I was happy to see her."

Brogan shifts in her seat, her mouth pulling into a tight line. "It could be your memory trying to come back in pieces."

I lean forward, pulse quickening. "So you think I'm remembering something?"

She hesitates. "Maybe."

"Do you know what it means?" I press. "Why she was at my game? What happened between us?"

She looks down, fiddling with the zipper on her hoodie. "I think maybe it means you should give it time. Rushing it won't help."

"That's not what I asked," I bite out, my frustration getting the better of me. "You know something so just tell me."

She lifts her head, expression torn. "I know you and Avery were getting close. Closer than I expected, and I didn't say anything before because..."

Her words trail off and it grates on my nerves. "Because what, Brogan? Just tell me, damnit."

"Because I wasn't sure it was a good idea," she admits. "She's my best friend, Cal. But whatever was happening with you two, it was intense and fast. I just don't want either of you to get hurt."

I stare at her, stunned. "So what? You just thought if I never remembered, it would be easier for everyone?"

She shrugs. "I thought maybe a clean slate would hurt less than reopening old wounds."

A bitter taste creeps up my throat. "Whose wounds, Brogan? Yours, or ours?"

She doesn't answer.

I turn my face away, heart pounding. If the only thing I remember about Avery is a kiss strong enough to ignite a flash of who we were, then maybe I was never meant to forget that part of myself anyways.

"Just take it day by day," she says. "There is no need to rush anything. Your memories will return when the time is right."

"What memories, Brogan? What are you not telling me?" My voice hardens. "You and Avery are best friends. You have to know something."

"I didn't," she says quickly. "You two were so secretive about everything. Whatever happened between you and Avery, it wasn't something you talked with anyone about."

I grind my teeth. "So you're telling me I had something going on with her and no one noticed?"

"I didn't say that," she mutters. "But, yeah. It kind of snuck up on you both, I think. Avery mentioned something right before the crash. Said things were shifting between you two and she didn't know what it meant, but she wanted to find out."

That strikes something in my chest. "And then I crashed."

She nods. "And everything reset."

I drop my head back against the pillow. "Fucking great."

Brogan stands and smooths her sweatshirt. "Look, I wish I had more to tell you. But whatever you two were, it was quiet and just between the two of you."

I don't say anything because I'm not sure what to say. There is so much history with Avery, so much buried pain that I can't imagine how we even began working forward from that. Was it just us hate-fucking? Because her lips on mine gave me an instant hard-on.

Could it have been more and there was a reason we were staying quiet? What does she know about me? Does she know about the Ice Lords?

Brogan leans over and kisses my forehead, but I can't even look at her.

"I've gotta head out," she says. "It's my last week of cheer practice, and Coach will have my head if I miss."

I nod, eyes drifting to the window.

"I'll come back tomorrow. We can talk about it more then, okay?"

"Sure," I say, even though nothing feels settled.

Once the door shuts, I push myself up higher in bed. My body aches in ways I didn't even know were possible. It's not the sharp pain like I had right after the crash; it's deeper now, like I've been hollowed out and slowly stitched back together with pieces that don't fit.

There are blackouts—empty spaces that echo. And Avery is the biggest one of all.

I can still feel that damn kiss. At first, I thought I was dreaming, but the moment her lips touched mine, something cracked open. It was a rush of heat through my chest, and her name echoing through me.

I saw her at my game. And I liked what I saw. I wasn't angry or plotting her demise; I was genuinely happy.

She was in the arena, wearing one of my hoodies like it belonged to her more than it did to me. Her eyes lit up every time I hit the ice. I fucking felt her there. There's no way in hell it was just a dream.

I can't explain it, but something about her lives inside me, beyond the amnesia and damage. It's like that kiss tried to remind me of what my mind forgot.

And that's the scariest part because I remember hating her. I remember thinking she was beautiful, dangerous chaos who stormed into my life and shattered it without warning.

I remember promising myself I wouldn't let her in again, but I must have. I must have healed those parts of myself that despised her so much. And fuck, maybe she's the one who helped me pick up the pieces. Maybe she's the one who made me feel whole again.

Brogan's voice echoes in my head. *"It was intense and fast."*

Sounds about right.

If I let myself believe this and I follow that flicker of memory, I don't know what I'll find. All I know is, I can't just forget again. Not with that kiss still burning on my lips, and certainly not with my heart fighting to remember a relationship my brain forgot.

Chapter Fourteen

SEBASTIAN

She's walking out of the hospital doors when I pull up, and the second she spots me, her jaw tightens like she's already bracing for a fight.

Perfect.

I stop the car directly in front of her and roll down the window. "Get in."

She levels a glare at me. "Excuse me?"

"You heard me." I lean over the center console and push the door open. "Aidric's driving your car home. Now get in."

Her laugh is short and humorless. "That's cute but I'm not some stray you can force-feed and leash."

"No, you're a target," I snap. "And I'm done watching you self-destruct in real time so get in the fucking car."

For a second, she just stares at me, fire burning behind her eyes. Then she sighs and climbs in without another word. Her arms cross and she folds in on herself, turning toward the window and keeping her body as far from mine as possible.

I hate it.

The ride to the house is oddly quiet. No fired insults, no eye rolls. She just stares out the window, lips pressed tight, hands fidgeting in her lap.

Something's wrong. And I hate that I notice—hate that I care.

When we pull up to the house, she drags her feet like she's headed to her own execution. The silence is deafening now. This isn't the sharp-tongued, relentless Avery I know. This version of her feels wrong. It's the one I was worried about, the Avery I see before she breaks down on herself, questioning everything, including her sanity.

I grab her bag from the back seat and push the front door open. The house is its usual blend of chaos, but still quieter than usual.

"Come on," I say, leading her upstairs. I toss a warning look at a couple of guys eyeing her ass as she goes up. *Great.* As if I didn't already have enough to worry about.

I'm starting to think maybe this was a terrible idea. Something tells me I'll be keeping an extra close eye on her while she's here. I know these guys, and they're starving for a feisty and hot as fuck girl like her. The perfect bullet to the heart for any hockey player looking for a challenge.

When we reach the guest room, Avery looks inside, nose scrunching. "Let me guess, this the house fuck room?"

I smirk. "Not officially, but it's happened a time or a hundred."

She scoffs. "There is no way in hell I'm sleeping in that germ-infested, cum-soaked bed."

"Suit yourself. Couch is all yours."

Instead of responding, she steps out into the hallway and glances toward the last door. "I'll take Callan's room."

I blink. "Terrible idea."

"Don't care. You kidnapped me, deal with the consequences." She shrugs, heading to his door.

I pinch the bridge of my nose. "Avery—"

"You said I'd be safe here," she cuts in as she walks down the hall. "And I'll feel safer in *his* room."

I want to argue, but it's a battle I won't win, so I don't even try.

"Fine." I step around her and open the door, dropping her bag beside his desk.

She stands at the foot of his bed, arms limp at her sides, staring at the space like it might swallow her whole.

Then she drops to her knees and covers her face with her hands.

Shit. I knew something was off.

"Hey." I move fast, crouching in front of her. "What's going on?"

Her voice breaks. "I kissed him."

I freeze. "What? You kissed who?"

"Callan. In the hospital." Her voice echoes out between sobs and I have no clue what to do. "He was asleep and I kissed him because..." She sniffles. "I thought maybe it would help him remember."

I look away, jaw grinding. She's holding onto hope like it's the only thing keeping her upright, and I can't lie to myself, a piece of me doesn't want him to remember. Not the crash, or Evan, Not the lies we've buried—and more importantly, her.

If he remembers her and everything they were, then I lose whatever sliver of her I've started to get close to.

Fuck. What am I even thinking right now? Am I seriously admitting to myself that I'd rather my boy lose two months of his life just so he doesn't remember falling in love with the girl who grates on my nerves more than anyone ever has in my entire life?

"I plan to do it again," she whispers, snapping me out of my thoughts. "And again and again, until he remembers me."

I force a breath. "That's a terrible plan, Little Lamb."

"It's all I've got." Her shoulders lift. "I'm losing everything. I can't focus on class. I have no independence because I'm never safe. My mom is locked away from the world and my dad is playing house with Barbie while pretending nothing else exists."

She rubs her fingers on her temples. "And I know it sounds

insane, but for a second, I swear he looked at me like I was someone worth remembering."

I can't respond to that without saying something I shouldn't. So, I just pull her against me. She doesn't fight it. Instead, she presses her face into my chest and lets me hold her. I don't like the way it feels holding her. It's too natural. Too comfortable.

My arms hold her close as she cries, shaking her head slowly as if she can't believe what is happening around her. To be fair, it is a pretty warped shitstorm, but here she is, in my arms, and for some fucked-up reason that makes everything blowing up around us not feel so intense.

Avery pulls back, wiping at her cheeks like she's angry at herself for crying in front of me. She doesn't say anything, just gets to her feet and brushes off her jeans.

"I need to do some homework," she mutters. "Then I'm crashing early."

"Yeah." I nod, stepping back to give her space. "Sounds like a good plan."

She doesn't look at me when she crosses the room, yanking her bag open and shuffling through it until she finds her laptop and a notebook. She sits on the edge of the bed, already trying to shut the world out again, so I take the hint.

"I'll be downstairs if you need anything," I say.

She just nods without even looking up.

I hesitate in the doorway, feeling like I need to say more, but instead, I leave the room and her.

When I get downstairs, low music floods through the house. There are a couple stray chicks sitting on the coach with some of the guys who are playing video games, but none of it touches me.

I walk into the kitchen, grab a bottle of water from the fridge, then lean back against the counter and pull out my phone to send a text to our society's group chat.

Me: Emergency meeting tomorrow night after practice. Dress code, casual. No ceremony. No excuses.

I hit send.

Read receipts begin to pop up and dots appear, likely with guys ready to throw out reasons why they can't make it, but none of them send. They know better.

Ground rules need to be laid out now that Avery is staying here. But more importantly, it's time for us to stop reacting and start hunting. Whoever's behind this shit has taken too much already and I'm done watching from the sidelines.

Normally I prefer to sit behind a screen and plan my attack, but not this time. Someone hurt one of our own and threatened Avery. For that, I'm going to strangle the fucker with my bare hands as I watch the life drain from their eyes.

No one messes with my family.

CHAPTER FIFTEEN

SEBASTIAN

Before I even reach the bottom step, the scent of burnt toast hits me. With my bag flung over my shoulder, I round the corner into the kitchen just in time to see Jeremiah—one of our newest society members and a shitty ass hockey player—leaning one shoulder against the fridge, smirking like the smug bastard he is.

Avery's bag is on the counter next to her notebook, coffee in her hand.

"Don't tell me that look is just for your professor," Jeremiah says, eyes skating down her legs with zero shame.

Avery raises a brow. "You're blocking the fridge and I need creamer."

He doesn't move, just smiles wider. "You want cream, sweetheart? I've got plenty."

My jaw tightens, fists clenched at my sides.

I watch from the entryway as Jeremiah slinks a little too close to Avery, boxing her in like he thinks she might flirt back if he breathes close enough.

"For someone staying in a house full of guys," he says, "you sure know how to make a man feel ignored."

Avery's face doesn't even twitch. "For someone with a functioning brain, you sure don't know when to shut the hell up."

For a second, I prepare to intervene and put this asshole in his place. But Avery is tough as fuck and can take care of herself. That doesn't mean Jeremiah won't pay for this little interaction later. But for now, I just stand, watch, and plot.

Avery steps sideways around him to grab her backpack off the counter, but he reaches out and snares her wrist.

My teeth grit, ready to lunge at him, but Aidric appears out of nowhere. Without a word, he grabs Jeremiah by the throat and slams him back against the wall so hard a painting crashes to the floor.

Avery stumbles back, completely thrown. But not as thrown as I am because Aidric, of all people, is actually defending her.

"What the hell?!" Jeremiah croaks, clawing at the hand around his throat.

"Shut up." Aidric's voice is deadly calm. "You don't get to talk to her. You don't even get to look at her."

"It's fine, Aidric," Avery says calmly.

"She's under this roof because we allowed it," Aidric growls, eyes locked on Jeremiah. "Say one more thing, make one more move, and I swear I'll crush your windpipe just enough to remind you who the fuck you're dealing with."

I step in, placing a steadying hand on Aidric's shoulder. "He gets it," I say evenly. "Take it easy, man. We're already under a microscope."

Aidric holds the choke for one more beat before shoving him back. Jeremiah wheezes with his hands on his throat.

Avery is still frozen, her grip white-knuckled around her bag strap.

"You okay?" I ask her gently.

She nods, even though her pulse is visibly hammering in her throat.

Aidric doesn't even glance at her, just turns and walks off like that entire outburst didn't just happen.

I watch him go, wondering what the hell just happened.

Avery looks at me. "What was that all about?"

I arch a brow. "Welcome to the hockey house, Little Lamb."

She swallows hard, glances once at Jeremiah, then storms out of the kitchen.

The front door swings shut behind her, and the second it does, I shift my attention to Jeremiah.

"Keep your hands to yourself," I grit out. "And if I catch you giving her a hard time again, I'll be the one making your life a living hell."

He laughs like he thinks this is all a joke, but I don't. I let the silence do the talking so he can see how serious I am.

"She's not yours, man."

"No," I say, stepping around him to grab a coffee cup, "but she sure as fuck isn't yours either."

He mutters something under his breath and heads toward the living room, probably to bitch about me and Aidric to Slade.

I don't care because no matter how much I try to convince myself that Avery Castle is a complication I don't need, every time I see her, I'm reminded that complications like her are exactly the kind I crave.

These guys will fall in line; I'll ensure it. Some of them forget who holds the power in this house—in the Ice Lords Society—and I love having the chance to remind them exactly who I am.

⚔

After practice, I didn't even bother showering at the rink. I needed air and distance—fast. Now I'm back in my room, sitting on the edge of my bed as I lace my boots tightly, hoping the pressure around my ankles will ground me.

Coach was on a warpath tonight, barking through every drill, tearing into every missed pass like he wanted to gut us. The guys are running on fumes. I can feel it in the heavy silence and in the frustration that simmers under the surface. Even Aidric is losing his edge.

The way he came to Avery's defense today still has my head spinning. We've all claimed to hate her a time or twenty, but Aidric meant it. The guy fucking hates everyone. So him stepping in and laying hands on Jeremiah wasn't just impulse, it was protection.

It has to be Callan's absence. It's taking a toll on all of us. Not just on the ice, or the Society, but in the house, too. The space he's left behind is so obvious it's fucking painful.

My phone dings beside me and I glance down.

> Aidric: Chamber in 10. The others will be down shortly after. Bring your war face.

Avery is at the archery range with Benson, so I don't need to worry about her snooping around tonight, and at least with Benson there, I know she won't get herself killed or do something fucking stupid like she always does.

Downstairs, Aidric is waiting for me at the staircase that leads to the chamber. He tips his chin. "Ready to fuck shit up?"

A devious grin pulls at my mouth. "Always."

"Good," he says. "Because without Callan, we're playing blind. I want Eaton Rapids' best player out before Friday's game."

I raise a brow, but he doesn't elaborate. Whatever he's cooking up, I know it'll be dark.

We head down, and as soon as we hit the bottom step, we stop cold.

"What the fuck," I hiss.

Spray-painted across the walls in dripping black paint are random threats:

You will pay.

I'm coming for you.

Rot in Hell.

Each phrase is loud and personal, like whoever did this wanted to be heard and feared.

On another wall, the Ice Lords' crest is slashed out in red. Then, scrawled across the back wall in are the words…

You were kings. Now you'll crawl.

Aidric drags his hand over his jaw, but he doesn't speak because it's my role to be his voice in this sacred space.

I walk to the nearest wall and run my fingers over the paint. "It's fresh. Probably less than a few hours old."

Aidric lashes out and kicks a chair across the floor, breaking it in two as it crashes into the wall.

A chill slides down my spine. We've always had enemies, but no one's ever had the balls to breach our house, let alone The Chamber.

I yank out my phone and open the backdoor security app I coded myself. One camera is fixed on the main entrance to The Chamber so I scroll through the feed, scanning each empty frame during practice hours.

At first I'm certain I'll come up empty-handed, but then a single frame glitches, and when it clears, the door is slightly ajar.

"Something's not right," I mutter, pulse spiking.

Aidric steps beside me as I switch angles to the hallway cam. That's when we see a cloaked silhouette, masked and moving fast, headed straight for the back wall.

"There," I say, tapping the screen. "That's the old boiler hall."

Aidric narrows his eyes.

My throat tightens. "No one uses that corridor. Surface level was sealed off years ago. Only the founders and us even know it connects to The Chamber."

The footage glitches again and when it returns, the figure is gone.

"They didn't stumble in," I say. "They knew exactly where they were going. If it's not one of us, it's either someone who used to be, or someone who's been watching us for a long fucking time."

Aidric stares at the red-slashed crest on the wall, rage simmering behind his silence.

I save the footage, mark the timestamp, then set a motion alert. The moment that corridor so much as breathes, I'll know.

One by one, the others file down the steps. But I raise a hand, stopping them before they can speak. "I swear on Edison Einhorn's grave," I say, voice razor sharp, "if one of you did this...if someone in this room betrayed us, I will bury you where you stand."

I look at each of them, hoping like hell there isn't a snake in the bunch. Loyalty is everything in this society and if one of our own members is the one behind all the shit happening lately, I'll kill them with my bare hands before feeding their corpse to the wolves.

Maintaining professionalism, I clear my throat and cross to the room, stepping onto the altar, along with Aidric. "This," I say, gesturing toward the walls, "this isn't just an act of vandalism, it's a declaration of war."

Whispers ripple through the room and I raise my hand again, silencing them.

"I don't know who did this," I continue, "but they got in. They found our sanctuary and they want us exposed and crawling." I glance at Jeremiah, who has the good sense to avert his gaze. "And speaking of crawling," I say. "Some of you seem to have forgotten what loyalty looks like."

Jeremiah's throat bobs. "I didn't—"

"Don't finish that sentence unless you want to clean this room with your fucking tongue."

Aidric stands behind me like a statue, silent and unmoving as he watches.

"As Lord Speaker, I'm invoking rite protocol," I announce. "Tomorrow night, we will reconvene for inspection. Everyone will arrive in full ceremonial cloak and mask," I continue. "No excuses. You show up, or you don't show your face here again."

My eyes sweep across the circle, landing on each of them

because I want them to feel this in their bones. "Someone out there is impersonating us. Or worse, they *are* one of us."

I let that sink in while they look from person to person, distrust blooming.

"We will inspect every mask and every cloak, along with every name and role." I pause. "Show up, stand tall, and wear your legacy on your goddamn face."

Aidric shifts slightly, his silence amplifying every word.

I pause for a beat before continuing. "And now, the other matter." I step forward, squaring my shoulders. "Avery Castle is staying here."

A few brows lift, murmurs rippling through the room.

"She was marked, that makes her one of us. Whether you like it or not, she is under our protection and she's completely off-limits" I lock eyes with Jeremiah. "Cross a line, and you'll wish the person coming after us got to you first, just like they did Callan."

Jeremiah scoffs, leaning back like he's above it all.

"Jeremiah," I say. He meets my gaze, jaw tight. "I want every inch of this room cleaned by tomorrow night."

"You're kidding." His eyes are large, disbelief written into his features.

I step down, right into his space. "Do I look like I'm kidding?"

He tries to hold my stare but fails miserably. "I was just being friendly."

"Then consider this me returning the favor," I say through my teeth. "By not breaking your goddamn jaw."

Slade claps him on the back, chuckling. "Better get started. The bathroom's probably next."

"Quiet," I shout. "We're not finished here. We play Eaton Rapids in four days. That means we've got two days to crush their streak before they crush ours."

Aidric moves beside me and slips a folded piece of paper into my hand without a word.

I glance down at the words scrawled across it and my jaw clenches. Rolling my neck slowly, the tension cracks loud in the silence, then I lift my eyes to Noah, another one of us who seems to be running his mouth a little too much.

"Noah. We need you to take out Hershman, their star player," I say. "We're not just taking down their team; we're dismantling their foundation."

Noah lifts a brow. "Meaning?"

"Meaning this isn't about scoring goals anymore. It's about destruction."

I flick the paper with my fingers, then tap it once.

"Start with their anchor. Dig into his personal life and find weaknesses, family drama, cheating rumors, a girlfriend with wandering eyes—anything that sticks."

Noah's eyes narrow. "What if nothing sticks?"

I smirk, handing the paper to him so he can read it on repeat until the job is done. "Then you make it stick. Fabricate, leak something, tip the press. We don't need the truth; we need to bury them."

Noah swallows, nods once, then grabs the paper from my hands.

My eyes sweep the room again, letting the weight of the moment press down on everyone. "No mercy," I say. "Not on the ice, not off.

Aidric grins beside me, hands folded in front of him as he stands tall.

"We're done here," I announce. "I'll see everyone after practice tomorrow, seven p.m. sharp."

They waste no time getting out of here. Our fellow Ice Lords file out fast, shoes scuffing against the concrete, whispers trailing behind them. Jeremiah lingers at the end of the line, and I take advantage of the moment.

"Jeremiah!" I shout up the stairs. "Fetch your cleaning supplies. You've got a long night ahead."

He mutters a curse under his breath then vanishes.

I laugh before letting the silence stretch around Aidric and me. As I look at the space, *our* space, anger simmers in my blood, but it's shifting now, giving me the fuel I need to take this fucker down.

I glance at Aidric, the exhaustion etched across his face mirroring my own. "Drink?"

He snaps his fingers and points toward the stairs without a word.

We go up in sync, moving through the main floor then up the staircase off the hallway, not stopping until we're at the top floor.

I push open the heavy door and enter the Lords' Lair. Aidric heads straight for the fully-stocked bar, grabbing a bottle of bourbon. He pours two shots into a crystal glass and slides it down the polished bar top without looking at me. Then he pours his own, swirling it slowly.

"Secrets are slipping," he finally says.

I take a sip, letting it burn down my throat. "Whoever left that message downstairs knows exactly what they're doing."

Aidric downs his bourbon in one gulp, the glass hitting the counter with a hard clink. "Then we end it now."

His words hang between us, me wondering how the hell were supposed to end it, and him likely forging a plan.

"I ran into Klein at The Effin Bar," he says grimly. "He was sniffing around again. He knows more than he's letting on." He pauses, jaw tight. "And he still has my fucking rock."

My stomach twists. That rock might not mean shit to anyone else, but to us, it means everything.

Aidric pushes off the bar and begins pacing, the tension in his movements unmistakable. "I want it back."

"You planning to ask politely?" I chuckle.

He shoots me a look. "Fuck that. I'm breaking into his office."

I blink. "Seriously?"

"One hundred percent. I'm done waiting. It feels like that's all we fucking do anymore. We get the rock; we lock our secrets down, then we find the traitor and gut him."

I throw back the rest of my drink and set the glass down beside his. "You're not going in alone," I say, voice hard. "You go, I go. Or..." I let the pause linger. "We send someone else. Jeremiah or Noah could use a little humility."

Aidric's mouth twitches. "Tempting, but nah. A little risk sounds like fun. We do this ourselves. Tomorrow night, after the meeting. Offices will be closed and we'll have an easy in, easy out. It's the North Ridge Police Department, not the goddamn NYPD. Should be a walk in the park."

Something primal rises in my chest, my adrenaline kicking in high gear. It's been too damn long since I've gotten my hands dirty—too long since we've stopped playing defense and started hitting back. Like Aidric said, we've been standing still, watching control slip through our fingers while someone out there plays god with our lives.

Not anymore.

"Let's fucking do it," I say, slapping my palms against the bar top. "Let's take back what's ours."

Aidric leans against the bar again, eyes narrowing. "We need to distract the girl. Last thing we need is her tailing us and blowing the whole thing up."

I nod. "She's got that archery competition coming up. Told me she might drop out because her head hasn't been in it. But if I pull some strings, I might be able to get her booked at that new indoor range in Chesterfield. There's not a doubt in my mind she'd go. I'll send a couple of the guys to watch from a distance. She'll be none the wiser."

Aidric's eyes glint. "Do it. She'll probably drop to her knees and suck your cock as a thank you."

I huff a laugh. "Wouldn't go that far."

He raises an eyebrow. "But you wouldn't stop her."

I look down at my glass and bite back a grin.

Fuck no I wouldn't.

Chapter Sixteen

AVERY

I don't remember falling asleep. One second I was scrolling through photos of Callan and me, and the next, I was out cold. His bed still smells like him. It's softer than mine, a little bigger, too. And somehow, despite the way it shatters me, it's the only place in this damn house I feel content.

The ache hits before I can stop it, missing him, not just by my side, but intimately too. Once you've had sex with a guy like Callan, stopping feels impossible.

The throbbing need for him builds slowly at first. It pulses low in my stomach, slow and hot, a hunger I've been pretending I don't feel. I squeeze my eyes shut, but all I see is Callan. His bright eyes, messy hair, full lips I swear I can still taste. His voice, his touch, the way he used to look at me like I was the only girl in the world. It fucking wrecks me.

God, I want him.

My thighs press together instinctively, chasing friction that doesn't come. Heat coils tighter and I give in to the pull. My hand drifts low, slipping beneath the hem of my shorts and into my aching center. I find my sensitive clit and stroke in slow circular motions until tension crackles up my spine. My back bows off the bed a little as I move with my fingers, chasing what I need.

I imagine it's Callan's mouth on me, sucking like it's his favorite taste. Desire builds deep and I arch my hips, muscles tightening as I edge closer. I'm dripping and needy, a desperate mess that would have him smug as he watched me beg for it. I close my eyes tight, biting down a moan.

"Oh God, Callan," I whimper, muscles clenching. I'm so close, that bittersweet euphoria waiting just beyond the edge of the cliff I want to fall over.

But then, I freeze when I hear the sound of footsteps. I turn my head slowly and, leaning against the doorframe like he owns the place, is Sebastian.

His eyes are dark and dilated as they devour me, the dim light from the bathroom making his silhouette look more sinister. My gaze drinks him in, still half asleep and drunk on lust. I can't miss the way his hands flex as if he is trying to maintain control, his nostrils flaring in an emotion I can't read. His chest is bare, aside from the black ink tattooed across it. But most impressive is the bulge pressing against his joggers that tells me exactly how long he's been watching.

My breath catches. "Get out," I whisper, but even I can hear the tremble in my voice.

He doesn't move or speak. He just drinks me in like I'm something filthy and sacred all at once. I watch him lick his bottom lip as if he were begging for a taste, just how I imagined Callan looking at me just a minute ago.

Heat floods my cheeks and my limbs go rigid. Maybe if I play it cool and pretend I was only napping, I can salvage this.

I shift onto my side, tugging the blanket higher. "You watching me sleep now?" I mumble, hoping I can use sarcasm as a shield. "That's not creepy or anything."

He doesn't take the bait, just leans a shoulder against the frame, jaw ticking. "You talk in your sleep."

I scoff. "I do not." Turning in the bed, I try to hide my damp fingers as I look at him.

"You did just now," he says, tone raspy. "You said his name."

I freeze.

My throat tightens. I don't have to ask whose name because I already know.

"Of course I did," I snap defensively. "This is his bed and I'm wearing his fucking hoodie. His scent is still on the pillow. It's only natural I'd talk about him in my sleep."

"You weren't sleeping." He grins, biting that lip my gaze was fixed on just a second ago.

"Was so."

Sebastian steps into the room and kicks the door shut with his heel. The click of the latch sounds louder than it should.

My heart jumps while his expression hardens. There's something behind his gaze, jealousy maybe?

I sit up slowly, pulling the sheet with me. "What do you want, Sebastian?"

His breaths are short, eyes dropping to where the sheets are twisted around my legs. They linger far too long and I shift under the weight of his stare. The heat between my legs roars back to life as if his presence alone fuels the desire I didn't get to finish.

His eyes flick up, locking on mine. Something in them smolders, like he walked in and caught the end of my undoing and now he wants to pick up where I left off. And fuck me, maybe I want him to.

My mind is still half asleep, half with him. I'm probably not thinking clearly, and right now I'm not sure I want to. Is it awful that I want him right now, that I want him to make me forget and feel good just like he did in the woods?

"You're being awfully quiet," he says as he comes closer and closer. "That's not like you."

I gulp, clutching the sheet tighter. "I have a lot on my mind."

"Yeah?" He takes a step closer, thighs touching the bed right beside me now. "Like Callan?"

I flinch. "Don't go there."

"Why not?" He trails a finger down my heated cheek. "You're

living in his room, sleeping in his bed and masturbating to his memory."

My breath hitches and I pull away from his touch. "Fuck you."

"No need," he says, voice dark and steady. "Looks like you're already doing that to yourself."

He's so close now I can smell him and his scent twists my insides. Even when we were out in the woods, when I was terrified and confused and covered in dirt, his scent made me feel calmer, safe. Even if Sebastian is the furthest thing from safe there is.

"Did you come in here to start a fight?" I bite, lifting my chin. "Because if so, congratulations. You win."

He leans down, one hand planting firmly on the bed beside me. "I didn't come to fight, Little Lamb. You're the one always looking for a battle."

"Don't call me that," I whisper, not strong enough to speak louder because his presence causes that ache I was chasing to build.

"Why not. Afraid you'll start to like it?"

I blink up at him, heart racing. I should shove him away or scream at him to get the hell out. But I don't. Instead, I stay frozen, burning from the inside out.

His gaze falls to my lips.

"Tell me not to do it," he murmurs.

"Don't do it," I echo, heart hammering.

Neither of us moves; he just hovers there, breathing my exhale and staring me down.

Then just when I expect him to kiss me, he jerks his gaze away and curses under his breath, "fuck."

I relax slightly, exhaling a pent-up breath, just before he returns, crushing his mouth against mine in a brutal, blistering kiss.

It's not gentle, and it's not sweet. But it is all-consuming, the same way it was in the woods. Doubt doesn't filter in when he's this close because all I can see, all I can feel is him. *And I need more.*

I gasp into his mouth, fingers fisting in the front of his shirt as I drag him closer. One of his hands moves to the back of my head, fingers tangling in my hair as he kisses me deeper. When he pulls ever so slightly, turning my head to get a better angle so his tongue can swipe in, I whimper into his mouth and he devours it like a wolf in desperate need of his next meal.

His hand drops from my cheek, and in a swift motion, his arm scoops under me, lifting me effortlessly as the sheet falls away. Suddenly, I'm in his lap, straddling him and every thought that isn't about him burns to ash.

His mouth crashes over mine and we get lost in each other. His hands grip my hips, dragging me against the hard line of him, over and over, like he's trying to grind the doubt right out of me.

He tears his lips away just long enough to trail his mouth along my jaw, down the column of my throat, grazing it with his teeth. "You think you hate me now," he growls, voice wrecked, "wait 'til I have you begging."

"Arrogant bastard," I hiss, clawing at his shirt until he's free of it. "Shut up and get to work or I'll be the one making *you* beg."

He chuckles, a sound that goes straight into my chest, lighting me up with a spark of joy I needed more than I needed my next breath.

In one motion, he flips me beneath him. His lips find mine again, his body pressing down like gravity itself is pushing us together, giving us no choice but to cave to this burning need. My legs wrap around his waist like they were made for it. Even if my brain is screaming to stop, my body is doing exactly as he said it would, begging for more.

Sebastian growls into my neck, and something in him snaps when I arch into him while his hard cock presses to my center. He releases my wrists only to slide his hands under my hoodie—Callan's hoodie.

His eyes darken as he shoves it past my ribs. "Take it off," he commands.

I hesitate, one hand clutching the fabric. For just a second I think about telling him no, I debate on breaking this up right here and now and pretending that this passion between us doesn't exist. But when he senses my hesitation, he growls, "now!"

All my doubts fade into thin air because the way he's looking at me right now, that predatory gleam in his eyes, is exactly what my body has been craving.

Desperate for more, I do as I'm told and yank the hoodie over my head, tossing it to the floor. His eyes drag over me like a brand, his hands claiming me again.

This was a terrible time not to have on a bra or panties, but judging by the look in his eyes, it's more like perfect timing. He would've taken them off anyway, so maybe I've just saved us both the trouble.

"Fuck, Avery," he grumbles, equal parts irritation and awe. "You're...breathtaking."

My heart stutters because that might be the first compliment Sebastian Banks has ever given me, and I don't know what to do with it. I'm not sure how to accept softness from someone who's made a game out of grating on my nerves. He can look at me like he wants to own me— that's one thing—but the admiration in his gaze is not something I'm used to. In fact, I've only ever seen this in Callan, but how Sebastian does it holds an edge of darkness I want a piece of too.

In the next breath, he resumes kissing his way down my throat, his breath hot and taunting against my skin. His hands trail lower, dragging across my breasts, my waist, my thighs like he's mapping a territory that's already been claimed.

"I can taste how much you want this," he whispers into my ear, sending shivers down my spine. "You touch yourself thinking about him, but it's me you see."

I inhale sharply, nails raking down his back. "You're so full of yourself."

Even though he might be right, I'll never admit that to him. It would give him too much power, and when it comes to the dynamic between the two of us, I can never let him hold the leash. I don't trust him not to use it to yank my heart out.

"Maybe so." I feel him grin against my throat, hips grinding into mine. "But you still haven't told me to stop."

Because I can't, asshole. I want this too bad.

But I don't say that. Instead, I let guilt simmer beneath the surface.

His lips brush mine again. "Say it," he dares. "Say you hate me."

"I hate you," I gasp, eyes fluttering closed, body arching into his thrusts. His hard cock feels so good between us, my legs spread as so he can press into my clit harder.

"I know," he says, kissing me again. "Now, Little Lamb, hate me louder."

My breath hitches as he grabs my wrists and pins them above my head. My heart pounds so hard I'm sure he can feel it against his chest. His mouth hovers above mine just enough to make me ache.

"Tell me to stop," he says, voice low and hoarse. It's like he's having a battle with himself, torn between what is right and wrong in this moment. But if there is one thing I know about Sebastian, it's that he has no problem making the wrong choice. And right now, I sure as fuck won't give him a reason to.

This man is sin—poison flooding my veins with a dark promise, but I have no plans to get rid of it. As much as I know this is dangerous territory, I can't find a way to stop.

I lift my chin and kiss him like the answer to all of my problems is written in the taste of his mouth, and not my damnation.

His hand slips beneath the waistband of my shorts, fingers sliding over my soaked cunt like he's been there before—because he has. Two fingers plunge deep and the moan that leaves me is nothing short of obscene.

I swear I forget how to breathe. My body bows off the bed as sounds of pleasure slip from my lips.

Sebastian drinks in every sound. "Look at you," he breathes, eyes locked on mine. "Pretending you don't want this when we both know you *do*."

I dig my nails into his back. "Don't flatter yourself. You're a convenient mistake."

He lets out a dark laugh, mouth brushing mine. "Then let's make it one hell of a mistake."

In the blink of an eye, his fingers slip out of me and his hands drop to my hips. He grips the sides of my shorts and yanks them off in one swift motion. The air feels cool against my soaked pussy and I suck in a sharp breath.

Before I can fully inhale, he buries his face between my thighs. His tongue drags up my center with devastating precision before he flexes the muscle, swirling slow, deliberate circles at my entrance while his thumb presses unrelenting against my clit.

A moan claws its way up my throat as his fingers plunge back inside me. He builds a rhythm, mouth and hands in sync, working me like he knows exactly how to make me shatter to pieces.

He hums against me, a low vibration that rips through my core. My legs tremble, fingers fisting the sheets, and I'm so fucking close I could scream.

Every movement, every breath, I fall deeper and deeper into his trance. It makes me forget about the world, my problems, the stalker, my fears of turning into my mother, and the worry that Callan will never remember me.

With Sebastian between my legs, nothing else exists.

And when he says my name low and rough right against my pulsing center, I come undone.

He doesn't stop, doesn't even let me breathe. He chases the sound of my breathing, the tremble in my thighs, and the heat of my skin. And just as the last wave crashes over me, he pulls out his fingers.

I shift, panting and aching for more because he left too soon. Just when I think he's finished with me, he shoves down his joggers and boxers. Those stormy eyes land on mine, hunger so clear I'm almost afraid he will tear me apart. And that fear doesn't ebb when my gaze roams down his body.

My jaw nearly hits my chest as I drink in his huge cock. It's no wonder this guy has such big dick energy. I'm literally speechless.

He flashes me a wink, heat flooding through me. Stepping forward, Sebastian leans over me, chest brushing mine. For a second, I think he's going to kiss me again, but instead, he reaches past me to the nightstand, yanks open the drawer and pulls out a condom like he knew exactly where to find them.

My heart jumps into my throat, knowing what's coming next, and also knowing I don't have the strength to stop it because I want him so fucking bad right now.

I watch as he slides the condom on like a tight glove. He wastes no time climbing on top of me and my traitorous legs part immediately. With his face hovering over mine, he looks into my eyes and for a heartbeat, I think I might see sincerity lurking there, like maybe he's going to ask if I'm sure, which I am. *Fuck yes, I am.*

But instead, he doesn't make me say it; he just glides the head of his cock to my entrance and slips inside.

He eases in, inch by inch, stretching me apart until he's fully seated inside me. Our breaths sync, hearts pounding to the same rhythm. For a moment, we don't move. We just stare at each other, eyes locked like we're both waiting for our minds to catch up to what we're doing.

When my mouth parts, a wave of hesitation comes over me, but he doesn't let the idea take root in my mind. His fingers curl around my waist, grounding me as he begins to move. His head falls to mine, forehead to forehead. He's slow at first, like he's trying to memorize the way our bodies fit together. The muscles in his arms strain, veins bulging in a way that has me licking my lips.

My hands slide up his back, pulling him closer—deeper. And when I finally give in, letting him have a piece of me I swore I wouldn't, he realizes it immediately.

His jaw clenches, and a groan escapes his throat as he buries his face in the curve of my neck.

"You feel..." His words trail off and he groans again, punctuated with another thrust that has me seeing stars. "God, Avery."

We fall into a rhythm, that's not fast or furious. Just a slow, deep roll of our hips.

He kisses me again, this time softer, like the fight between us has shifted into something far more dangerous and real.

The bed creaks beneath us, the headboard tapping against the wall. *Callan's bed.* My heart cracks with the thought, but then Sebastian hums against my skin and it drives the guilt somewhere I can't reach.

His hand slides up my thigh, gripping tight. "Fuck," he breathes, teeth grazing my jaw. "You're driving me insane."

Our chests stick together, fused by sweat. I tilt my hips, meeting each of his thrusts, and the pleasure builds again. My senses are on fire—his scent, the scrape of his stubble against my skin, the low growl in his throat when I moan his name.

"Don't stop, Sebastian," I whisper, voice frayed.

He pulls back just enough to meet my eyes. "Wasn't planning on it."

Driving into me again, he goes deeper this time, picking up his pace. My head falls back against the pillow, lips parted, body trembling.

His forehead drops to mine, eyes wide open as he watches me. "I shouldn't want you like this," he breathes.

His words hit like a match to gasoline, rearranging everything I thought I knew. We're here, doing this, but...Sebastian wants me? In which way? Sexually? Emotionally?

I don't respond because I'm not sure what I should say.

His eyes darken, and for a second I think he's going to pull away. But instead, I act first. I don't know how to give him words, but I wrap my hand around his neck, keeping him close to me. I make it clear that I don't want this moment between us to end; I don't want him to walk away. And the moment I do, he captures my mouth with his again in a desperate, hungry kiss.

This isn't just lust. It's grief and rage. It's both of us burning the house down and pretending we're not the ones who lit the match.

My entire body feels like it's been zapped to life, tingles shooting through my veins. I clench my walls around him, muscles tensing, and he lets out an airy groan. "Avery..."

I heave, breaths coming in stutters, and I cry out. My second climax hits harder and I gasp into his mouth, breaking apart around him.

"Give it to me, Sebastian. Give me all your hate."

He follows with a growl, hips stuttering as every muscle in his body locks down tight. He surges deep, pausing for a moment as he comes. His body shivers with the intensity of it and when he puts a hand between us, rubbing my clit while he pumps in and out in shallow thrusts, I come apart again.

My voice shakes, and he watches the tremble of my lip, the intensity of this moment clear as day. And the second I come down, he relaxes his body on mine. He pins me there, under him, and it's the most comforting thing I have felt since the night I called Callan in a panic.

For a moment, the room is nothing but the sound of our breathing.

I turn my head, eyes fixed on the ceiling as silence wraps around us. I'm in Callan's bed, tangled in his sheets, naked, and freshly fucked by his best friend. Someone he considers family.

The weight of what we just did slams into my chest like a goddamn wrecking ball, and Sebastian must feel the hit too because he lets out a long sigh that has nothing to do with pleasure.

He rolls off me and sits on the edge of the bed, running both hands through his damp hair. "Well...that was a shit idea," he says, not looking at me.

I feel a pang of humiliation in my chest, but I just blow out a dry laugh. "Yeah. But we did it anyway."

He glances over his shoulder, something unreadable in his expression. "You okay?"

I nod. "You?"

"Doesn't matter," he mutters. "We've already crossed the line. There's no going back now."

I don't know what this means or how we come back from it. But I know one thing for certain, this isn't over. Not even close.

Minutes of silence pass, both of us trapped in our thoughts. I pull the sheet tighter around me, swallowing the lump in my throat. I refuse to cry because who the hell cries after sex? I won't be that girl.

It's not like I cheated on Callan because we were never official. But in my heart, it feels like I did. Not that he'd even care. He doesn't remember our deep talks or the way he looked at me like I was more than the chaos I brought into his life. He has no idea that when he crashed, my heart was in that car too.

Sebastian speaks suddenly, breaking the silence. "Don't drop out of the competition."

I blink, caught off guard. "Huh?"

He leans forward, elbows on his knees, head hanging low. "You should do it," he says. "It means a lot to you and you've worked hard for it."

I sit up slowly, pulling the sheet over my chest. It's not because I feel vulnerable, but because I'm confused as to why he's talking about this now. And even more so, I'm confused as to why he cares enough to say it at all.

"Why are you bringing that up right now?"

He shrugs but keeps his eyes fixed on the floor. "You said you were thinking about dropping out. You shouldn't."

The tone in his voice cracks right through my defenses. "Why do you care?"

I need to know. I need to see if this meant more for him just like it did me.

"I don't," he says point-blank, giving me my answer. "But you do. So much so, I pulled a string or two and got you time at that new indoor archery range over in Chesterfield tomorrow night."

My eyes widen, his actions not connecting with his words. Who helps someone follow their dreams if they don't care about them?

"Are you serious?"

I'm caught somewhere between wanting to hug him and wanting to shove him off this bed. His mood swings are starting to give me whiplash.

"Dead serious."

"Why would you do that for me?"

He shrugs again, still refusing to meet my eyes. "Moment of weakness. Don't get used to it."

I tilt my head, studying him. He isn't tense and his body isn't in the fight mode we bring out in each other. And for once, I'm not either. I just had amazing sex, came two times, and now I get to go practice my favorite sport in one of the most state of the art places this side of the country.

"Well, for what it's worth, that was actually really nice of you. So, thanks."

He pushes himself to his feet, still avoiding looking at me. "Don't mention it."

I watch him, unsure what version of Sebastian this is—the villain, the savior, or the one in between, weighed down by guilt.

Then, just before he turns to leave, he surprises me again and leans down, pressing a chaste kiss to my forehead.

"Night, Little Lamb."

Something twists in my chest. My stomach flutters, heart squeezing with an emotion I can't place, or one I don't want to. *I don't like it.*

When the door clicks shut behind him, I collapse back onto Callan's bed with a breathless laugh.

What the actual hell just happened? And what in the world am I supposed to do next?

Chapter Seventeen

SEBASTIAN

"Aim, Banks!" Coach shouts as I miss yet another pass. "What the hell was that?"

I grunt, slamming the heel of my stick against the ice as I skate back to the center.

Fuck.

Once again, I can't get her out of my head. I can't stop thinking about this morning and how she snuck out of the house while I was at the gym like she was purposely avoiding me. Her first class isn't until nine, so there was no reason for her to leave an hour early. She just slipped through the cracks like we didn't tear each apart piece by piece in Callan's bed last night.

Aidric said he was stopping by the hospital to see our boy before class. I told him I might go later, but I doubt I'll make it. I don't even know what the hell I'd say. *Hey, man. Sorry I fucked the girl you were hooking up with in your bed last night.*

Just the thought makes my gut twist. The guilt is a slow burn, acid chewing through every part of me. Seeing him will only make it worse, make this connection I keep telling myself they didn't really have all the more real.

Last night, I barely slept. And today, I sat through every class in a haze, thinking about her. *Avery fucking Castle.*

Her voice, her mouth, the way she said my name right before she came apart under me. How we both held a question in our eyes neither of us was ready to answer. How I tenderly kissed her forehead and told her goodnight like it's not the first time I've ever done that with anyone.

And when I wasn't thinking about that, I was focused on the meeting tonight, replaying the checklist over and over like it might keep me from spiraling.

Break into Klein's office, retrieve the rock, and seal the cracks of this shitstorm before we get exiled from the Ice Lords, or worse.

Sounds simple enough, until it's not.

I skate harder, try to outrun my thoughts. *Clear your head, Banks. Get it the fuck together.*

That's exactly what Coach and all my teammates are thinking. It's exactly what I need to do. So I fight like hell and push the thoughts aside. For a few minutes, it works. The feel of the ice under me turns familiar, my stick in my hands a muscle memory as I chase the puck. The smell of the rink, the bright lights above, and the taste of the guard in my mouth center me.

For the next few plays, I'm in complete control. Instead of letting everything around me suffocate me, I shove it all out the door of the arena and focus on the only thing that used to matter in my life. Hockey.

Coach finally blows the whistle, ending practice, and I'm the first one off the ice. I hit the locker room like a ghost, ripping my helmet off and dropping my pads. Sweat clings to my skin and nothing around me seems to resonate at all. My body's here, but my mind's still stuck somewhere between her mouth on mine and my cock buried in her pussy.

My fists clench as I yank my jersey over my head. If I'm lucky, I'll be too busy with school, the Ice Lords, and hockey for the guilt to catch up to me. But knowing my luck lately, I'll be bleeding from it by midnight.

I swipe a towel across my face, ignoring the way my ribs ache with every breath.

"You hitting the gym tomorrow?" Slade asks as he slams his stick into its case.

"Yeah," I grunt. "Bright and early. You?"

He nods once. "Could use the extra conditioning."

"Cool. I'm leaving the house at six o'clock on the dot. Don't bail on me this time."

"Wouldn't dream of it," he says, but we both know it's a lie because Slade hasn't seen the crack of dawn since preseason.

I sling my bag over my shoulder and head for the door, wanting nothing more than to get home, shower, and collapse on my bed before the meeting that I know will test every ounce of my patience.

I'm halfway to the door when a fist slams into my shoulder, jarring me sideways.

"Snap the fuck out of it," Aidric hisses.

I clench my jaw and roll my shoulder, turning to meet his glare. 'What the hell, man!"

"You've been out of it for days," he grumbles. "A fucking freshman could've nailed that pass you botched today."

I don't respond, just keep moving toward the exit.

"Did you even go to see Callan?"

I stop, spine straight, and my hand gripping my bag a little tighter. "No," I say without looking at him.

Aidric scoffs. "Unbelievable."

He steps in front of me, but I hang my head low. It's not because I'm intimidated by Aidric, not in the least. It's because I'm ashamed of myself and if I look into his eyes, he'll know what I did.

"Fucking look at me, damnit." His voice thunders across the locker room.

I force my chin up, jaw clenched.

"Callan's getting out Friday," he says. "They're sending him to a short-term rehab facility for a few days and he'll probably be back in the house next week." His stare sharpens. "That means if his memory's still gone, the girl *goes*. He comes first."

The breath I didn't realize I was holding punches out of me. *Next week? Fuck.*

Aidric's eyes narrow. "You need to figure your shit out before he walks back through our door."

I don't say a word back. I just give Aidric a stiff nod before pushing past him and heading out the door.

As soon as I get back to the house, I go straight to my room. I peel off my sweat-drenched shirt, kick off my shoes, and strip down, heading for the shower.

The hot water hits my back like a slap and I grit my teeth through it. I need to wash this fucking day off. Shitty thing is, the day's not even over. I've still got a bunch of bullshit to take care of tonight.

Man, I miss the days when all I had to worry about was hockey, school, and the depraved shit we do as Ice Lords. Now, all that depraved shit is backfiring and I'm dodging bullets left and right.

Fifteen minutes later, I step out of the shower, steam curling around my shoulders as I dry off and toss on black pants and a fitted black shirt. Fury still burns in my veins as I get dressed and I can't figure out how the fuck I'm supposed to get rid of this feeling. Part of me wants to storm back into Callan's room and fuck Avery until she forgets any name that isn't Sebastian Banks.

But that's insane, so I shove that idea away because it can't happen. I hate her. She hates me. And that's how it needs to stay.

I go back in my room and put on my ceremonial cloak, brushing my fingers over the crest stitched into the shoulder.

Finally, I pull the bone-white, hollowed-eyed mask over my face, the gold crest of the Ice Lords on the bottom right cheek.

When I look in the mirror, I don't see Sebastian Banks, I see the Lord Speaker, and tonight, my voice will echo. It will speak with authority, branding itself into the very bones of our members. And if they dare betray us, they will pay.

I head down to the chamber, bypassing a few of the guys who are waiting to go down themselves.

I pause on the steps to check a text from one of our insiders who ran the blood on the arrow. I'm hoping like hell it's good news.

> Mark: Sample doesn't appear to be of human origin. Probably animal blood. If you need anything else, let me know.

Damn. I was counting on that giving us something. But we'll find a lead eventually.

We have to.

I forward the text to Aidric and keep walking, each step grounding me more than the last because beneath the chaos and secrets is the place where we rule. Down here my thoughts aren't riddled by a little lamb; they're solely focused on the Ice Lords

When I get to the bottom of The Chamber, I assess the place where the red paint marked a declaration of war. A few stains still line the walls, but it's cleaner now. Jeremiah did well.

Aidric's down here when I arrive, standing tall at the altar, his own mask in place. We watched the video feed at least a hundred times, but the figure was too well-hidden and what we had to work with was too short.

I nod to the back door where I added a new camera, a small one on a video feed no one knows about. Aidric glances that way behind the mask then gives me a penetrating stare. I know him well enough that I can guess exactly what he is saying without words.

Next time we will catch the fucker.

I take my place beside Aidric, waiting as the others file in. I count each one, watching and searching for nerves. Some come in quickly, knowing their place and finding comfort down here. The Ice Lords take care of each other as long as we don't betray one another, so our seasoned members know this isn't a place to fear. But a few of the newer ones are hesitant, moving slower and less sure.

Once everyone is here, Slade closes the door with a click,

silencing the room. The wind that had been echoing through the vents stills, as if even the air knows to obey the authority this place demands.

"Brothers," I begin, voice sharp and commanding through the mask. "Tonight is not about rituals or rank—it's about loyalty."

Meeting the gaze of each member, I continue. "We've been compromised. This, paired with what happened to Callan is much more than a simple threat."

The silence that follows is heavy, weighted by what isn't being said. It's not the same without Callan, and I know they all feel it.

A sharp inhale breaks the silence, but no one speaks. I step off the altar and begin pacing the space slowly. "Someone broke in, defaced our revered sanctuary, and threatened our legacy. This isn't just an insult; it's a declaration of *war*."

I stop in front of the first member, chin tilted high. "Inspection begins now."

Aidric steps off the altar, folding his arms and watching like a silent predator.

I approach the first Ice Lord. "Mask," I order.

He removes it, and I take my time memorizing each detail, running my gloved finger over the plastic, searching for signs of wear. When I see it's clean, I nod and hand it back to him.

One by one, I move down the line, checking masks, lifting cloaks, and brushing gloved hands across shoulder seams. I watch for every twitch, every suspicious movement.

When I reach Noah. I jerk the edge of his cloak aside and see a faint scuff along the end. It's barely noticeable, but it's there. Then, along the edge of his mask, it looks like someone dragged it across brick or gravel.

I tilt my head. "Interesting," I murmur. "Where'd that come from?"

Noah shifts uncomfortably. "Must've dropped it."

"Bullshit." I grab his collar and yank him forward. "These masks don't leave this house without permission. And they don't get scuffed unless someone's running."

He opens his mouth to defend himself, but I raise a finger. "Shut it. You'll speak when you're spoken to."

I move on with every intention of returning to Noah.

When I've finished inspecting everyone's attire, I return to the altar. "If someone in here is hiding something, I will find out," I growl. "And if I do, I won't ask questions. I'll rip your fucking throat out and drag your body across every inch of The Chamber walls, before feeding your blood to our forefathers as payment for your betrayal."

The room holds still; nobody dares move.

"Meeting adjourned...for now," I seethe. "But you're not off the hook. Surveillance is going up until trust has been restored. Every inch of this house will be monitored. No one and nothing is off-limits."

"Does that include your little pet, Avery?" I hear.

"Who said that?" I snap, turning swiftly, anger burning ten times hotter than before.

Cloaks part until one is left in the center and I walk toward them with menacing steps, my eyes giving way to the predator that lies beneath the mask. I reach out and rip the mask from the asshole's face, tossing it across the concrete at our feet.

Jeremiah.

"Didn't you learn your lesson before? Or do you need more chores to do to keep you in line?"

His jaw is clenched tight when I shove him in the chest. "Answer me."

His breaths are heavy, and his eyes drift to Noah before snapping back to mine. But I don't miss the look. If he thinks his buddy is going to save him from my wrath, he's sadly mistaken.

"Since you seem to be so obsessed with what is mine, maybe I should remind you about the evidence we hold that can send you to prison."

Jeremiah's skin turns pale, and the defiance in his eyes quickly turns to regret. He might not have felt so sorry after scrubbing the walls, but reminding everyone here of what the Ice Lords can really do is where I hold the power.

My finger presses into the center of his chest, applying steady pressure until he winces. "Say her name again, look at her again, and I will *ruin* you."

"Out!" I order and Jeremiah runs like the little rat he is.

The others waste no time getting the hell out of here, but before Noah can follow, I bark, "Not you, Noah."

He freezes, then turns slowly.

"Take off your mask," I command as I walk toward him with slow and deliberate steps. "Funny how the only damaged mask just happens to be yours."

He opens his mouth to argue, but I cut in. "Sit."

Noah obeys, dropping onto the edge of one of the chairs, hands clenched in his lap like a scolded child.

I crouch so we're eye level. "Now," I say evenly, "let's talk."

"I didn't—" he starts, but I cut him off with a raised hand.

"You think I give a fuck what you didn't do?" My tone stays cold. "What I care about is how your mask got scuffed, why your cloak smells like smoke, and why you've been acting like a nervous little bitch for days."

I pause before continuing. "So here's what's going to happen. You're going to leave your location on at all times. We want access to your phone, your car, anything of importance. If you take a shit in a different building, I want to know. If we see so much as a blip out of pattern..." My eyes gleam behind the mask. "We'll take that as confirmation."

Noah swallows hard. "You think I had something to do with the graffiti?"

"It wasn't graffiti," I snap. "It was a message. A message someone sent, and if wasn't you, then you shouldn't mind us watching, right?"

"No," he stutters. "Not at all."

His skin is whiter than a sheet, and if I didn't know any better, I'd think he might cry right here.

I lean in, my voice just above a whisper. "Do you know what we do to traitors, Noah?"

His eyes widen, but he doesn't respond.

"We don't expel them—we *erase* them."

Aidric leans over Noah's shoulder, breathing down his neck as I say, "Have you started your orders?"

He hesitates for a second, then nods. "Yeah. I started digging into Hershman's grades. There's potential there. Looks like the athletic department has been overlooking them for some time while keeping him on the ice."

"Good," I say. "Expose it. I want results before the puck drops in tomorrow's game."

Noah gulps. "I got it. I won't fuck it up."

I smile coldly and stand. "See that you don't."

Aidric opens the door slowly and gestures for him to leave.

Noah stumbles to his feet and bolts up the stairs like he's running from fire.

Once he's gone, I look at Aidric. "He's cracking."

Aidric nods.

I clench my jaw. "We need to keep squeezing until something breaks. I'm not sure if Noah has it in him to do something this insane, but I suspect he knows more than he's saying. After the Evan incident, he seems skittish."

Once we're upstairs, Aidric goes to the kitchen to grab a beer, but I barely make it two steps into the hall before Slade's slapping a hand on my shoulder.

"Hey, man. Got a sec?"

With a quick breath, I nod and follow him down the corridor.

He waits until we're alone before speaking. "Look, Seb. I get it—structure and order and all that bullshit. But this shit feels less like a brotherhood these days and more like fucking boot camp."

My brows lift. "You got something you want to say, Slade? Say it."

He sighs, rubbing the back of his neck. "Yeah. I do. This isn't what we signed up for. Treating us all like we're traitors. Being an

Ice Lord used to mean something. Now we're just jumping through hoops, policing each other, tracking phones like fucking federal agents. Everyone's walking on eggshells lately and all we wanna do is play some hockey and win the games."

My jaw ticks, but I keep my voice steady. "We're at war, Slade. One of our own is lying in a hospital bed. Nothing that's happening is coincidental; it's intentional. Whether you realize it or not, someone out there is targeting us and someone inside might be helping them. We can't just pretend this isn't happening."

His lips press into a tight line, and I step closer.

"I don't like this any more than you do. But what happened downstairs was necessary. Every single one of us is a liability until we know we can trust each other again."

Slade shifts his weight, still looking uncertain. "I just don't wanna lose what this used to be."

"Neither do I," I tell him truthfully. "But the only way we keep what we built is by protecting it with control, discipline, and a hell of a lot more paranoia than we're used to."

Slade exhales and drags a hand through his hair. "Alright. Let's just not forget what we stand for. We break rules, not each other."

A faint smirk tugs at the corner of my mouth. "I'll keep that in mind. Now go get a drink and cool off."

He nods and disappears down the hall, and I stand alone for a moment, thinking about what he said.

I fucking hate this as much as everyone else does, but it's just temporary until we bury the son of a bitch that's hunting us. The Ice Lords have always been a brotherhood for me; it was the family I chose when I didn't have one.

I will restore it to its greatness one day; I just have to take out a traitor first.

Chapter Eighteen

AVERY

Damn. This place is top-notch. It smells like polished wood and fresh-cut turf.

I still can't believe Sebastian set this up for me, but even more so, I can't understand why he did it. Sure, the time slot is later than I would've typically chosen, but the gesture is thoughtful in a way I never expected from him.

My boots squeak as I step onto the mat, bow in hand, tension strung tight along my spine.

There are only a few people here—two casually shooting a few lanes down and two watching me.

Killian and Drake, a couple guys from the house, are standing near the vending machines, trying and failing to look casual. I can't even be mad because I know, without a doubt, Sebastian ordered them to be here. It just means he either cares, or he's unhinged and obsessed. Maybe a little of both.

Every time I move, the guys jerk their heads, eyes following me like I'm a bomb they were assigned to babysit. But as soon as I get into a rhythm, they seem to settle and stare off into the distance.

They look bored, so maybe I'll change that.

I nock an arrow and raise it. The sound of the string tightening less than an inch from my face is almost therapeutic. With a long exhale, I shoot and the arrow slices through the air, striking the bullseye with a satisfying thud.

"Oh no," I call out dramatically. "Are you two here to kill me or just to stare until I spontaneously combust?"

Killian stays awkwardly still. Drake smirks. "Just here to keep you safe, Castle."

"From what?" I ask. "Target practice trauma?"

They exchange glances but say nothing. I give them a fake gasp and widen my eyes. "Wait, is this where I die? Oh my God, is this the scene where the girl gets taken out during archery practice?" I strike a pose like I'm drawing an invisible bow, overly dramatic.

They chuckle under their breath, probably wondering if I've officially lost it. Maybe I have. It's hard to tell these days. But the whole act brings a smile to my face, something I've been missing lately. When was the last time I just laughed and joked around for the fun of it?

I shoot again, hitting the bullseye and just as I lower my bow, my phone buzzes in my pocket. I pull it out and slightly glance at the screen to see that it's Brogan.

I step off the turf, and answer. "Hey."

"Hey," she says softly. "Just checking in."

"Just practicing for the comp on Sunday. Sebastian got me..." I trail off before I say too much. The last thing I need is her accusing me of cozying up to him again. "Just practicing," I say, flat.

"Right," she drawls, reading me like a damn book. Her tone shifts. "I didn't want you to hear it from anyone else but Callan's being transferred to rehab on Friday."

My heart skips. "Rehab?"

"Yeah. Just a short-term place for PT. A few days, maybe a week."

"Where?" My eyes gather with tears I refuse to let fall. The thought of Callan struggling through PT while I stand out here laughing and joking around makes me feel heartless. He was hurt because of me, and here I am, living my life while he sits in limbo.

"Same facility Evan's in."

My stomach twists hard. "Oh."

"Speaking of Evan," she adds, "have you seen him lately?"

Guilt barrels into me like a freight train. "No," I tell her truthfully. "Things have just been so busy."

"No judgment," she says. "I haven't been by much either. He's still catatonic anyways. The doctors don't know if, or when, he'll even come out of it."

I nod, even though she can't see me. My chest feels tight, my mind racing with all the secrets I know.

"I'll go soon," I say quietly.

"Callan's been asking about you," she adds, her voice softer now, like she's unsure she should even be saying it.

I press my fingers to my forehead, my heart hammering. "Does that mean I can see him?"

She pauses for a beat before saying, "maybe wait until he's settled in. Let him adjust a little bit."

"Right," I mutter. "Yeah. I get it."

After a long silence, I shift gears to lighten the mood because I can't do this with her right now. It hurts too much.

"Hey, did you hear the Lords are playing in Callan's honor tomorrow night before the big event Friday?"

"I did," she says, her voice lifting a little. "Hayes is dreading it, though. Not exactly thrilled about sitting through a Lords' game, but since they played earlier this week, he's coming."

I laugh. "Perfect. You can be my emotional support human."

"I got you, babe. Wanna grab drinks at Legends after, like old times?"

"Hell yes," I beam. "I could use a mojito or five."

"Perfect. Let's meet at the dorm at six and ride over together?"

"Can't wait."

I hang up and take a deep breath, trying not to focus on all of the things Callan is going through.

No. I won't go there. This is progress. Callan has been asking about me; he's getting moved to rehab—things are looking up.

I shoot for a while longer, letting the rhythm of the bow center me. When my lane lights blink off, I exhale and roll out my shoulders. It feels good to have gotten so many shots off and I feel like I really did improve my aim a bit. The longer lanes and smaller bullseyes seem to challenge me more.

As I head down the hall toward the exit, I hear footsteps behind me, and when I turn cautiously, I see Killian and Drake.

I almost forgot they were here. "You two following me?" I smirk, resuming my pace as they fall in line behind me.

"Nah," Killian says too fast. "Just figured we'd grab something to eat. You hungry?"

I stop walking, eyeing them both. Their expressions are too casual, like they practiced being relaxed and forgot how normal people behave.

"Or we could hit a movie," Drake adds. "Something chill to kill some time."

Killian elbows Drake in the side and it's not subtle at all.

My eyes narrow. "Why are you two suddenly my social planners? Better yet, why do you need to kill time?"

They glance at each other and both shrug.

I cross my arms. "What the hell is going on?"

"Nothing," Killian says, which is exactly what someone says when it's definitely not nothing.

They're acting far too strange. It's like they're trying to keep me busy, or away from something.

Son of a bitch.

Sebastian and Aidric are up to something and they don't want me anywhere near it. So much for being in this together.

"Are you fucking kidding me?" I hiss. "Sebastian doesn't want me going back to the house, does he?"

"Look, we're just doing what we're told," Drake mutters, holding up his hands in surrender.

"Yeah," I snap. "And failing miserably. Next time you're given orders to watch someone and keep them occupied, don't make it so damn obvious."

I spin on my heel and head toward the doors, ignoring their halfhearted attempts to slow me down.

Whatever they're doing, I'm going to find out. And God help them if they thought they could keep me in the dark.

The second I walk into the hockey house, I notice how quiet it is. The lights are low, there's no music or rowdy laughter. More importantly, no sign of Sebastian or Aidric. Considering they are staples of the house and here anytime they don't have class or hockey, that's suspicious alone.

"Shit," I whisper, closing the door behind me. "Where the hell could they be?"

I head straight for the stairs, taking them two at a time, not even hesitating as I push open Sebastian's bedroom door.

Of course it's unlocked. The bastard can plot a covert mission like he's James Bond but can't be bothered to lock his own damn door. I don't know if it's confidence, or just stupidity, but I'm taking advantage of it.

It's my first time in here, and I sort of expected more. This space is minimalistic and tidy, like he thinks the chaos he causes won't touch this place if he keeps it orderly.

My gaze snags on a small box on his bookshelf with a tube of lipstick on top. *That's odd.* One of his whores must've left it behind.

There's fire in my steps as I snatch it and march into his adjoined bathroom. Without pause, I twist the top off, revealing a blistering shade of crimson. Pressing it to the spotless mirror, I scrawl out an angry, to-the-point message.

Liar!

I step back, tilt my head and admire my work. Is it a little crazy? Yes. Do I regret it? Hell no.

I put the cap back on the lipstick and toss it onto the sink.

As I'm walking out of the bathroom, still irate about this entire situation, I decide to leave just one more message.

I go back into his room, and stalk to his desk.

Yanking open a drawer, I find a notepad and tear out a page. Then, I grab a pen and write:

**Thanks for the range time, asshole. Hope
your secret mission was worth it.**

If Sebastian wants to play stupid games, he can win stupid prizes.

The worst part isn't even the lie. It's the fact that he made me believe, for a second, that he actually gave a damn.

I walk out, close the door behind me, and return to Callan's room with my head held high. I thought we were getting somewhere, learning to trust each other. He said we were going to figure this out together but then leaves me in the dark the first chance he gets.

Well fuck that and fuck him. If Sebastian wants to go off script and do his own thing then I will too. One thing is for damn sure though, I'm done playing games.

CHAPTER NINETEEN

SEBASTIAN

THE STREETS ARE SLICK WITH RAIN MEANING WHEN THE temps drop tonight, everything will be a skating rink by morning.

Aidric kills the headlights a block from the North Ridge Police Department and rolls to a stop behind a row of maintenance trucks. From here, the station looks small and harmless, but we both know better.

"You ready?" I ask, tugging on a pair of black tactical gloves.

Aidric pulls a dark mask over his face, voice flat. "This place is a fucking joke. We get in, get the rock, and get the hell out."

We move like shadows. Aidric's stride is steady and fearless like this isn't his first break-in. Which, granted, it's not.

We circle around the back toward the loading dock. It's dark and deserted with one overhead bulb flickering. We already checked the security here and the feed is embarrassingly easy to hack. I was able to adjust their field of vision a little to the left so we won't be in the frame.

Aidric crouches and pulls a lockpick set from his inner jacket pocket. "Just gimme a sec," he says, already getting to work.

I keep my eyes on the alley, heart thudding like a war drum. The cameras are taken care of, but we still need to be mindful of anyone lingering around the building. The police station is just an office and isn't used overnight, so we should be safe.

Less than a minute later, the door creaks open. "We're in," Aidric says flatly.

I scan the lot once more, then slip inside behind him. The air smells like old paper and burnt coffee. It's dead quiet, meaning either the security guard is slacking or Aidric was right, and this place really is a joke.

We move fast and low, ducking past the front desk and a couple wall-mounted cameras that clearly haven't been serviced in years. Down the hall, we find the corridor marked *Administration*.

"Klein's office," I whisper, nodding to a door at the end.

Aidric doesn't hesitate as he pulls out a small flashlight, wedging it into the crook of his neck so the angle beams just right. He picks the second lock even faster than the first and we slip inside and close the door behind us.

The office is cramped but meticulously arranged. Towers of files are stacked on the desk, the corkboard above webbed with red string, pins, and notes. My breath catches when I see a photo of Callan's mangled car taped dead center with the brake line circled in red.

My stomach drops.

Aidric heads for the bookshelf. "Start looking," he growls. "I'll check the shelves."

I move toward the desk, eyes scanning every detail. I tug at the top drawer but halt when I realize it's locked.

"Hey," I whisper. "Gimme the pick."

Without hesitation, Aidric tosses it over and I catch it midair. A few quick turns, and the drawer pops open.

Inside, I find more than I bargained for—a hella thick folder labeled ***ICE LORDS*** in bold marker.

My pulse spikes.

I flip it open and find documents—transcripts, photos, initiation logs. My name, Aidric's. Jeremiah's, fucking Slade's. It's all here.

Then, I see a faded photo lying where the file was in the drawer. It's old, yellowed at the edges. It has to be twenty-five, thirtyish years ago. Three members wearing masks and cloaks. I flip the photo over, and my breath leaves my lungs when I see three names scrawled in cursive ink:

Klein. Redmond. Church.

Aidric's last name.

"Holy shit," I whisper, holding it up. "Dude. He was one of us."

Aidric glances over, brows furrowed. "What?"

He drops whatever he was holding and marches toward me, snatching the photo from my hand.

"Flip it over," I tell him, and his eyes going wide the instant he reads the names.

"That's my dad," he says quietly. "And Klein."

His face hardens like stone. "Son of a bitch," he grits out. "He was an Ice Lord."

"Jesus," I breathe. His vendetta against us makes so much more sense now.

Aidric rakes a hand over his jaw, eyes darting. "That means this fucking detective knows everything about us."

"It also means he knows about the back entrance to The Chamber. This asshole is either hunting us," I say slowly, "or someone else is and he's trying to get ahead of it."

I slide the photo back into the folder and slap it shut. "We take everything."

"Already ahead of you," Aidric says, holding up the rock.

My breath rushes out. "You found it?"

"Hiding in plain sight, behind a fucking nameplate. Idiot thought it was safe in here."

I grin. "We came for one secret and walked out with a hell of a lot more."

Aidric moves toward the door. "Then let's move before it gets us fucking killed."

We don't talk as we retrace our path and slip out the back door, vanishing into the night like ghosts, but my mind is racing.

Klein was one of us. Which means this shit just got personal.

Back in the car, Aidric grips the steering wheel like it insulted his mother. His jaw is clenched, eyes locked on the wet road as rain continues to drizzle across the windshield, freezing at the edges and turning to sludge as it traces a path down the glass..

I stare out the passenger window, watching the world blur past like we're trying to outrun it.

"What are ya thinking?" I finally ask.

Aidric doesn't look over. "I'm thinking we let Klein sweat this out, don't give him any clues that we did this."

I nod, jaw tight. "I agree. Let him walk into that office, see the wreckage, realize the file and the rock are missing. We make him feel exposed. He'll know it was us, and he'll come."

"He'll panic," Aidric says with a dark smile. "Panic makes people stupid and sloppy."

"He's already sloppy," I mutter. "But now he knows we know, and that shifts the playing field in our favor."

A long pause stretches between us.

"We watch him," Aidric adds. "Every move, every call. If he runs, we follow."

I nod again. "He'll show his hand sooner or later."

Aidric relaxes in his seat, wrist draped over the steering wheel. "This might actually work in our favor," he says. "Klein can't touch us now—not without torching himself in the process."

"Didn't think of it that way. But you're right." I crack a grin and lean my head back against the seat. "We are un-fucking touchable."

We fall into silence again as Aidric takes a sharp turn onto our street. The house looms ahead beneath the stormy sky. I pull out my phone and send a quick text to Avery.

> Me: How'd it go at the range, Little Lamb?

I can see that she reads it instantly, but no dots pop up to say she's typing.

A minute passes, and no response. I frown slightly, thumb hovering over the screen. She always replies, even if it's just to tell me to fuck off.

"Something wrong?" Aidric asks as he kills the engine in the garage.

I shake my head slowly. "Not yet."

We head inside and the house is mostly dark aside from a faint glow coming from the kitchen. Aidric heads toward The Chamber door, mumbling something about locking the stone in the tunnel room.

I take the stairs two at a time, file tucked under my arm. My night just filled up. I plan to go through every page of this file until I know exactly how deep Klein's reach goes.

But first, I need to change and get this nasty, cop-office stench off me.

When I push open my bedroom door, I freeze when my eyes catch the bathroom door open with the light on. I step inside and immediately see the word "liar" written in what appears to be red lipstick on my mirror.

I drag a hand down my jaw and stare, a humorless laugh slipping out before I can stop it.

This is so impulsive, so chaotic, and so perfectly her.

I'm not even sure what I did this time. Could she be jealous that a girl I hooked up with left her lipstick here. Nah. Avery wouldn't give a shit about that.

Either way, she's pissed about something.

"She's gonna be the death of me," I mutter under my breath, the corners of my mouth twitching.

I leave the message where it is. Hell, maybe I'll keep it there forever as a reminder of the hurricane I invited into my life.

I go to my desk and flop the folder down, noticing another note from my little lamb.

***Thanks for the range time, asshole. Hope
your secret mission was worth it.***

I stare at it for a long moment, a dry chuckle falling out of my mouth again. This time, it's a little humor, a little guilt, and a whole lot of *fuck.*

I sit on the edge of the bed, elbows on my knees, hands under my chin.

So that's what this is about. She figured out the range time wasn't a kind gesture, but a calculated one. Probably thinks I only fucked her as a distraction, too. Which is the furthest thing from the truth.

So much for keeping secrets from the girl who reads between lines like they were written for her.

She's pissed, and honestly, she has every right to be. For some reason I find it adorable that she got so upset about me keeping her in the dark. I imagine her storming in here, her face scrunched up in fury as she looks around my space, seeking revenge.

She could have stolen all of my underwear, taken my pillow, wrecked the whole place just to prove a point. But she didn't. Even in her anger, she was calculated and methodical.

And for some odd reason, I actually feel bad for not telling her about tonight. Not because this got her upset, but because maybe she deserves to know. This person isn't just going after us, they threatened her too. And that's what I can't seem to figure out.

How is Avery connected to this adversary we're up against?

The question plays on repeat in my head before I shake it and get to my feet. Answers aren't going to come from sitting around doing nothing. Now I'm gonna have to kiss some serious ass to get Avery to trust me again, so we can find this fucker together.

Chapter Twenty

AVERY

I avoided Sebastian like the goddamn plague this morning. He texted twice so far and I've ignored them both. I timed everything perfectly to avoid crossing paths in the house. If I heard his voice, I went the other way. If I heard his footsteps, I disappeared. No way in hell am I giving him the satisfaction of rubbing what we did in my face. And if he thinks he can lecture me about the lipstick on his mirror after everything he's done, he can go straight to hell.

Maybe next time he'll learn to lock his door.

I'm skipping all my classes today because, really, what good is a degree if I'm not alive to use it? The only thing that matters now is staying ahead of whatever's coming. I'm done being passive. It's time to take action.

Before I can really get into the dirty work, I need to make sure everything is set for Callan's benefit event on Friday.

I spent the entire morning back in my dorm with my laptop, a stack of flyers, and what is now three empty coffee cups. If I can't fix the disaster that is my personal life, at least I can make this event one for the books.

The masked benefit is being held at the arena, and while the

Lords team handled most of the arrangements, there were still a few details left hanging.

I scroll through my checklist again, making sure everything has been assigned, confirmed, or completed.

- Catering: confirmed.
- Ice time and lighting transitions: double-checked.
- DJ's song list: delivered.
- Tribute video: Brogan's emailing it later.

All that's left now is for me to find something to wear.

It's so easy to get lost in the tasks and disappear inside the details. Honestly, I don't mind helping with the event one bit. I love a good distraction. It keeps me from unraveling completely because if I stop moving, I'll think about Sebastian. Or Callan.

So instead, I keep working—for control, and for the version of myself that still believes in clean slates. Because I know there will be a day that all of this anxiety and fear will be a distant memory, and I have to convince myself to keep working toward that.

Once I'm certain everything is finalized, I pack a few essentials Aidric missed when I was forced into the hockey house: my hair straightener, my dildo, and a box of tampons. After stuffing them in an old backpack, I fling it over my shoulder and give the room one more sweep. Time to head out and complete my next task of the day—figuring out how the hell I can get fingerprints scanned on a hockey puck without triggering an investigation.

I drop my face into my hands, rubbing my temples like I can massage the confusion out of my brain. None of what I'm reading makes any sense.

I've been holed up in the library for the past hour, scouring every possible way to get fingerprints analyzed quietly. Every search I make on my laptop or phone back at the house could be tracked and maybe that makes me paranoid, but after everything that's happened, I'd rather be paranoid than blind.

As of right now, there is only one person who can help me out in this matter, and I really don't want it to come to that because I know he'll tell my dad. But, after everything I've researched, I know I can't do this one on my own.

Standing up, I grab my phone and scroll my contact list until I find "Uncle Dave."

As it rings, I pace the thriller section with my phone pressed to my ear and my heart in my throat. I stop in front of a shelf and run my fingers down the spine of a murder mystery novel, wondering how their story ended.

The line picks up, and I flinch.

"Avery," Uncle Dave answers, warm and surprised. "It's been a while."

"Hey, Uncle Dave," I say, using the name I've called my dad's best friend since I was old enough to say it. "I was wondering if I could ask a favor?"

There's a pause and I wonder if this is too weird. I haven't talked to him in years so calling for a random favor is probably the last thing he expected. But after a moment, he responds, "Of course, sweetie. Anything for my favorite niece. Is this about your mom?"

"Not this time," I tell him truthfully. "It's something... intense."

After my mom ended up in the center, Uncle Dave dove into research trying to help us find all the best resources for her. However, when my dad felt like it was time for him to move on and Uncle Dave supported him, I felt betrayed, and it's the main reason we haven't talked in so long.

"Are you in some sort of trouble?"

"No," I lie without hesitation. "Nothing like that. I just need to run a set of fingerprints off a hockey puck. It's sort of silly, but there was this prank and I was hoping maybe you could help me out."

There's a pause. "You want prints?"

"Yes," I whisper. "No questions asked, please. Just a precaution."

He exhales and my heart rate kicks up. This is really the only option because Detective Klein can't get wind of what I'm doing and the guys can't know either. If he can't do this, then I'm not sure what I'll do.

"Kid–" he tries, but I cut him off.

"Please don't," I warn, knowing where he was going. "If you can't do it, just say so. But please don't try to get information out of me. I really can't say anything more"

He sighs and I can picture him pinching the bridge of his nose like he normally does when he's frustrated. "Okay. As long as you're sure. You know you can come to me if something's really going on."

"I know. And thank you." I force a small laugh. "But really, I'm okay. I just need this favor."

"Alright," he says, not sounding convinced. "Text me when you're nearby."

"Will do. Thanks again. You're the best."

"I know," he says with a smile in his voice. "Talk soon, sweetie."

There's no way in hell he's not going to press when I see him, but I'll deal with that conversation when it happens. I hang up and let out a long breath, readying myself to do what I have to do next.

First, I have to get that damn puck. I haven't seen it since Sebastian and I dug it up in the woods, but I did see him go down to The Chamber with it. Breaking into their creepy ritual room and stealing it back shouldn't be that hard, right?

I pick up my bag and start heading out, smiling at the librarian as I leave.

"Have a nice day," I murmur.

She nods, barely glancing up from her computer, and I slip out the main doors.

The sun's dipped behind the clouds and the roads are slick as hell from the freeze we got overnight. Every stop light drags; every red brake light feels like a sign from the universe telling me to turn back.

By the time I pull into the driveway, my jaw aches from clenching and my nerves are vibrating. The guys are all at the arena getting ready for the game, so this should be a no-brainer.

I don't waste time. I get out of my car and slip through the front door, careful not to let it slam behind me, then I make my way toward the basement. It's strange when the house is quiet; the guys usually make it feel full of life. But now it's silent and eerie, as if I'm walking to my death.

I hold my breath as I twist the knob to the door, and to my surprise, it isn't locked. Making my way down the stairs, my hands trail over the cool stone, trying to center myself as I make it to the bottom.

The Chamber is completely empty, just that weird stillness that makes the air feel too thick to breathe. I waste no time making my way past the altar to the hidden key. If I'm lucky, it's still where I found it last time.

Behind the curtain, the surgical trays gleam under the light, lined with tools used in psychological and physical warfare.

It's strange how this place doesn't faze me anymore. The first time I saw all of this, I was literally preparing to be under these knives at some point. Now, I find myself wondering which one I'll use when we catch our stalker. Because I have no doubt they'll be strapped down right here, bleeding for their sins.

Bypassing the horror show, I head straight for the far wall. Sure enough, the key dangles from the same rusty nail driven into the stone. You'd think after everything that's happened, these guys would have started guarding their secrets better. But it seems ego wins over logic in this house. Typical fucking men.

I step out from behind the curtain and head for the door to

the room that holds the Ice Lords' secrets and, if I'm lucky, the puck.

I slide the key into the lock and twist. The door creaks open and I immediately see that the glass case I shattered has been replaced, like it never broke into a million pieces all over this very floor. It feels unsettling, seeing how quickly they can put back together the pieces I destroy.

My eyes scan the area and damn, luck is on my side. Sitting right on the dusty bookshelf is the puck. I walk over and pull the gloves out of my pocket, careful when I pick it up, noticing that it's still smeared with that dried red stain, marked with Callan's number. I slip it into a plastic baggie before looking over the shelf again.

I don't know what I expected, but it isn't what comes next. My chest tightens when I see a rock sitting there, out in the open. Not just any rock—*the* rock. The one that the guys have been giving me shit about that Klein confiscated.

My brows pinch together as I try to process what I'm seeing. They told me that Klein having it was the reason Callan wasn't safe. They said it would burn us all.

They fucking lied.

All this time, they've had it while feeding me bullshit lies. I'm not sure why, but it hurts more than I expected it to. Part of me knew I shouldn't trust them, but another stupid part of me was starting to.

And to think I was taking my walls down for Sebastian. I confided in him about my mom and my fears. I fucking had sex with him. All the while, he's been lying to my face. First about the time at the indoor range, and now this.

I feel sick with regret and so much pain, but I refuse to let myself process it right now because it's too much. The weight of everything threatens to make my knees buckle, but I won't go down with these assholes. So I lock my legs and glare at the rock.

Without thinking twice, I slip both the puck and the rock into the inner pocket of my jacket, pressing them tight to my chest. It feels satisfying to know I won something, that I beat them at the game they set me up to lose. They thought I was a subservient girl who would fall in line, but they didn't look deeper. Avery Castle isn't someone to be messed with.

With determination pumping through my veins and a rejuvenated sense of purpose, I turn toward the door just as a soft ding breaks the silence. A sharp sense of deja vu runs through me. Same room, same sound—and sure enough, same voice.

"We've really gotta quit meeting like this, Little Devil," Aidric says, sweat gleaming around his hairline.

He stands in the doorway in all black compression wear, chest rising like he ripped off all his hockey gear and ran straight from the arena just to catch me in the act.

"Something I can help you with?" he asks casually.

"Nope," I say, lifting my chin.

They told me multiple times that we're in this together, but Aidric is the only one who's been clear from the start about not really wanting me here. With him I know I can show no fear or he'll use it against me. So I slip on my mask that says, "don't fuck with me" and move forward.

"Move," I snap, brushing past him. My shoulder knocks into his, but he only smirks, falling in step beside me.

"You tripped the alarm."

"Huh?"

I look up, and *now* I see them. Damnit. How could I have been so blind? There are cameras mounted in every corner that weren't there the last time I was down here.

"Wasn't doing anything wrong," I lie, schooling my face.

Aidric steps forward, slamming the tunnel room door shut with his foot, then circles me slowly. "Funny, because it looks like you took something." He stops behind me, fingers grazing the curve of my hip. "You really need to get better at hiding your sins, Little Devil."

His hand slides inside my jacket and I freeze. He won't understand my plan and out of all of them, he is the least likely to ever trust me. But when he pulls out the rock by itself, I try not to look too relieved. The weight of the puck is still pressed against my ribs, and I let out a short breath of relief he doesn't pick up on.

I almost laugh at him for being the worst detective ever because he totally missed the second half of the evidence.

He holds the rock up, inspecting it like he can't place where he knows it from when we both know that's a load of bullshit. "What have we got here?"

I shrug causally. "That would be the rock you used to threaten me. The one Detective Klein had. But apparently he didn't, and you've been lying to me this whole fucking time."

"Not lying," he croons, bending down so he can chuckle right in the crease of my neck, his breath hot against my skin. "Got this gem back last night. Question is..." He moves his hand below the waistband of my leggings and presses the stone between my legs, rubbing it forcefully against me. "Why the hell do you want it?"

The rock is cold against my skin, a stark contrast to the heat in my flesh, but I don't flinch. I just lift my chin and smirk.

"Spite," I say coolly. "Proof that we're not a team and you bastards are still pulling strings behind my back."

His hand presses harder, grinding the stone with deliberate cruelty against my clit as he steps in so close his breath grazes my lips.

"I've got a fucking game to win," he growls, voice low and lethal. "So why don't you take your smart little mouth and that tight little ass upstairs and stop sticking your nose where it doesn't belong."

I click my tongue and tilt my head, pretending to be unfazed even as my legs open a little wider.

"Is that a confession, Aidric? Do you want to repent for your sins," I whisper, eyes narrowed. "We're really not on the same side, are we?"

In one swift, unapologetic motion, his thumb drives into my pussy, forcing a broken gasp from my mouth. At the same time, he holds the cold rock against my clit, grinding it with slow, punishing pressure.

"I don't have any sins down here, Little Devil. Wanna know why?"

I shake my head, my jaw locked so tight I don't think I could form words. My body is at war—stuck between being angry and wanting to close my eyes and just fall into the pleasure of the moment because everything feels so fucking bad all the time right now.

"Because here, in this room, I'm a god."

I laugh out loud, startling him a bit. "I thought you were a *Lord*," I say mockingly.

"You and I both know that's the same thing." He swirls his finger around my entrance, the wetness obvious as he spreads it.

"Look at you," Aidric murmurs, his breath ghosting across my cheek. "Breaking rules and stealing relics like you're immune to consequences."

I hold my chin up, but my eyes fall closed as he gets impossibly closer, his lips touching mine when he exhales long and slow.

"You can't help yourself, can you? This is the part that's thrilling for you." He bites my neck, pushing his finger in deeper, and I gasp. "You're dripping down my hand like you want to be punished for it."

I try to move, but he cages me in, chest to chest, his free hand curling around the back of my neck.

"You want this, don't you?" he taunts, rotating his finger in maddening circles inside me. "You act like you hate us but your body doesn't lie."

His grin twists, devilish and amused as his voice dips to a growl. "Tell me, Avery, were you hoping this little rock might give you some kind of power over us?"

He pushes deeper, adding another finger. "You already have it. Every goddamn one of us is watching you, and here you are, looking to get punished, soaking my hand for stealing what was never yours."

The shame should be burning through me right now, but it isn't. Aidric wants to push my buttons and if how he and Sebastian dealt with me before on the altar is any indication, he thinks this is the way to do it.

So I'll let him take what he wants because I still have what I really came for.

I roll my hips into his movements, shamelessly grinding into him. If he wants to make me feel good, who am I to stop him? He says I deserve a punishment, but this is far from punishing.

"Still think you're not one of us?" he whispers darkly. "Because if this is how you fight back, I'd say you've already been initiated."

I can't stop the tremble in my legs or the way my breath comes out in ragged bursts. My back hits the stone wall as Aidric steps into my space like he owns it, like he owns *me*.

The rock presses harder against me, and he pushes two more fingers in until I...*fuck*.

My body jerks, coming undone under his touch. And even though I hate him with every fiber of my being, I can't deny how good he makes me feel.

I gasp, lips parting, fingers clawing the wall behind me as if it might ground me, but nothing could prepare me for the moment he presses his mouth to my neck and bites down like a savage.

Pleasure rips through me, my sounds echoing off the walls around us. I squeeze my eyes shut, refusing to look at the way his large body towers over me. When he's done and I'm nothing but jelly, he steps back, just enough for air to fill my lungs again, and when I finally open my eyes, he's watching me with that satisfied smirk he wears so well.

Slipping his hand out of my pants, he lifts the rock to his nose and inhales it like the sadistic asshole he is.

His gaze stays locked on mine as a dark laugh rumbles low in his chest. "Would've let you keep it," he says. "But I think I like watching you come on it more."

Then he flings it in the air and it spins under the lights before landing perfectly in his palm.

My lips are still parted when he turns his back and starts to walk away, slow and unhurried, like he didn't just wreck me in five minutes flat.

"See you at the game," he tosses over his shoulder.

The Chamber door slams shut behind him and silence swells in the space he left behind. My heart is still slamming against my ribs, my skin flushed.

I press a hand to my chest, fingers brushing the inside pocket of my jacket. Sighing in relief when I feel that the puck is still there. I bite down on my bottom lip, tasting blood and fury."

See you at the game, asshole," I whisper.

CHAPTER TWENTY-ONE

SEBASTIAN

"Tonight's game will be played in honor of North Ridge's own, Callan Cromwell." The announcer's voice booms across the speakers, shaking through the arena. My pulse thunders to the sound of the crowd cheering for my brother, the guy who has had my back for three years now.

The people in the stands explode with a cheer some of the ice girls were shouting earlier, a sea of signs and jerseys lifted high with Callan's name and number.

From the bench, I glance up, scanning the rows until I see Avery sitting next to Brogan and Hayes. She's bundled in Callan's old team hoodie, a cream-colored crochet beanie sitting on top of her dark hair. Her cheeks are flushed from the cold, lips parted slightly as she watches the rink with focus. Her own sign is in the air: *Fight like hell #11. We Love you.*

Guilt flares and my throat tightens when I see it. He's not even back yet and she's still his. It shouldn't bother me, and I'm not usually one to fight over a girl. Hell, I don't even fight for them when I have them. But Avery is different for some reason and the fact that Callan can't even remember they fucked and she's still doing all of this for him pisses me off more than it should.

The only silver lining lately is that Callan's memory loss doesn't seem to pose a threat to the society. Aidric said he talked to him and told him things might resurface out of order. Callan shrugged it off and said nothing could surprise him after the shit he already remembers.

The announcer's voice cuts in again, pulling me from my thoughts.

"And don't forget, tomorrow night, join us right here for the masked benefit skating event hosted in honor of Callan Cromwell."

Applause floods the rink as the ice girls skate in a choreographed sequence. Music blasts through the speakers and the screen flashes with our logo and each player's name and number.

Aidric goes out first, like always. Then it's my turn. I skate fast, circling once before lining up for the first play. The chill of the ice hits my face like clarity, all the tension and rage inside me turning to fuel.

When the puck drops, we're off. Blades scrape, bodies collide, and the roar of the crowd becomes white noise.

Eaton Rapids is hungry and ruthless, but we hit back harder, not giving them an inch.

I launch forward, weaving between defenders with my heart slamming against my ribs. My stick connects with the puck and I send it ricocheting toward Aidric. He shoots, but the goalie blocks it, sending it to their star player. I skate in front of him, distracting him so Aidric can slam him against the boards, pinning their center in place and regaining possession.

The guy grunts, trying to shove him off, but Aidric doesn't budge. I clap him on the back when the team starts driving forward, and he instantly turns to face the action.

We play with everything we've got. Like something's chasing us. Like we've got something to prove. Because we do. We're the fucking Lords—Ice Lords. This is why we exist.

Every time I hit the ice, it's not just about the win; it's about control. We own hockey; we own all of the people who bet and play games behind the scenes. Without us, sports would be back in the mafia's hands, the way it used to be.

But not anymore. The Ice Lords took out all of the families controlling and rigging hockey games, making the fans miserable in the process. Colleges suffered, national teams struggled, and the sport was no longer fun until we stepped in.

The Ice Lords are a legacy of strength, built on the belief that no matter how big you are, we'll always find a way to keep the game in the players' hands, even if that means rigging a few matches along the way.

Eaton Rapids is out for blood tonight, so we're gonna make damn sure they choke on their own.

By the end of the first period, we're up 2–1. My lungs are on fire, sweat dripping down my neck and soaking into my collar.

As we switch sides, Aidric skates over and leans in. "She was in The Chamber."

I freeze for half a second, blades skidding on the ice. "What the fuck? Is that where you disappeared to earlier?"

The idea of Aidric cornering her down there alone makes my stomach twist. There's no telling what he said or did.

He nods. "She found the rock again. I caught her on the way out."

I exhale heavily. *Of course she did.* She's always trying to be three steps ahead, and I'm always two steps too slow. I don't even know if I'm more pissed at her for sneaking around, or at myself for always underestimating her.

Aidric shrugs and skates off like it's just another problem to shelve for later. It's really not a big deal. She's already seen the rock, already knows it exists. It's just that now, she's probably got a lot of questions as to why we have it and Klein doesn't.

The second period starts and I let everything go, hitting the ice like I'm trying to destroy it. Like I can outrun the image of her with that sign, sitting with Brogan, like she's part of Callan's life and I'm just a shadow in the background.

By the end of the second, we're up 3–1. I've scored once,

assisted once, and flattened their defenseman so hard, the boards shook and blood flew. I did exactly as I promised and made sure he choked on it before his buddies helped him off the ice. But the fucker was baiting me and got in my way one too many times with that cocky grin on his face.

Intermission hits, and it feels like time is flying. I head into the locker room, grab my jug of water, and chug until my throat burns.

Dropping onto the bench, I rip the tape off my stick and start wrapping on a fresh layer. Retaping always helps keep my hands busy when my head won't shut up and right now it's fucking screaming. I can't stop picturing Avery alone with Aidric in The Chamber.

Was she scared? Did he touch her? What else could she have been looking for down there?

Slade plops down beside me, breathing hard, helmet hanging from one hand.

"Yo," he says, voice low. "You hear the rumor?"

I don't look up. "What now?"

"Brogan told me Callan might make an appearance at the event tomorrow."

My hand stops mid-wrap. "What?"

"Yeah." Slade glances around to make sure no one's listening. "Apparently, if he's feeling strong enough, the doctors are letting him come by for a bit to see the crowd, feel the love or whatever."

I stare at the black tape, jaw tightening. "Does Avery know?"

Slade shrugs. "Don't think so. Brogan made me swear not to say anything. Said she doesn't want to get anyone's hopes up if it falls through."

A dry laugh scrapes my throat. "Yeah. Good fucking luck with that. Callan is one stubborn fucker."

Avery can smell a secret from a mile away, especially if it involves her precious Callan. There is no way she doesn't already know.

Slade eyes me sideways. "You okay?"

"Fucking fantastic," I mutter, finishing the tape job with a final rip and slamming the roll into my bag.

Callan's my boy and fuck...of course I want him back. But lately, every move we make is for him. Every fucking thought is wrapped around Callan. Especially when it comes to Avery. Callan is all she sees, and all she wants. Him coming to the event tomorrow will be a goddamn miracle to everyone else, but a grenade to the chest for me.

I take another long drink, drag a towel over my face, and lean back against the locker.

Coach walks in, clapping his hands. "Strong period, Banks. You're flying tonight. That's the shit I need from you."

I nod, not really hearing the rest. Something sharp twists in my chest and I press my shoulders hard into the locker behind me, like it might help dull the edge. But even here, away from the ice and the crowd, she's still in my blood.

The buzzer sounds, echoing through the room and snapping me back to reality. I rise with the rest of the team, grab my stick, and follow them out.

As we step back onto the ice, the sound of music and chants rushes in, but even in a packed stadium, I'm drawn to her. She's standing at the glass, eyes locked on mine, and for a second, the weight lifts and nothing else exists.

I've been trying to ignore what's building between us. Pretending it's just adrenaline or obsession. But fuck...I think it's more than that. I feel something for this girl—something I don't want to. I just don't know yet if it's about wanting control, or needing her in a way that scares the shit out of me.

I break our stare first because if I look too long, I think I'll have the answer to my question. And I'm not ready to face that yet.

By the time the final buzzer sounds through the arena, my lungs are heaving and adrenaline is still ripping through me like a storm.

We fucking did it. North Ridge wins, 4-2.

The guys gather around, sticks raised, gloves in the air. Callan's name echoes from the stands, signs waving like a tribute to a fallen king. For a second, I let myself feel the pride, the relief, the kind of win that makes it all worth it.

But I'm not looking at the scoreboard for validation of our win—I'm looking for her.

She's already making her way toward the exit, Brogan at her side, her dark hair tucked beneath that damn beanie, the one that makes her look too sweet for the way she wrecks me.

I cut across the tunnel and intercept them near the corner of the stands.

"Avery."

Her steps slow and she doesn't even look surprised that I found her.

"We're heading to The Effin Bar, wanna go?" I ask, feeling like I already know the answer.

She blinks at me once. "No. We're going to Legends."

That's it. There's no smile, no sarcasm, not even a spark of heat in her eyes.

I nod, jaw flexing. "Right."

Brogan gives me a knowing look, one that says *don't push it*, before she loops her arm around Avery's and guides her out through the crowd.

For a second I think about chasing after her, then I remember the notes she left me and I assume she's still pissed. Not to mention, she got caught red-handed tonight by Aidric and there's no saying what he did to crawl under skin. And as much as it kills me not to follow her, I know when to give a girl space.

That doesn't mean I'm letting her out of my sight though. I spot Drake leaning against the tunnel wall, laughing with a couple of the rookies. I nudge him with my stick as I pass.

Tipping my chin toward Avery, I say, "Go keep an eye on her at Legends. Make sure she doesn't do anything reckless."

Drake's smile fades just enough to show how much he doesn't want to do this, but I couldn't care less.

"Got it."

I don't need him to report back; I just need to know she's okay.

Chapter Twenty-Two

AVERY

After a quick stop at the dorm for an outfit change, Brogan and I are living it up. The bass is thumping, lights are low, and my third mojito is going down way too easy.

I'm surprised Legends is so busy, considering the Devils didn't play tonight. Nonetheless, it's shoulder to shoulder in here.

Brogan and I managed to snag a high-top table near the back, tucked enough into the corner that I don't feel like I'm being watched by half the damn room. I've heard the whispers about how I'm staying at our rival team's hockey house and no part of me is prepared to deal with that drama tonight.

Brogan clinks her glass against mine with a smirk. "To hockey wins, hot boyfriends, and holidays we'll probably regret."

I laugh, the sound bubbling out of me with more ease than it should. "God, I needed this."

"You and me both," she says, downing half her drink. "Hayes is already blowing up my phone. He's mad I left without him."

I raise a brow. "And yet, here you are."

"Yup." She grins, leaning in. "Because if I'm going to survive bringing him home for Thanksgiving, I need at least four mojitos and a best friend reminding me I'm not insane."

"You're not insane," I say, slurring just a little. "You're just...emotionally ambitious."

Brogan throws her head back laughing. "That is the nicest way anyone's ever said I have commitment issues."

We giggle like idiots for a solid thirty seconds before she looks at me...really looks at me. "So, are we gonna talk about it?"

I blink. "Talk about what?"

"You've said Sebastian's name like six times in the last five minutes. And I know that glazed-over, smitten look. That's not nothing."

I groan and drop my head into my hands. "Don't say his name like that. It makes my stomach do things."

"Oh my God," she gasps. "You like him."

"No, I don't," I snap, too fast. "I...hate him. So much so it makes my teeth hurt. At least, most days I do."

"But?" Brogan leans in, laying an arm across my shoulder.

"But sometimes..." I pause, swallowing another mouthful of mojito while I try to find the right words. "I guess sometimes he says things, or does things, that don't feel like the version of him everyone else sees. And that version gets under my skin, makes me question things. Makes me feel...like maybe there's more to him."

Brogan is quiet for a beat. "And Callan?"

My heart lurches. "Callan has my heart, he really does. But Sebastian...it's like he keeps poking at it. Chipping away at something I thought was already spoken for. There's this coldness to him, but every now and then, I catch a glimpse of what's underneath, and I can't help but wonder if he's like that for a reason. Like maybe he had a rough past."

I don't even know why I'm telling her all this. Must be the... three? No, four mojitos. *Definitely four.*

If it were any other guy, she'd already know every sordid detail. But this isn't just any guy—this is her brother and his best friend, and that makes this whole situation messy.

Brogan nods slowly, drawing her finger through the condensation on her glass. "Ya know, you're not the only one who's wondered why he is the way he is."

My brows pinch together. "What do you mean?"

She hesitates, eyes flicking toward the bar before settling back on me. "Callan mentioned it once, real offhanded, but it stuck with me. He said Sebastian's dad was bad. Like really emotionally vicious and manipulative. It was just him and Sebastian—no siblings, no soft place to land. Callan said hockey isn't just a sport for him; it's his way of surviving. It's the only thing that's ever really been his and he throws everything into it because it's the one place he has control."

The words hit like lead in my gut. So much about him slides into place, like I had all the pieces to the puzzle in front of me and I just needed to turn them over to see where they fit.

"Jesus."

"I'm not saying it excuses how he acts, but it explains a hell of a lot. Like why he pushes people and thrives in chaos." She shrugs, sipping her drink while watching the door for Hayes. "Maybe it's because that's all he's ever known."

I lean back in my chair, ice swirling in the bottom of my glass, heart beating too loud in my chest.

"Shit," I whisper. "That actually makes me feel worse."

Brogan smiles softly. "Yeah, welcome to liking complicated men. It's a full-time job."

We order another round and fall into a lighter chat about professors and Hayes' taste in music, but my head is still stuck in the conversation about Sebastian.

I stare into my drink and think about him. Not just the asshole he wants everyone to see, but the boy behind the mask. The one who was forced to learn early how to survive an emotional war.

My own childhood wasn't perfect, but at least I had two parents who showed up and made me feel like I mattered. At least I did for a while.

No wonder Sebastian clings to control like it's the only thing keeping him upright. No wonder I can't shake him. Because despite having a good upbringing, I also have a lot of trauma. My mother doesn't know how her words have destroyed a part of me I don't know if I can ever get back, but Sebastian knows that feeling. The rejection and the hurt speak deeper to us.

So why is he still lying to me? Why is he trying to push me away? And why do I run every time he gives me an out?

Brogan and I somehow end up on the dance floor, clutching our fifth drink and each other, laughing like we don't have a care in the goddamn world. The music pulses through my body, and everything feels soft and light. My head spins, but in the best way.

"Brogan," I giggle, gripping her wrist as we stumble through a sway. "This might be the happiest I've been all week."

She throws her head back, blonde waves bouncing. "Same girl. Same."

We keep dancing, engulfed in laughter when I nearly trip over her foot. At some point, someone hands us shots. I don't even know what it is. Could be tequila, could be rocket fuel. I'm too far gone to even care. I toss it back, shrieking at the burn. Definitely tequila.

Just as I lower the shot glass, I see Drake. Or is it Killian? Nope. That one is Drake, and he's alone this time, lurking by the bar like he's pretending to enjoy the scenery, but I know better.

I stumble toward him with a crooked smile, dragging Brogan behind me. "Well, well, well," I slur, pointing at him. "If it isn't one of the Lords' little guard dogs."

Drake raises a brow, clearly trying not to laugh. "Castle."

"Don't 'Castle' me. Did Sebastian send you? Or was this Aidric's idea?" I sway a little, bracing myself on the bar. "Or are you just here because you missed me?"

"You're drunk," he says, more amused than annoyed.

I lean in dramatically, finger on my lips. "Shhh. Don't ruin the mystery."

He sighs and pulls out his phone. "I'm calling Sebastian."

"Ohhh, betrayal," I croon, clutching my chest. "Right in front of me? That's cold, Drake."

He ignores me, muttering nonsense into the phone. "Yeah, she's here." He looks at me, expression stoic. "Oh yeah, she's wasted—drunk, dancing, slurring."

I laugh. "Tell him I said he's a manipulative dick with cute dimples."

Drake pockets his phone, grinning like this is the most entertaining thing he's seen all night. "He's on his way."

"Of course he is," I grumble, going up to the bar to order another drink like I haven't already had enough. "Why wouldn't he be?"

Brogan pulls at my side and I turn to see her, cheeks flushed from dancing. "Hayes is on his way to pick us up."

"Apparently I need to wait," I deadpan. "Sebastian's coming."

Brogan gives Drake a look that could cut steel, then loops her arm around mine. "Come on. Let's go outside and get some air."

Before I can even order another drink, I'm being steered outside.

"Hey," I whine. "I needed another one of those drinks before I have to deal with my enemy."

Brogan rolls her eyes and pushes me through the doors.

"Sit," Brogan says as she lowers us both to the curb. We plop down like teenagers after prom, heels in hand and faces tilted to the sky. I rest my head on her shoulder, eyes fluttering shut for a second.

"You know," I murmur, "you're a good best friend."

She bumps my knee with hers. "And you're a train wreck."

We stay like that, with our heads together, streetlights casting shadows overhead, until two cars pull up at the same time.

Brogan seems to care, but I don't. Honestly, I just want her shoulder back because I was about to fall asleep.

I blink a few times, trying to clear the fog when I see Hayes step out of his car. He glances at me then...Sebastian.

"You better not let anything happen to my girl's best friend," Hayes says, voice stern.

Sebastian scoffs and shakes his head, exhaling a long breath. "Relax. I'll keep her in one piece."

Hayes doesn't look convinced, but Brogan kisses his cheek and runs her hand down his arm, calming him. "He'll take care of her because he knows I would cut off his balls in his sleep if he didn't."

Sebastian winces and Brogan winks at him, but it isn't friendly. *God I love her.*

I squint up at Sebastian, who's standing over me now with that unreadable expression of his.

"Well," I say, wobbling to my feet. "If it isn't Prince Charming in all his moody glory."

He steps closer, catching me by the elbow when I stumble. "Let's get you home, Little Lamb."

"Ugh," I groan. "You're lucky I'm drunk or I'd fight you on that nickname."

"Good thing you're drunk then." One of his smiles I love so damn much greets me, and I find myself walking to his car without making him struggle to catch me. This is the Sebastian that confuses me, the one who makes me question what I want out of life. Because before him, I only wanted Callan. Yet, I can't say the same now.

Callan is still important to me and I want him too, but is it normal to want two men with your whole soul? Because I feel torn and at this point, even though I'm mad at Sebastian, I can't imagine my life without his sarcastic comments in it.

Life before the Ice Lords was boring and I was just walking through it, content to stay on my path. But with them, I feel like there is a thrill to life. And while it could do with one less stalker, I think I might like the exhilaration these men add to my life.

Chapter Twenty-Three

SEBASTIAN

With her arm slung lazily over my shoulders, I guide Avery across the parking lot. Her steps are clumsy, but at least her heels are in her hand so she won't break an ankle in them.

"You came for me," she hums, her cheek resting on my shoulder. "My sarcastic knight in shining armor."

I grunt, unlocking the passenger side and opening the door. "Yeah, well, your damsel routine was getting pathetic."

She gasps like I've insulted her. "Rude. I was acting perfectly fine. I'm not even drunk."

"Oh yeah? From what I heard, you were practically dry-humping the jukebox."

"I was feeling the music," she slurs, laughing as she sways. "Big difference."

I ease her into the seat and reach for the seat belt, but her hands grab at my shirt, yanking me closer.

"I missed you tonight," she whispers, lips brushing my jaw before I can stop her.

My pulse spikes. "Avery..."

She giggles again. "You smell so good. What is that? A little bit of ego and a whole lot of attitude?"

I stare at her lips as I answer, trying not to get too wrapped up in this moment. She's drunk, that's all this is.

"Yeah, well, you smell like too many mojitos with a side of regret cocktail."

"Don't act like you don't like it." Her hands drift down my chest, stopping just above the waistband of my jeans. "Still hard as a rock under there?"

I curse under my breath and gently peel her fingers away. When her face falls, I laugh to try to ease the tension.

"Okay, drunk girl, let's not get arrested in a parking lot tonight."

I drove here the second Drake called me. Grabbed my keys and left the party. I hadn't been drinking tonight because I was worried Avery might need me, whether she knew it or not.

"Why not?" she pouts, leaning back as her dress rides higher up her thighs. "I think you'd look hot in cuffs."

Jesus Christ.

I slam the door shut and circle around the front of the car, dragging a hand down my face.

This girl is going to fucking kill me.

Now all I can picture is her cuffing me to the bed and having her way with me. That image quickly changes to me doing the same thing to her, having her spread under me and bare.

I take a few calming breaths, willing my insane hard-on not to make an appearance no matter how hard it pushes against my jeans. By the time I slide into the driver's seat, she's messing with the volume, singing the wrong words to a song she thinks she knows.

"Buckle up," I say, reaching over to clip her seat belt in place like I was trying to before. Our faces are inches apart; her lips parted slightly, and her glazed eyes locked on mine. I thought this position might be easier to help her buckle, but it's like no matter where I go, I can't escape the heat between us.

"I like you better like this," she whispers. "All bossy and frustrated. It's pretty hot."

I groan. "Jesus, Little Lamb. You're going to wake up with a mountain of regret."

"Nope." She grins. "Regret is a thief with nothing to offer."

She chuckles to herself, flipping down the visor to look in the mirror.

"Well, except more regret."

I shake my head, start the engine, and pull out of the parking lot, white knuckling the steering wheel and hoping like hell I don't do something I might regret—like pull over and fuck her in the back seat. How can she be such a mess and still so perfectly *her*?

She hums again, curling into herself as if she were in a bed and not my car. "Tell me a story."

"No." My answer is firm. The only story I could even think to come up with right now is all the ways I want to fuck her, all the ways I want to make her mine. But I can't do that, so I stay quiet.

"Fine. Then I'll tell you one."

"Please don't." My fists tighten on the steering wheel. The only thing her voice is doing is making me harder.

"I had a dream I didn't have to choose."

"Choose what?"

"Between Callan..." She yawns dramatically. "And you."

My jaw locks. I don't even know what to say to that because I didn't realize there was a choice to be made. I just figured there was only Callan for her, and seeing her in his hoodie tonight confirmed it for me.

But when I look over at her curled up in his jacket, her eyes are on me as if she expects me to say something insane like "choose me" or "choose us both."

She sighs dramatically, finally settling down as street lights blur past the windows. Her hand finds my arm, fingers curling around my bicep. "You came for me," she whispers again, eyes closed.

"Yeah," I say quietly. "I came for you, Little Lamb."

Before we even hit the highway, she's out cold.

I glance over at her slumped against the window, mouth slightly open, and I can't help the dry chuckle that escapes me. Drunk off her ass, but still beautiful and still a whole lot of trouble.

By the time we pull into the driveway, she hasn't stirred once. I kill the engine, pocket the keys, then reach over and shake her gently.

"Avery, wake up."

She doesn't so much as flinch.

I get out and walk around to her side. Thankfully with her silence, my dick has calmed down.

I stand there for a second, watching her through the window. When I finally move, I open the door slowly, sure to catch her head before it falls. Then I unbuckle her seat belt and cradle her against my chest.

"You sure love being a pain in my ass," I murmur as I lift her.

"Let's get you inside," I say as I slide an arm under her legs, supporting her back with the other. I lift and she rolls into my chest.

Pausing for a second, I savor the moment of being in her presence and not hearing her run her mouth. And for half that second, I actually miss it.

Kicking the car door closed, I carry her to the house. Just as I raise my foot to go up the first step, she lifts her head.

"Put me down, Sebastian," she grumbles. Her head lolls back before snapping forward again in protest.

"Not happening. I'll put you down when we're inside." I make it two more steps before she shoves at my chest, breaths panting.

"I don't feel so hot. I'm gonna—"

Warm liquid erupts from her mouth, trailing down my side and splattering across my shirt and jeans. I grit my teeth, jaw flexing hard as I breathe through my nose.

Fucking perfect.

She groans miserably into my chest. "I tried to warn you."

Her body starts to shake. "I—I'm sorry."

The last thing I need is her spiraling, so I hold her tighter, pretending I don't feel the wetness clinging to my clothes.

I adjust my grip on her as I kick the front door open with my foot. "You're lucky I like you."

Her shaking stops, and she lifts her head from my chest. "You do?"

I don't answer as I carry her in.

Thankfully everyone is still out celebrating our win so the house is dead quiet. The last thing I need right now is more whispers and rumors circulating about how I'm spending too much time with "Callan's girl."

I carry Avery straight upstairs, almost tripping over someone's empty fucking beer can on the steps. When our maid isn't here, this place turns into a dumpster and I can't stand it.

Once we're at my bedroom door, I nudge it open with my shoulder and take her straight to my bathroom.

Avery groans as I set her down on the closed toilet lid. She looks like hell, but hell has never looked so tempting.

Her lashes flutter open and she rolls her lips, trying not to laugh. "My last mojito is dripping on the floor."

"No shit." I peel off my puke-soaked shirt and toss it into the trash. I'll try to salvage my jeans, but the shirt has too much on it for me not to lose it trying to get it out.

She stares at me with unfocused eyes, then lets out a tiny laugh. "You're still hot though."

Biting back a smile, I shake my head and start the shower. "Come on, drunk girl. Let's wash the night off you."

I lift her to her feet, but her coordination is a mess. She ends up sitting back down, defeat in her eyes. Gently, I push the hair out of her face.

"I'll help you," I say, lifting the bottom of her dress. When she doesn't curse me, I pull it up and over her head as she sways, using the wall for balance.

I leave her underwear and bra on, not wanting her to feel exposed.

Steam starts to fill the room and I help her to her feet again. She sways as she reaches behind her back, trying to unsnap her bra. "Little help with this too?"

"Just leave it..."

She chuckles. "Come on now, Seb. It's not like you haven't seen my tits before."

That's a true statement; however, she was stone-cold sober the last time. I do a lot of fucked-up shit, but taking advantage of drunk girls isn't one of them.

"Just keep it on. I'll throw it in the dryer."

"Fine," she stammers. "You won't do it for me, I'll do it myself." She slides one of the straps down her arm, then the other before spinning her bra around until the clasp is at her chest. Then, with a flick of her finger, it falls, right along with my sanity.

My heart jumps into my throat when two perky breasts spring free. "Goddamn," I mutter under my breath.

Just when I think we're good, she steps out of her panties and I'm suddenly reminded of how good she tasted a couple nights ago. My eyes quickly correct themselves, pinning to her gaze instead of her body.

"You good now?" I ask.

She nods, but I'm not convinced.

"Take these off and get in with me," she says, unbuttoning my pants.

My brows lift. "You want me to shower with you?"

Her gaze drags down my body and back up. "You're a mess too. Why not?"

I exhale, biting the inside of my cheek. "Alright then."

What was it she said about regret? Right, it's a thief. I'll be reminding myself that every hour on the damn hour tomorrow because I'm about to shower with Avery and I'm not going to touch her for a second longer than necessary.

I tug my jeans and boxers off and step into the shower first, then gently pull her in after me. She stumbles once and I catch her, both hands locking around her waist. Our naked bodies press together, and that heat that always seems to come alive between us burns like an inferno.

Water runs over us and I look down into her soft honey eyes, savoring every moment with her.

"I got you," I whisper, holding her close. I told myself I wouldn't do this, but I'm keeping her upright, so it can't be that wrong. She melts into me, her warmth seeping into my bones. She feels too perfect against me.

Leaning in, she buries her face in the crook of my neck, like she wants to disappear—or fall asleep.

I reach behind her and grab a loofah before squirting a couple drops of my sandalwood and pine tar body wash on it. Once it's lathered, I run it down her spine and over her arms, watching as suds paint her skin.

Bracing herself on my arms, she takes a small step back, just enough to look down. Her brows pull together in confusion then she looks up at me, lips jutting into a pout.

"Am I not hot enough for you, Sebastian?"

I bark out a laugh, caught completely off guard. "Excuse me? What the fuck would make you think that?"

She squints, clearly offended. "I might be drunk, but I know an erection when I see one, and I don't see one. You think I'm hideous, don't you?"

"Not a fucking chance," I snap, voice low and firm.

"In fact..." I pinch her chin and force her to look at me. "I think you're probably the most gorgeous girl I've ever laid eyes on. And I probably shouldn't even be saying that because you're not my girl—you're *his*."

The heat in her eyes fades, but her pout doesn't. She just stares at me, water dripping down her face like tears she won't let herself cry.

"I'm not his either," she says quietly.

My chest tightens. "You will be," I say, even though the words gut me. It's the truth, though. Callan's going to get his memory back, and when he does, they'll fall back into place and pick up where they left off. And I'll still be here, watching, but never front and center. Never with her.

Whatever this twisted thing is between Avery and me will fade into the past. With any luck, it'll become nothing more than a memory I can push down so far it stops clawing at me.

But even as I think it, I know I'm lying to myself. The physical part will be easy. It's the emotional shit that's going to wreck me.

I hold her under the spray until the worst of the mess is gone, then I hold her there a little longer. Her body is warm and soft against mine, and the silence between us is louder than any confession.

My arms are aching, but I don't let her go. Not yet.

When she starts to fade, her body leaning heavier into mine, I reach back and turn the shower off.

Reaching out, I snatch a towel off the hook and wrap it around her gently. Still naked and soaked, I step out first, guiding her carefully onto the bathmat. Her skin shivers against the cool air, but she doesn't complain.

I grab a second towel and run it down her arms silently because the words in my head are a mess and none of them feel safe enough to say, even if she won't remember in the morning—I will.

I wrap the towel tighter around her shoulders before adjusting one for myself around my waist. She waits for me to guide her back into my room. "Come on, Little Lamb. Let's get you dressed."

Once we're inside, I pull open my dresser and grab one of my t-shirts. Gently, I slip it over her head, and my eyes linger for a second as I admire my number on her chest.

She looks down and giggles. "Fancy."

I open the top drawer and grab a pair of boxer shorts for her. She steps in, one foot at a time, wobbling slightly.

"You do realize I'm starting to sober up and could probably dress myself?" she says with a crooked smile. It isn't teasing, more like she is wondering if I've actually noticed.

I did, but I don't want to let her go. Taking care of her feels right, and I'm not ready to stop. Grinning up at her, I tilt my head. "Oh yeah? Ready to run away from me again?"

Just then, she stumbles sideways, and I immediately reach out and wrap an arm around her waist before she tips.

I smirk. "What's that you were saying?"

She scratches her head and says nothing, biting back a grin. There's no saving herself with that one.

"And that's exactly why I'm walking you to Callan's room. Last thing we need is you taking a wrong turn and crashing down the stairs."

I turn to toss on a pair of boxers, dropping my towel and feeling Avery's eyes on me the whole time. When I stand to guide her back to Callan's room, she steps away from my touch and slowly walks backward toward my bed, sitting on the end.

When I don't say anything, too stunned to really process what's happening, she smiles and lifts her legs up. I step forward to try and refuse, but it's like she knows me too well.

Wasting no time, she pulls the blanket over her, curls into my pillow, and exhales like she just completed a marathon.

I blink, confused. "What the hell are you doing?"

She turns her head, eyes half-lidded but somehow still managing a pout. "Sleeping in your bed," she says simply, like it's the most obvious thing in the world.

I raise a brow. "Why?"

"Because it's warm. And because this house is big and empty and creepy and I don't want to be alone tonight." Her voice softens. "I promise I won't make a move unless you do."

I sigh, dragging a hand down my face. "You're impossible."

"I know." A hair falls in her face, still wet from the shower. Without thinking, I move to push it behind her ear, my fingers lingering on her face for a second longer than they need to. She closes her eyes and for a brief second she looks like an angel—the perfect little lamb.

Reluctantly, I slide into bed on the other side. "It's been a long-ass day, so we're just sleeping. Nothing else."

She lifts a pinky under the blanket. "Pinky swear."

I don't take it, but I settle in anyway, lying on my side so we're facing each other. Reaching back, I turn out the light and we're plunged into darkness.

After a long silence stretches between us, she whispers, "Did you know sea otters hold hands when they sleep?"

"What the hell?" *This chick is so random sometimes.*

"It's true. I saw a video once. They hold hands when they sleep because it stops them from drifting apart."

I can't help the laugh that rumbles low in my chest. "Jesus, Avery. You're really gone."

I can just make out the faintest smile on her lips in the dim lighting as my eyes adjust. "Maybe so, but you laughed and that counts for something."

The next thing I know, she's reaching for my hand under the covers, her fingers wrapping around mine. I hold back for half a second, then lace my fingers with hers until our hands are locked together. It feels good—too good. Like this is something we should've been doing all along.

"Don't let me float away," she says, her voice so low I can hardly make out the words. But they ring in my head, loud and clear. And because I'm a glutton for punishment, I squeeze her hand, assuring her that I won't let her go far. Not from me. Not from us.

I stare at her as her lashes flutter closed, lips parted slightly. I don't move a muscle. I just watch her. I don't know how this became my reality—her in my bed, in my head, in every goddamn part of me.

And I'm not sure what scares me more. The fact that she's here, or the thought of waking up without her.

Chapter Twenty-Four

AVERY

My head feels like it's been stuffed with cotton and left out in the sun too long. But my body feels safe and warm, more comfortable than I've felt since before Callan's accident. That's when the room around me registers; a scent I'd know anywhere is wrapped around me, and a presence that is equal parts frustrating and enamoring. When I lift one eye open, Sebastian is right there.

I groan, the sound scraping my throat. *Shit.*

My first instinct is to untangle my hand from his, slip out of this bed, and run like hell. But then he grazes the soft spot between my thumb and index finger, and I melt a little deeper into the sheets.

His eyes are still closed, lips parted slightly. He looks...peaceful. Which is rare for Sebastian. He's usually always braced for a fight.

I can't deny he was a perfect gentleman last night. I remember every single detail.

He showed up for me. Brought me back here and took care of me. Not once did he try to take advantage of the situation. If anything, I was the one coming onto him.

A wave of humiliation ripples through me. God, I was so

forward. Maybe a little dramatic and annoying. Scratch that, I was *definitely* annoying.

Still, it was a good night. And waking up next to Sebastian isn't so bad.

One eye opens and the corner of his mouth tugs up in a lazy grin. "Morning, Little Lamb."

I tuck my chin down, saving him from my rancid breath. "Morning," I whisper, my voice hoarse from sleep and mojitos.

He doesn't say anything right away. Just stares for a second, eyes roaming my face like he's memorizing it. Then he lets out a breath and stretches, his hand still loosely wrapped around mine.

"Head pounding?" he asks, his smile deepening with a hint of amusement.

"Feels like there's a damn jackhammer in my brain," I admit.

He chuckles and squeezes my hand once before finally letting go. "Come on. I've got an extra toothbrush so you can scrub the puke residue off your tongue."

I groan and cover my face with the blanket. "I still can't believe I puked."

"Oh, you did," he says, already climbing out of bed. "You also called me a knight and begged me to shower with you."

"Stop talking," I grumble from under the covers.

"Just speaking the truth." His laugh follows him to the bathroom.

Dragging myself out of bed, my bare feet pad across the cold floor into the bathroom. Sebastian's already at the sink, brushing his teeth in nothing but a pair of gray joggers.

He smirks at me in the mirror before reaching into the drawer and pulling out a toothbrush still in its packaging. He tosses it to me and points to his toothpaste on the counter.

I catch it against my chest. "Do you stockpile these for all your sleepovers?"

He spits, rinses, and wipes his mouth with a towel. "You're actually the first person to sleep in my bed in at least a month."

I bark a laugh as I unwrap the toothbrush. "Wow. A whole month. You poor, deprived thing."

He shrugs one shameless shoulder. "What can I say? It's been a dry season. Hockey keeps me busy."

I shake my head, smiling as I brush my teeth beside him, watching his reflection. "You always this charming in the morning?"

"Only with the ones who puke on me."

I nudge him with my elbow, foam forming at my mouth. He glances at me and smiles just enough to knock the air out of my lungs. It's strange how normal this feels, how comfortable I am here.

Once I'm finished, I go to drop the toothbrush in the trash, but Sebastian grabs it before I can.

"What are you doing?" I ask with a sideways glance.

He drops it into the toothbrush holder beside his with a crooked smile. "Just in case."

My stomach flutters a little bit, but I shove the feeling aside.

Taking a step back, I catch my reflection in the mirror. I look like death warmed over, but I have to admit, Sebastian's shirt looks pretty damn good on me. Can't say the same for his boxers, though. They're clinging to my hips like they're hanging on for dear life.

Once I finish brushing my teeth, I meet Sebastian's gaze in the mirror.

"I need to go somewhere today," I say, turning to face him fully.

His brows lift. "Where?"

I shake my head. "Can't tell you that yet."

He folds his arms, chest tightening. "That doesn't work for me, Little Lamb."

"I'm not asking for permission, Sebastian," I say softly. "I just need you to trust me. Don't send any of your other goons after me. Just let me do this on my own, please."

He stares at me for a long beat, tension radiating off him.

Then, finally, he sighs. "You get into trouble, you call me immediately."

I nod. "Promise."

He doesn't smile, but his eyes soften just a sliver.

I give him a grateful look and head to Callan's room. The scent of his cologne still lingers faintly, and for a moment, guilt pinches deep in my chest. My hand trails across the mattress and I picture Callan here, grinning up at me with one arm tucked behind his head.

Part of me misses him, but part of me is still back in that room with Sebastian.

Refusing to let the intrusive thoughts get to me, I slip into the attached bathroom and take a quick shower, rinsing off last night's chaos and this morning's emotions. Once I'm dressed in a pair of bootcut jeans, sneakers, and a Rosewood hoodie, I head out quietly without saying goodbye again.

⚔

The drive to my uncle's office is long and quiet. It's actually pretty nice, something I've been needing but didn't realize until I finally broke free of the hockey house. My hangover hums at the base of my skull, but it's manageable, thanks to the gallon of water I chugged before leaving.

My phone buzzes from the holder on my dash and I glance over to see that my dad is calling.

My stomach flips. Hopefully Uncle Dave didn't mention anything about me bringing fingerprints to him.

Reluctantly, I answer, trying to sound composed. "Hey, Dad."

"Avery," he says cheerfully. "How's everything been?"

Small talk. My worst subject.

"Been good," I tell him. "How's...your new life."

He pauses, likely letting my sarcasm slip before saying, "Everything is well here. I just wanted to talk about Thanksgiving plans."

"Oh. Yeah, umm...I don't think I'll be able to make it this year."

There's a beat of silence. "You always come home for Thanksgiving."

"Well, this year's different," I say, trying to keep my tone even. "I have a lot going on."

He hums like he doesn't believe me. "Dina is going to host and she was hoping to finally meet you."

"Wonderful. Will her darling little daughter be there, too? Or is it her dad's holiday?" Sarcasm drips from my tone. I don't want to meet them. I don't want to play this game where we act like my mother doesn't exist and isn't just a short drive away.

"She'll be there. In fact, Grace has a cheer competition the day after Thanksgiving. You should see this routine, Ave. The girl's got talent."

I grip the wheel tighter. "Yeah, well, I have a competition this Sunday."

He hasn't been to my last two shooting competitions, but he's seen Grace's routine enough to know she's talented. It's like he left me in the past with my mom and I don't want to be a pity call anymore.

"Right. Right. You mentioned that." He clears his throat. "I'll be there."

I force a breath. "Sure you will."

Silence stretches, thick and awkward.

"Have you been up to see Mom lately?" I ask.

Another pause. "Haven't had time," he says too quickly. "Work's been chaos."

"Of course. Grace's backflips take priority."

"Avery."

"I gotta go," I interrupt. "Enjoy your Thanksgiving. Maybe I'll see ya at Christmas." I don't wait for his reply. I end the call with my jaw clenched.

I'm not going to let my dad or his new life get to me. I've got my own shit to take care of.

When I get to Uncle Dave's office at the forensics laboratory in Eaton Rapids, I stretch my arms up, hitting the roof of the car as I release a drawn-out yawn.

It's been a while since I've taken a ride with the windows down and wind in my hair while pretending for a minute that life isn't a full-blown dumpster fire. It was going well until my dad called and now I feel a little derailed.

I kill the engine and drop my keys into my crossbody purse before heading inside. Hopefully this helps my mood because I'm getting sick of always being pissed off or hurt. The only one who seems to make me feel like I can laugh is Sebastian, and even then half of it is pure sarcasm.

Uncle Dave is already waiting in the hallway outside his office. He looks the same with his salt and pepper hair shaved short and a matching light stubble on his chin. His arms are crossed over the chest of his pressed polo shirt and I immediately notice that familiar smile on his face. Anytime I pouted as a kid, that smile could pull me right out of it.

"Hey, kiddo," he says, pulling me in for a quick hug.

I wrap my arms around him and let myself lean into it for a second, just long enough to feel like that carefree girl again. "Good to see you, Uncle Dave." I smile. "Thanks again for doing this."

"Like I said, anything for my favorite niece." He ushers me inside his office, and I dig into my purse, pulling out the hockey puck sealed in a plastic baggie.

"It's been handled by a few people," I explain, handing it over. "I jotted down their names and included them in the bag. If there are any prints that don't match, I need to know."

He nods, examining the puck through the bag. "You really think someone's just pulling a prank?"

I hesitate, then nod. "Yeah. Just...humor me, I guess?"

He gives me a long look but doesn't push. "Alright. I'll run it myself. Should have something in a couple days, maybe sooner."

I wrap my arms around him again. "Thank you. This really means a lot."

Uncle Dave moves around his desk, caging me into another hug that threatens to have me crumbling right here. The pressure of the hockey house, Callan, my father, my mother. The weight of everything around me feels like too much.

He squeezes me tight and when he lets me loose, some of that pressure seems to fade. "Be safe, Avery. And call me if anything feels off."

"I will," I promise, stepping back.

As I head out, I exhale slowly, the weight of it all starting to come back with every move I make. I climb into the car, start the engine, and head back toward the hockey house. The benefit event is tonight, and I've checked all the boxes on my list of things to do. All except one...

Figuring out what the hell I'm going to wear.

Chapter Twenty-Five

AVERY

Stopping in front of the door to the rink, I slide the black lace mask over my face. It does little to hide my identity, not that I'm trying. Tonight isn't about anonymity; it's about celebration.

I smooth my hands down the front of Callan's hockey hoodie, a shiver trailing up my spine.

After yelling at my wardrobe for twenty minutes, I finally settled on something simple. I went with the hoodie—because it's Callan's and tonight is for him—paired with fitted jeggings and white Converse. Not that the shoes matter because once the event starts, I'll be trading them in for skates anyway.

The moment I step inside the arena, I'm hit with awe. I showed up an hour early to make sure the guys didn't screw this up, but they've already done a stellar job.

The stadium has been completely transformed. Twinkling bulbs dangle from the rafters, casting a golden glow across the ice. A velvet archway is at the entrance to the rink, framed by silver lanterns and frosted pine. Teal and black banners line the walls, each displaying Callan's number.

Even the benches have been reupholstered with black satin, and a tribute wall near the far end displays photos from his best games, candid snapshots with friends, and there's even notecards with a box for guests to write messages of encouragement to Callan.

My heart catches in my throat when I look up and see Callan's face on the Jumbotron, his smile larger than life and his number blinking in the corner.

I press a hand to my chest. My heart still aches for him fiercely. But this time apart has really shown me things I didn't expect. It reminded me of how deeply I still love him and how much I still want him, despite everything that has happened.

Callan has been the boy I was in love with since high school, and he became the man I was falling for when we finally opened up to each other. It feels like we were cheated out of our time together and I have a strong feeling I'll be burying my face in his pillow to cry tonight from how badly I want him back.

I had only just gotten him before he slipped right through my fingers. Yet, even with the surety and the ache pulsing through me, there's someone else I long for, too.

Sebastian walks up beside me, wearing his own matte black mask with silver trim. His shoulder brushes mine, and I feel the jolt before he even speaks.

"Digging the mask," he says, a crooked grin on his face. His eyes roam my face like he's trying to remember what I look like without it.

I smirk. "Yours isn't bad either. Mysterious and brooding—very on-brand."

Members of the Lords team dart around the arena, some in skates, others in sneakers, stringing up last-minute decorations, adjusting spotlights, and taping off sections of the ice. One of them curses as a banner slips sideways, and another tosses him a roll of tape mid-skate. It's organized chaos and, somehow, it works.

"Is there anything I can help with?" I ask, glancing around.

His eyes flick back to me. "As if coordinating all this wasn't enough?"

"Now that I see everything in action, I realize I didn't do nearly enough." I gesture to all of the guys working like bees in a hive to get it all put together and make my vision come to life.

Sebastian throws an arm over my shoulder, pulling me close like we're old pals. "You did plenty."

Scanning the room, he observes everything. "Well, we've got the DJ mic-checked, the lights queued, and the finger-foods are rolling in soon. Slade and Killian are making sure the skates are organized by size at the rental tables, and Aidric's...well, who the fuck knows what Aidric is doing." He chuckles. "Unless you feel like giving motivational speeches or lacing up hockey skates for strangers, I think we're good."

"Motivational speeches aren't exactly my strong suit."

Sebastian opens his mouth to speak, but before he can, Slade skates past us backwards, pointing two fingers at Sebastian. "We've got a lighting glitch at the west end. You or me?"

Sebastian groans. "I'm coming."

He starts to step away, then leans in just enough for me to hear. "Stick around. I've got something I want to show you later." His voice is barely above a whisper, but the promise in it sends a flicker of heat down my spine.

"Should I be worried?"

He smirks again, already moving. "Terrified."

I shake my head, smiling as I watch him disappear. Whatever this night turns into, I already know it's going to be unforgettable.

Making my way toward the skate rental booth, I weave through a mix of familiar and unfamiliar faces, some in masks, some not.

The sound of the DJ testing the system comes through the speakers, followed by a few static thumps and mic taps.

I get to the booth and stand in line, which, of course is a mile long. Just as I take a step forward, inching ahead, a hand grips my arm and yanks me sideways.

"What the hell—" I start, but then I see that it's Aidric.

"Didn't peg you for the skating type," he mutters, dragging me straight to the front of the line like he owns the damn place.

"And I didn't peg you for the lurking type," I snap, elbowing my way into the narrow space between the counter and the pissed-off people behind us.

"Now gimme your damn shoes."

I shove them into his chest, thrusting a gasp out of him, and he snarls.

Without even looking at my size, he slaps his hand on the counter. "Size six, hockey skates."

I scoff. "Actually, I'm a seven and a half. And I wasn't planning on joining the damn team tonight."

He gives a short, humorless laugh. "Not in skates you're not. And you're not doing spins and tricks, Little Devil. So unless you plan on breaking your ankles out there, hockey skates are your best bet."

I arch a brow. "I knew that."

What I don't know is how he even knew my size without looking inside my shoe. Now that's a little creepy. Maybe Aidric is my stalker.

He smirks. "No you didn't."

Aidric grabs a pair of black skates with white laces from the guys behind the counter. "She's a volunteer with the event," he tells him before shoving the skates into my chest the same way I did to him.

A sharp breath escapes me. "You're insufferable, you know that?"

"Maybe so, but I'm also not wrong. You need these so you can help organize shit."

I sit down on the bench and he lingers like a fucking mosquito out for blood.

"Ya know," he continues, arms crossed over his own Lords' team hoodie. "I'm curious to see how the night goes for you. Being here for the guy you claim to love, but hanging around with the one you're fucking on the side."

I lift my chin, forcing a smirk when I really wanna grit my teeth. "You sound jealous."

Aidric's eyes narrow slightly, then drop to my lips before flicking back up. "If I wanted you, Little Devil, I'd have you."

I bark out a laugh. "Right. Because that's worked so well for you in the past."

"It did, did it not?" He taps his chin, gaze pointed at the ceiling. "I seem to remember my fingers deep inside your cunt not long ago."

My cheeks flush and my breath shutters. "Jesus Christ, Aidric. Why don't you just tell the whole goddamn arena?"

"Might as well, the truth always comes out eventually. You should know that by now."

"I don't even care." I shrug. "I'm not ashamed of my sex life. The only thing I'm ashamed of is that I ever let you touch me. But I can promise you, it won't happen again."

He grins and a chill actually creeps down my spine. "We'll see about that. Keep on pretending you're in control, but I promise you, this will all blow up in your face eventually. The question is, who will be standing next to you when it does?"

Once I've got my skates on, I push past him.

"Try not to fall on your ass," I hear him say from behind me.

I turn and wave my arms out wide, taunting him as I shout. "Trust me. If I go down, I'm taking you with me, asshole."

He grits his teeth, but I walk away with a pep in my step, refusing to give him an inch.

When I reach the edge of the ice, I'm surprised by how many people are already out there. The DJ has the music going, lights dimmed with strobes dancing across the rink. Most of the Lords, who were running around earlier handling last minute details, are now skating and laughing.

I step one skate out, clutching the wall like a lifeline as I try to find my balance. It's been forever since I've done this, and my confidence is shaky at best. Part of me considers staying on solid ground with my shoes on and my pride intact. But this is for a good cause—for Callan. It'll be fun.

Just as I ease my second foot out, trying to find balance, I feel two hands on my waist.

"You've got this," Sebastian says behind me.

I tilt my head just enough to catch his face over my shoulder. That crooked smile and that damn confidence.

A laugh bubbles in my chest. "I'm not so sure about that."

"Sure you are," he says. "Now let go of the wall and let me help you."

I hesitate, and he catches it right away.

"Just trust me, Little Lamb," he adds, eyes locked on mine. "I've got you."

Trust Sebastian? That used to feel impossible. But lately he's been...different. There's a softness beneath the sharp edges—a quiet way he's been showing up for me without asking for anything in return.

Maybe he's not just the cold, ruthless guy I pegged him for. Maybe he's just a guy who was dealt a brutal hand, trying to make it as a hockey player.

Yeah, I think I can trust him—at least with this.

"One foot at a time," Sebastian says. "Don't fight the glide."

I try to follow his lead; my body stiff at first, but he steadies me. Each time I wobble, he's there with his hands firmly on my waist, his body close enough that I can feel the heat of him through our layers.

"Okay." I laugh nervously. "Maybe I don't totally suck."

He smirks. "I'm gonna take full credit for that."

We keep going, lap after lap, until our rhythm becomes second nature and I forget how terrified I am. The music shifts to something slower—"Unsteady" by X Ambassadors—and, for a moment, it feels like we're the only ones on the ice.

He skates backward in front of me, holding my hands. "You're actually not bad," he says, one brow raised.

"I'm a fast learner."

"Mmm," he hums, pulling me closer. "Or maybe you just trust me."

I don't answer because I don't need to. He knows.

By the time the ice starts to get packed, my legs are burning and my cheeks ache from smiling.

"I need a break," I say, panting softly. "My ankles hate me."

He laughs and nods. "Come on, Little Lamb."

He leads me off the ice and helps me settle onto a nearby bench, crouching down to unlace my skates.

For the next hour, he barely leaves my side as we mingle, sip hot cocoa, and chat with donors and friends. Anytime someone tries to pull me away for too long, he finds an excuse to bring me back.

I don't know what this is between us. But tonight, it feels like something real. Something that won't disappear the second our masks come off.

We're about to get our skates back on to give the ice another go when Aidric skates up to the wall. "Incoming," he mutters under his breath, eyes darting behind us.

I follow his gaze and spot Detective Klein walking down the stands in our direction. He's looking smug as hell in a black trench coat and simple silver mask.

"Well," Klein says smoothly as he approaches us. "Quite the turnout. I'll admit, you boys know how to throw a spectacle."

Aidric's jaw clenches as he steps off the ice, towering us all with his skates on. "What the hell are you doing here?"

"It's a public event," Klein says smoothly. "Why wouldn't I attend?"

I step to the side, watching the tension unfold with my heart lodged in my throat. The last time I saw Detective Klein, he was in my dorm, grilling me with questions. To say I'm on edge would be a massive understatement.

Sebastian's voice drops "Cut the shit, Klein. What do you really want?"

Klein steps closer, lowering his voice. "I've seen your little heist work firsthand. Impressive, but sloppy. Breaking into my office was a bold move. But have you ever considered that maybe I'm not the enemy."

Aidric scoffs. "Bullshit."

Klein's gaze flicks to me, then back to them. "You want to protect your people? Maybe I do, too. That rock ended up in the wrong hands. Perhaps I was simply protecting a sacred artifact."

A sacred artifact I had. Klein had no way of knowing it was actually safe in my hands. Even if at that time, it was debatable.

Sebastian narrows his eyes. "Why should we believe anything you say?"

Klein leans in slightly, his voice barely audible. "Because the enemy you're chasing doesn't wear a badge."

With that, he gives a tight nod and turns, heading back up the stands.

Sebastian and Aidric exchange a look—Sebastian's full of questions, Aidric's burning with suspicion.

"I don't trust him," Aidric grits out.

Sebastian exhales. "I don't either. But maybe we can't afford not to listen."

With a low growl, Aidric steps back onto the ice and skates away. Sebastian and I stare at each other for a long minute before he finally says, "Come with me. It's tense as hell in here, and I want to show you something."

With our skates slung over his shoulder, he takes my hand and leads me away from the rink, through the crowd and toward the arena entrance.

After a quick stop at the locker room to drop off our skates, he guides me into a narrow service hallway that smells faintly like popcorn.

"Where in the world are we going?" I ask as we start up a flight of stairs.

The corner of his mouth tugs up. "You'll see."

Once we're at the top, he pushes open a heavy metal door, and we're hit with a gust of cool night air. It swirls around us as we step out onto a secluded rooftop above the main entryway of the arena.

It's quiet up here, aside from the distant echo of music and laughter below. The stars spill across the sky like diamonds trying to show off just for us.

"This is my favorite place," Sebastian says, pushing his mask up onto his head. "You can see everything—the sky, the city, the whole damn world feels quiet here."

"It's breathtaking," I say, eyes on the sky.

I turn toward him, my heart pounding in my chest. The way that he looks around makes it clear just how special this spot is to him, and my stomach twists, not knowing what to do or how to act.

Sebastian and I don't do nice; we hardly tolerate each other. We do sarcasm and bickering. We do jabs and backhanded compliments. We don't do whatever this is.

"Why'd you bring me here?" I finally ask, my voice trembling slightly.

He hesitates, then closes the space between us. His hand lifts, fingers brushing against my cheek as he slides my mask up until it rests on the top of my head. "Because I wanted to share it with someone who'd appreciate silence in the midst of chaos."

I open my mouth to respond, but the words never make it out because in the next breath, his lips are on mine.

This kiss is nothing like the others. It's slow and deep, the kind that doesn't feel like a mistake or a game.

His hand cups the side of my face, fingers threading into my hair. I breathe him in, savoring the scent of everything I've been trying to resist. When we finally pull apart, I still feel the kiss deep in my chest.

With his hands still cradling my cheeks, I smirk as his thumb grazes my bottom lip. "So that's why you brought me here."

Sebastian shrugs, dimples cutting deep as a slow smile spreads across his face. "Nah," he says. "That was just a bonus."

I tilt my head slightly to the left, studying him. "What are we doing, Sebastian?"

His brows lift, a grin tugging at his lips. "Hmm," he muses, glancing up at the sky. "I think we're standing on a rooftop under the stars, feeling the bass of a party thumping under our feet."

I laugh softly, but steady my voice when I press, "That's not what I mean. What are we doing? Do you hate me? Want me? Like me? Loathe me?"

He meets my gaze head-on, his smirk unwavering. "All of the above."

My heart pounds as I stare at him. *God help me, I think I'm falling for him.*

It's not just the banter or the way he protects me; it's the way he looks at me when he thinks I'm not paying attention. Like I'm not some burden he's stuck with, but someone he chose to fight for.

And maybe it's reckless and wrong, but I think I'm falling for him.

Before I can stop myself, I lean in again, and this time he meets me halfway. Our mouths crash together, desperate and sure. His hands find my waist, pulling me in until there's no space left between us. I feel his undeniable hardness pressing into my hip and my breath hitches.

Sebastian groans into my mouth, like the sound's been hiding in his chest and finally breaks free.

I kiss him harder as the rest of the world falls away. My heart skips, all logic dissolving until it's just us. His warmth, our need, this burning passion we keep trying to fight but can no longer ignore.

Suddenly, my phone buzzes between us, cutting through the moment.

I pull back just enough to glance at the screen and see a text from Brogan.

B: Tribute video is about to roll. Where
are you?

My lips part, still brushing his. "We should go," I whisper.
"The video's starting soon."

Sebastian presses his forehead to mine, breathing hard.
"Right."

His hand slides down my waist until his fingers wrap around
mine, then we step apart and go back into the arena.

As we're going down the stairs, he glances at me with a look
that says, "this isn't over." And I feel it in my fucking soul.

Chapter Twenty-Six

SEBASTIAN

I glance over at Avery as we rejoin the crowd, masks back on. She looks at me briefly, a faint smile tugging at the corner of her mouth. I don't know what the hell this is between us, but I'm fucking reeling. That kiss...*Jesus*. It wasn't just heat. It was something deeper and that scares the shit out of me.

Even the way her hand fits perfectly in mine feels like I'm tempting fate by holding onto it.

We step back into the stadium, the floor thumping with bass, voices, and skates slicing the ice.

Aidric appears from across the rink, heading straight for us. His expression is carved from stone and his eyes are burning.

"I talked to my dad," he says, exhaling sharply when he reaches us. "He said we can trust Klein."

I let out a sharp breath. "You fucking serious?"

"Dead," he quips. "He said he's one of the good guys."

I blink. "Damn. Didn't expect that. Did he say anything else?"

Aidric shakes his head, frustration bleeding into his voice. "That's all he gave me. Just said, 'You can trust him,' and hung up."

Avery glances between us, letting go of my hand. "So now what?"

I drag a hand through my hair. "We're back at square one. No proof or leads. No idea who's fucking with us. Did your dad say why Klein's been questioning us?"

Aidric rolls his eyes. "Apparently he tests the loyalty of the brothers by seeing if anyone will spill our secrets then reports them to the society."

I chuckle. "Fucking sneaky bastard."

Just then, a ripple of movement at the far end of the rink pulls my attention. I turn, and there he is.

Callan.

Sitting tall in a black wheelchair with Brogan behind him, beaming like it's Christmas morning.

The air punches from my lungs. Beside me, Avery's breath catches, eyes locked on him like the rest of the room has disappeared.

I stare after her, something sinking in my chest as she rushes toward him. *Of course she does.*

Aidric claps a hand on my shoulder. "It's our boy!" He grins as he moves toward him. "Let's fucking go."

I follow at my own pace, slow and detached. Yeah, I'm happy Callan's here. He deserves every bit of love and loyalty the crowd is giving him. But damn, if it doesn't feel like every step toward him is a step away from her.

Just when I thought maybe Avery and I were finally figuring things out, the real hero returns. The one with the memory loss, the girl, and—whether he knows it yet or not—the heart she's still trying to give back to him. I fucking hate how much it costs me to admit that.

Before I can reach them, the lights dim and the tribute video begins.

Soft instrumental music flows through the arena as footage of Callan lights up the Jumbotron: him scoring goals, grinning at teammates, getting mobbed after a win. It's everything good about him—everything we're here to celebrate.

I stop moving, drawn in as I watch. But then, static crackles across the screen and the music shifts. The image flickers, and suddenly, it's not Callan anymore.

What the fuck?

The video shifts to security cam footage of the arena parking lot. A timestamp glows in the corner. This was the night we smoked the Saints.

My stomach drops. There we are: me, Aidric, Slade, Noah, Callan...and Evan.

Jesus Christ.

I remember that night too clearly. Evan ran his mouth about our win against Northwestern and accused us of cheating. Shit got heated fast.

Evan's hands are trembling as Aidric steps in, chest to chest. I jump between them, arms out, trying to de-escalate, but it wasn't enough.

Evan keeps spewing venomous threats and accusations and Aidric snaps, driving his fist right into Evan's gut. Evan doubles over, hitting the pavement hard.

Callan hovers over him, his face twisted with fury as he yells something I can't hear, but I know the words. I remember every damn one. *You wanna talk the talk then get up and walk the fucking walk.*

Evan fires back. "You're all fucking worthless! Watch your backs because I'm coming for you!"

The camera catches me grabbing him as he tries to stand then I shove him back down *hard*.

Suddenly, the screen goes black and whispers and accusations begin to spread through the arena like wildfire.

"Did you see what they did to him?"

"What the hell was that?"

"Do you think they're the ones who hurt Evan Sanders?"

My throat tightens. "What the actual fuck."

I turn to Aidric and his jaw is locked, eyes burning.

We've been hit again, and this time, we were slapped in the face with an audience to witness it.

I break into motion, heart pounding, fists clenched as I shove past confused guests, eyes locked on my group huddled near the edge.

They all look rattled.

"Was that real?" Brogan demands the second I reach them.

Aidric just shakes his head, still stunned, as he runs his hand down his jawline.

"I'm going to check the file," Brogan says quickly. "It wasn't on the final cut. I triple-checked." She narrows her eyes at us one by one. "But when I get back, I want answers."

She doesn't wait for a response, just spins and storms off.

Callan shifts in his wheelchair, knuckles white as he grips the armrests. "That night..." he says, voice low. "I remember that night. But I'm not sure I want to remember what came after," he adds. He blinks a few times, slow and strained, like something's trying to crawl back to the surface of his mind.

Aidric leans in, tense. "You remember what happened next?"

Callan doesn't answer right away. He turns his gaze to Avery. "I remember you in the locker room. You heard us talking. We threatened you."

Avery's eyes widen. "Callan?"

He closes his eyes briefly, then opens them, glassy and distant. "There was a...music box," he says slowly. "And a picture."

Avery's voice wavers. "What picture?"

"I had it," Callan says, blinking. "The one of you and your mom."

She shakes her head. "No, I found that. Someone took it and left it for me at Faraway Archery Range."

His brows pull together, the pieces refusing to fit. "Someone stole it from me." He blinks again, a tremble in his hand now. "I...I don't remember anything else."

None of us speak for a moment. The air is heavy with tension, the music still playing somewhere far off in the background like nothing ever happened.

Avery steps closer to Callan and rests a hand lightly on his shoulder. His breathing slows, but I can tell he's shaken—we all are.

There's no denying it anymore, someone's been playing this game longer than we realized and they've now gone from watching to acting.

A sudden scream slices through the air, startling all of us.

"What the hell was that?" Aidric snaps.

We all search for the source of the noise as a ripple of panic tears through the crowd.

"Come on," Avery says, already moving behind Callan's wheelchair. She grips the handles tightly and pushes him toward the commotion.

We follow, taking the wheelchair-accessible ramp toward the main entrance. The crowd parts in bursts of confusion and gasps and we get a perfect view of what has everyone freaking out.

A body lies crumpled on the floor, a growing pool of blood seeping beneath it.

My heart drops. "Holy fuck," I breathe. "That's...Julian."

He was a former Ice Lord we dismantled and ruined. Callan was supposed to finish him off in the woods after. But this isn't an old, rotting corpse. This is a fresh, recent kill.

I glance at Callan. His face has gone pale, eyes locked on the body. But I can't tell if it's recognition or just shock.

If the timeline of his memories serves accurately, he should remember Julian's demise. Or what should have been his demise.

"Shit," Aidric mutters under his breath, his jaw clenched.

The sirens of the arena's emergency system blare to life, red strobes pulsing through the space as security swarms in, ushering people back and creating a perimeter.

Avery steps forward, wrapping her arms protectively around Callan from behind. And this time, he doesn't flinch or shove her away. He just stares ahead, shaken and silent. By the look on his face, he remembers. Maybe not everything, but enough for that body to haunt his mind.

Hell, it's haunting all of us because as I look around, seeing all eyes pinned to us, whispers rippling through the crowd, I know... *they know*. Or at the very least, they're suspicious as hell.

Thirty minutes later, security is still trying to restore order and the crowd is dispersing, heading out the exit doors.

As we're shuffling away, movement down the corridor catches my eye.

I look closer and see someone wearing a black cloak and a mask eerily similar to our ceremonial attire.

I tense immediately. "There." I point.

We all watch as the figure turns into a side hallway, away from the chaos.

"That's not right," Aidric says, already moving.

"Stay with Callan," I urge Avery as I break off from the crowd and follow quickly. The second the figure reaches the far end of the hall, Aidric and I close in.

"Hey!" I bark, charging ahead.

The figure jolts and bolts, but not fast enough. Aidric grabs him by the collar and yanks him back. I rip the mask off...

"Noah?" I snap, staring at his flushed face.

He stumbles, breathing hard. "Jesus, man. What the hell?!"

"What the hell?" I echo, slamming my fist into his shoulder hard enough to make him wince. "What are you doing wearing this shit in public? Are you trying to get us all killed?"

"It's not real!" he protests. "It's a knock-off just for tonight."

Aidric grabs the edge of the cloak, inspecting the fabric. "It's close enough to get you mistaken for someone who shouldn't be seen. We have fucking rules for a reason."

Noah runs a shaky hand through his hair. "I didn't think it'd matter." His voice drops, cracking. "But Julian...and the video," he stutters. "We're screwed, aren't we?"

Aidric steps forward, slapping Noah across the face when he begins to full blown panic. "Fucking breathe, damnit. You're not helping anything by losing your head."

He glances down the hall, jaw tight. "Go back to the house now. No detours and no questions. We'll meet you there."

Noah nods frantically and takes off down the opposite hallway, ripping the cloak off as he goes.

As he disappears, I run my hand down my face. "This night just keeps getting better."

Aidric exhales beside me. "Something tells me this is just the beginning."

By the time Aidric and I make it back to the front of the arena, Avery is bent over Callan's wheelchair, her arms wrapped tight around him.

"Can I come see you soon?" she asks softly, her voice barely audible over the noise of emergency crews and guests being ushered out.

Callan nods, eyes tired but clear. "Yeah. I'd like that."

Aidric and I step up beside them.

"We'll keep you in the loop," I say, clapping a hand on his shoulder.

"Whatever this is, whoever did it, we'll figure it out," Aidric adds.

Brogan joins us, pushing through the thinning crowd. "That's enough," she snaps. "It's probably best if you all keep your distance for a while."

Callan shifts in his chair, clearly uncomfortable. "Brogan, come on. It's fine."

She doesn't look at him. Her eyes are locked on us. "It's not fine. Not when the last video people saw of you had these two idiots at your side, throwing punches and making threats. Then..." She gestures to the blood stain on the floor. "One of your teammates ends up dead at your own benefit."

"Brogan—" I start, but she cuts me off with a glare sharp enough to slice skin.

"We'll talk later," she mutters before grabbing the wheelchair and rolling Callan away.

Callan looks over his shoulder, giving us a faint smile and a small wave.

I glance at Avery. Her face is pale, her eyes wide and unfocused like she's still stuck in that moment with Callan.

I reach for her hand. "We need to get out of here."

She blinks, turning to me slowly. "What?"

"We need to go before someone starts asking the wrong questions to the wrong people."

"He's right. We all need to get the hell out of here," Aidric says as he takes out his phone and starts typing out a message.

A second later my phone dings and I know it's a message to the group chat. I don't even need to read it to know he's telling everyone to go back to the house.

Avery hesitates, but then nods, letting me lead her to the exit.

And to think I thought the night might end with me fucking Avery on the roof or in my bed. Instead we now have rumors spreading about us and a dead body on our ice. Not to mention Callan is starting to remember more and more.

I know I should be spending more time with him as his memories return. He shouldn't have to go through it alone, and one of us should always be there with him.

Avery takes my hand when we get in the car; her gaze locked ahead, but when I scoot closer in the back, she leans in and part of me hopes that maybe she won't pick Callan over me. She didn't run off with him like she probably could have. Instead she came with me and her hand is in mine, squeezing it like I'm her anchor to life.

And maybe, just maybe, she might be starting to be mine.

CHAPTER TWENTY-SEVEN

AVERY

I WAKE UP WISHING LAST NIGHT WAS JUST A BAD dream, but the ache in my chest tells me it wasn't.

Julian is dead and the video was real. The only silver lining is that Callan is beginning to remember.

Last night I was able to recall what he told me about Julian just before the crash. That he had orders from the Ice Lords to kill him and return with his tongue. My stomach turns just thinking about it.

I burned Julian's tongue.

Oh my God, that makes me an accomplice in some sick and twisted way. Callan didn't kill him—said he couldn't do it. But he did do enough to get slapped with an attempted murder charge. He told me he did the only thing he could. He cut out Julian's tongue and dumped him at a hospital, not even sure if the guy would survive.

Now we know he did. Except he wasn't able to survive whoever's hunting us.

Last night changed everything. This isn't some depraved prank or scary threat. Callan was targeted and nearly died, and now someone has. Part of me wonders if it's time to involve the authorities before we're next. The other part wants revenge and justice served the Ice Lords' way.

They deserve that honor. For the first time, I'll admit I'm on their side. I might not know what happened to Evan, but I believed Callan when he said it was an accident.

I sit up slowly, the morning light bleeding through the curtains as my thoughts race.

Callan looked at me last night like he knew I was more than a girl he used to hate, someone more than just his sister's best friend.

Then there's Sebastian. *God, Sebastian.*

The way he looked at me under the stars. The way he kissed me like it meant something. I still feel it in the pit of my stomach. My feelings for him aren't just a complication anymore; they're real. Messy and inconvenient, but real.

I tug a hoodie over my tank top, brush my teeth in the bathroom, and head downstairs. The house is quiet except for a few low voices drifting from the living room.

As I round the corner, I see Aidric, Slade, Killian, and even Noah, crowded around the tv, eyes locked on the screen.

A news alert flashes, freezing me on the bottom step.

"Local student found dead at charity hockey event. Police are asking anyone with any information to come forward."

I gasp, hand flying to my mouth.

Sebastian glances over his shoulder and when he sees me, he reaches out and curls his fingers, beckoning me. I walk to him and sink onto the couch, curling into his side.

He wraps an arm around me and I press my cheek against his chest, listening to the beat of his heart beneath the chaos. It's the only thing that doesn't feel like it's about to fall apart.

The room is quiet and still, except for the news anchor's voice cutting through the silence.

"...the victim has been identified as Julian Lorenson, a former North Ridge University student and member of the

university's hockey team. Authorities are currently investigating his death as foul play."

Aidric curses under his breath and runs a hand through his hair, pacing behind the couch. "Who the fuck's tongue did Callan bring us?" he mutters.

Sebastian looks at him and shrugs. "There's only one person who can answer that question."

I don't tell them that I can answer for Callan, because it's not my place to. Callan confided in me, and while I want to solve this puzzle as much as everyone else, I'm not about to reveal details that aren't mine.

Slade just stares at the screen, jaw clenched, arms folded tight like he's trying to keep it together.

Noah's shaking his leg so hard the floor vibrates. "We're screwed," he mutters, barely above a whisper. "We're so fucking screwed."

Killian looks over at him. "Shut up, man."

"No, seriously." Noah's voice cracks. "That video paired with Julian's body is our fucking death sentence. You think they're gonna believe this is just a coincidence?"

"They won't," Aidric says, his voice low and stern. "Which is exactly why we need to get ahead of it."

"Get ahead of what?" I blurt. "We don't even know who did this."

Sebastian's arm tightens around me. "Not yet. But we will."

I pull away slightly so I can see their faces. "You all saw what that video looked like to anyone who doesn't know the full story. It made Evan look like the victim and you all look like monsters."

Aidric's gaze snaps to mine. "We didn't push him off that cliff."

"I know," I say quickly. "But someone wants people to think you did. And now, that same someone wants people to think you guys killed Julian."

Aidric and Sebastian share a look. They don't even need words because I know exactly what they're thinking.

Callan. They don't know I know the full story, but we're all aware now that Callan didn't finish the job. He didn't kill Julian, but someone else did.

Sebastian shakes his head, eyes fixed on the screen. "Someone out there is trying to dismantle everything we built by twisting it and burning it to the ground."

"And they're doing a damn good job of it," Slade mutters.

The screen cuts to a shaky cell phone clip of flashing lights and a stretcher being wheeled out of the arena. Julian's body is covered, but I still have to look away.

"This is only going to get worse," Sebastian says finally. "And we can't afford to wait around for the next body."

Noah leans forward, elbows on his knees. "So what do we do?"

A long pause stretches through the room. Then Aidric answers, calm and cold, "We find the fucker before they find us."

I glance back at the tv, Julian's name now flashing across the bottom in a red banner.

A tremor works its way through me. Not from fear, but from rage. Whoever's doing this thinks we're just pawns in their game. But we're not, and I'm done sitting back, waiting to be picked off next.

I pull my phone out of the front pocket of my hoodie and type out a text to Uncle Dave, asking if he's got any information yet. Then I slide it back into my pocket and exhale slowly, trying to steady my nerves.

"Everything alright?" Sebastian asks, looking down at me.

I nod once, my gaze locked on the screen.

Noah stands, his knees nearly knocking as he rolls his neck, cracking the tension. "We gotta do something. We can't just stand by and wait. I'm not cut out for prison. I'll get eaten alive. And fuck," he whines. "I don't wanna die."

"Hey!" Sebastian snaps, loud enough to cut through the room. "Get your shit together, Noah."

Noah freezes mid-step, eyes wide and chest heaving.

"We're not gonna solve anything if you lose it," Sebastian growls. "So calm the fuck down."

Just then, the news anchor reappears on screen and Aidric's voice booms over the room. "Everyone shut the fuck up. We need to hear this."

"Authorities report the victim was killed by a single arrow to the chest. The fatal shot pierced directly through the heart. More details will be shared as they become available."

I shoot upward and Sebastian's arm falls behind me. "Oh my god!" I cry out, my breath caught in my throat, heart pounding fiercely against my rib cage.

My gaze snaps to Sebastian and his brows furrow, jaw tight. "Don't overthink it," he says, as if his words will suddenly stop me from doing just that.

"An arrow?" Noah says, voice trembling. "Who the hell kills someone with an arrow?"

Aidric's eyes dart toward me, and I know why. This is far too specific to be a coincidence.

In my next breath, Aidric storms out of the room.

"Where's he going?" I ask, but no one answers.

Everything falls dead silent as the news anchor continues, her tone graver than before.

"Sources indicate the victim had undergone a glossectomy and used a prosthetic tongue. However, it has been confirmed that was not the cause of death."

My stomach lurches and I shoot to my feet. "Jesus Christ. And I burned his damn tongue to ash."

My vision blurs and my knees buckle. Sebastian catches me fast, lowering me back onto the couch.

"Try not to panic," he says softly, cupping my face in his hands. "We'll figure this out."

"How?" I snap. "And when? We're running out of time."

Thunderous footsteps come down the hall right before Aidric

bursts back in, face flushed, chest heaving, and piece of paper crumpled in his hand.

"They were here," he growls. "They got into our fucking house *again*!"

My spine stiffens. Sebastian immediately unlocks his phone, fingers flying. "How is that even possible? I have cameras on every inch of this house."

While he scans the security footage, Aidric steps in front of the television, holds up the paper and begins reading.

"One. Two. I'm coming for you.

Three. Four. Don't you score.

Five. Six. Put down your sticks.

Seven. Eight. Forfeit Westgate."

"What...what does that mean?" I stutter.

"They want us to forfeit the game?" Killian blurts out. "No fucking way."

Aidric holds up his hand. "There's more." He reads the final line, voice taut. "Forfeit the game, or find out who's next."

Sebastian stands with fire in his eyes. "Hell no! Not only will we be playing, we'll be winning. Let's drag this bastard out of the shadows ourselves."

"We need a plan," Killian says, now on his feet. "A real one, because this psycho's getting bolder."

"How about a trap?" Sebastian suggests. "Let's give him the game he wants. High stakes and high visibility, but what he doesn't know is we'll be ready."

"Ready how?" Noah asks, still pale from earlier.

"We control the environment," Aidric replies. "Have eyes at every access point—the entrance, exits, locker rooms, *everything*."

I sit up straighter. "You're assuming he'll be at the game. What if he doesn't show?"

Sebastian's eyes find mine. "Then we draw him out another way."

My brows knit. "How? How are you going to stop him from going after someone else if you play that game?"

A beat of silence passes before Aidric says flatly, "You."

My stomach tightens. "Me?"

He nods. "You've always been his favorite target. If we're all at the game and you're alone, he'll come for you."

"No way," Sebastian mutters. "That's suicide."

"She wouldn't be alone," Killian cuts in. "We'd wire her with a mic and camera—real-time feed. Someone will be watching her location at all times."

I bark a dry laugh. "You want me to just go about my day and pretend I'm not being hunted by a deranged psycho who's been five steps ahead of us at all times?"

"This can work," Aidric says calmly. "Keep everything as normal as possible. Get coffee, read a book in the student center, take a walk through campus. Routine gives predators a boost of confidence. That's when we catch him."

The more I think about it, the more I think this could actually work. I have zero faith in Aidric, but I believe Sebastian will keep me safe. While I have no idea why I was the first person this stalker went after, I have to assume there was a reason. Maybe this isn't so much about the guys as it is about me. But I don't know who I could have pissed off so much that they would go to these lengths.

Fuck it.

We aren't getting anywhere sitting here and Uncle Dave is moving too slow so I really have no choice.

"I'm in," I blurt. "But I think we should get Klein involved. He's a detective and he's got experience. And Aidric's dad said we could trust him."

"But can we trust your dad?" Noah asks, the question fair.

"He's a legacy member of the Ice Society, just like Klein," Aidric replies, unbothered. "He wouldn't steer us wrong. The Ice Society gave him his job and the power he has; he wouldn't risk giving that up for bad intel."

"I say we go for it," Killian agrees. "Klein wants to help? Let him prove his worth."

Aidric exhales sharply. "We loop him in carefully. No police reports and no official case. He's only part of this for backup."

"We give him very limited intel," Sebastian says. "We bring him the plan and see if he can help us out without going full badge."

Killian nods. "We'll need someone to tail Avery in the shadows too, just in case the feed goes dark."

"Me," Sebastian offers. "I'll follow at a distance. He won't see me, but I'll see him."

"Hell no," Aidric scoffs. "We need you at the game if we plan on winning."

Sebastian curses under his breath, dragging a hand down his jaw. "Didn't think of that." He glances around the room before saying, "Drake can do it. He's benched with a wrist injury and I trust him with my..." He pauses and corrects himself, "with Avery."

I'm almost positive Sebastian was about to call me his girl. I wouldn't have corrected him either. Of course, I still consider myself Callan's girl, too.

Because why not be framed for murder and in a love triangle at the same time?

"So we've got a plan?" Aidric asks.

Everyone nods in agreement.

I stand, squaring my shoulders. "Let's flush this bastard out."

Chapter Twenty-Eight

AVERY

"I'm not going," I tell Sebastian with my arms crossed as he drops my boots on the floor in front of me.

He looks up, brows drawn. "You worked your ass off for this. You'll regret it if you don't go. Besides, you could use a little normalcy right about now."

"Normalcy?" A hollow laugh escapes me. "Nothing about our lives is normal, Sebastian. A man was just murdered, with what can only be assumed as one of my arrows. And now you think I should step out in front of a crowd of hundreds and show off how good of a shot I am?"

He doesn't answer right away, just studies me like he's trying to figure out where my resistance is really coming from.

I exhale hard and sit on the edge of the bed, burying my face in my hands. "I can't stop thinking about Julian and that video and how easily that could've been one of us."

He crouches in front of me, resting his forearms on his knees. "I know. But hiding isn't going to stop this."

My hands drop into my lap. "If I compete today, will you sit out of the Westgate this Friday?"

His expression flickers. "Avery..."

"I'm serious." My voice cracks. "What if this psycho sees the game as the perfect place for his next move? Or worse, what if he finds a way to hurt you guys on the ice?"

Sebastian runs a hand down his face. "I've been playing my whole life. That game out there is the only thing I've ever had full control over."

"I get that," I whisper. "But I'm scared, Sebastian. I'm scared something's going to happen to you next. I can't..." I swallow hard, eyes stinging. "I can't lose you, too."

He moves closer, one hand coming up to cup the side of my face. "You're not gonna lose me."

I nod, but it doesn't ease the panic clawing at my chest.

"I'm glad Callan's not here," I admit. "He's safe in rehab. Far away from all of this. But you're walking straight into the fire, and I don't know how to be okay with that."

Sebastian brushes his thumb across my cheek, his touch warm and grounding. "That's why we're doing this. So none of us have to keep living like this."

His words are meant to comfort me, but all I feel is dread. Because, deep down, I know he's not wrong. And I hate that he's still going to do it anyway.

I stare at my boots for a long minute, thinking about what he said and how playing hockey is the only thing he has full control over. In a way, I can relate. Archery is the only thing in my life I've had full control over. It's the only thing I do for myself.

When I look up at Sebastian, I see him watching me like he's waiting for me to fall apart. But I'm done falling.

I'm Avery fucking Castle.

"No," I say, my voice steadier now. "I'm not going to let this psycho destroy my future, or my life, anymore. And I refuse to let him have any control over the game you love so much."

His eyes search mine. "Does that mean...?"

"I'll compete." I inhale sharply. "I've worked too hard to let fear win."

His mouth curves into a smile. "I'll be there, watching you and cheering you on the entire time."

My heart twists a little and I nod. "Then I guess I better not choke."

The nerves hit me the second I step onto the range.

I've competed before, sure, but never with a target on my back like this. Today isn't just about a title, it's about proving to myself that I still own this, even after everything. Even after murder and masked figures and sabotage, I won't let this psycho take my future from me, too.

For a second, I catch myself scanning the crowd for my dad, but he's not there. It's possible he's just lost in the sea of faces, but deep down, I know better.

The sun beams across the rows of archers like a spotlight. My name is called, and I roll my shoulders before stepping into the box.

Steadying myself, I take a deep breath and the first arrow slices clean through the air, sinking into the bullseye. My second and third follow suit, dead center. My breathing is steady as I drown out the crowd noise, focusing on nothing but the sound of my draw and the snap of the string.

When the round ends, my score flashes on the board, and I advance to the next. My palms are sweaty when I walk back up the hill to wait for the reset.

"You fucking did it," Sebastian beams, and I throw my arms around him without thinking.

"Hell yes, I did."

The competition intensifies in round two. Our targets are pushed back and the wind starts to pick up. I plant my feet, exhale slowly, and adjust my aim just a hair lower on the second shot.

The arrow hits dead center, just like I knew it would.

It's the third round and still no sight of my dad. *Figures.*

I hate that I keep looking for him. Hate that I feel like some kid at a school play searching the crowd for a parent who never shows up.

I'm sure the girl next to me has her whole family here watching. She's got that polished, private-range-since-birth energy. There's something about the way she flips her braids and crinkles her nose at me that screams spoiled rich girl.

We both hit the center nearly every shot, neck and neck. I beat her by a single point, and when I lower my bow, the edge of her smirk falters.

With a flick of her ponytail, she grumbles, "Nice shooting."

"Thanks," I say sweetly, flashing the most insincere smile I can manage.

They announce a thirty-minute break before the final round, and my stomach growls like it's ready to compete next for how much food someone can eat in one sitting.

As I'm unstrapping my arm guard, Sebastian shows up holding out a sandwich like some kind of post-apocalyptic knight with deli meat.

"I got you turkey and provolone. If you wanted anything fancier, you're shit outta luck."

I take it and nudge him with my elbow. "This'll keep me from passing out, so I guess I'll keep you around."

We go into the clubhouse, taking a corner booth. It's quieter here, and for these few minutes, life feels normal.

"Three rounds in," he says between bites, "you're killing it."

"I feel good," I admit, unwrapping my sandwich. "My hands haven't even started shaking yet."

His gaze trails down my arms. "That's because you're tough as hell."

"Careful," I tease, "Flattery makes me cocky."

"Yeah, well, you've earned it." He smiles and it fills me with so much confidence I want to giggle. This is exactly why I think I'm falling for this man. No matter how much life is turning to shit around us, he still finds a way to make me forget. Not just that, but he makes me laugh, our banter feeling familiar and comfortable.

We talk as we eat, letting the weight of everything fall away while we're here. He tells me about a water balloon ambush Aidric orchestrated in high school that left the cafeteria floor soaked. I tell him about the Fourth of July Brogan and I nearly set ourselves on fire trying to make sparkler art.

We laugh, leaning in a little too close, and the weight lifts a little. The pressure doesn't disappear, but it feels manageable, like maybe we will figure everything out and it will all be okay.

Then my name echoes over the loudspeaker, and the spell breaks.

Time for the final round.

Once I'm back in my box, I square my shoulders like I own the whole competition. It's time to win this damn thing.

I nock my arrow and draw back, steadying my breath as the wind cuts across the field.

Focus and breathe, Avery.

I release, and the moment the arrow flies, I know it's off. It sails so wide, it doesn't even graze the target. I've never missed like that in my life.

Gasps ripple through the crowd, but all I hear is the thundering of my own pulse.

Something's wrong.

I shoot a frantic look toward Sebastian and he stiffens the moment our eyes lock, already reading the panic in mine. I see him start to move, but I force myself to turn back around. I can't let this shake me.

I nock another arrow, trying to keep my form steady, but the moment I draw, I feel it. The tension's off. My bowstring feels loose. I know this setup better than I know myself. There is no way this was an accident, or a coincidence.

Someone tampered with my fucking bow. It had to have been when Sebastian and I were in the clubhouse eating.

I grit my teeth and release again. This one lands closer, but it's still off-center. The placement makes my stomach twist and warrants another ripple of whispers from the crowd.

Don't let them see you sweat, Avery. Damnit. You can save this.

But I know I can't. What's done is done. Those shots were shit and there is no way I'm winning this.

My hands are clammy, the pressure mounting. I adjust my stance and draw one last time, whispering a silent prayer to whoever's out there watching.

Please. Please. Please.

This arrow flies cleaner, but it still doesn't land where it should. A near miss, and I know it's over.

A moment later, the scores confirm it.

Second place. Just like my last competition. Only last time, I wasn't nearly as skilled. This time, I had this in the bag.

I lower my bow slowly, swallowing the scream threatening to claw its way out.

When I turn back toward Sebastian, he's already there scanning my equipment with restrained fury. His hands curl into fists, but when his gaze meets mine, it softens and he shrugs.

By the time I reach him, he's fuming. "You were sabotaged," he says as I peel off my gloves. "But you almost won the whole damn competition and that's something to be proud of."

I shake my head, tears pricking the corners of my eyes. "Second place still means I lost."

The only small mercy in all of this is that my dad isn't here to see me fail.

"Bullshit. Under any other circumstances, you would've taken first. You're tough as nails, and I'm really fucking proud of you."

I glance over at him, a tired smile tugging at my mouth. "Thank you."

His words mean a lot, but the false peace we found earlier feels tainted now. It's not that I need to be the best in the world at archery, I just want to feel like I can still be good at *something*.

"Of course. And there's always next time because there *will* be a next time."

I nod. "Yep. And I plan to take first in the spring competition. Until then, I plan to destroy whoever did this."

Sebastian grins. "There she is."

"I'm in," I say, turning toward him. "*Really in*. No more secrets or hesitation. We work together and we bring this asshole down."

"Good," he says. "Because I wasn't going to do this without you."

We stand in silence for a moment, letting everything settle between us.

The words Brogan told me about him echo in my head. That hockey is his escape and that his dad was cruel. I see him differently now. Strong, yes, but also hardened by survival.

"Do you ever talk about...your family?" I ask gently.

Sebastian's jaw tightens, his eyes locking on something across the field. "No," he says finally. "And I'm not starting today."

I nod once, not pushing, but there's a heavy ache in my chest for everything Sebastian's had to carry alone.

Dragging my feet, I make my way to the crowd gathered as the winners are announced for each bracket.

When my name is called, I step onto the podium. The owner of Faraway Archery Range places a second-place medal over my head and it feels cool against my skin. The crowd claps, but the sound is more like an applause at a funeral.

Sebastian waits for me near the clubhouse, leaning casually against the railing. But his eyes track my every move. I approach him with my hand clenched around the medal.

"Let's get you home," he says, throwing an arm around my shoulder.

I don't say anything because nothing fits. I'm not disappointed in myself—I'm furious I didn't realize something was off with my bow until it was too late.

As we're driving down the road, I open my phone and see a text from my dad—the icing on the fucking cake today.

Dad: Sorry I couldn't be there today. Work got out of hand, and I couldn't step away. I'll make it up to you. Promise.

Grinding my teeth, I fire off a reply.

Me: Expect a similar excuse from me at Christmas.

There's no point trying anymore when he stopped a long time ago.

We ride back to the house in silence, but my thoughts are anything but quiet. Whoever did this thinks they'll win in the end, but they won't. A match has been lit inside me and I plan to burn brighter than they ever saw coming.

No one fucks with my bow and gets away with it.

Chapter Twenty-Nine

AVERY

This week has been grueling, to say the least. It's the final stretch before Thanksgiving break and my professors have really been cracking the whips. I've fallen behind in two classes, and more times than I'd like to admit, I've seriously considered dropping them. But then I straighten my damn crown, remind myself who the hell I am, and I keep going.

It's Friday now, which means it's the away game against Westgate. To say my heart's been lodged in my throat since I woke up would be an understatement.

Last night, Brogan cornered me, and we had a full hour long talk where she poked and prodded, trying to get the truth out of me.

She asked all the questions I had no good answers for, so I lied and told her I didn't know much. That I'd been kept in the dark, and honestly preferred it that way. It killed me to do it, especially with everything she's already had to carry, but it's for her own good. The less she knows, the safer she stays.

Just when I thought we'd wrapped things up with a neat little bow, she hit me with another question I didn't expect.

When am I returning to the dorm?

The benefit is over and there's technically no reason for me to still be holed up in the hockey house like a stray cat they took in. So, I told her I feel safe there right now, which isn't really a lie at all.

She didn't argue, but I could tell she wasn't sold. Her eyes narrowed, and she said she hoped I knew what I was doing. But the truth is, I don't. I feel like I'm just biding time lately.

"We're heading out," Sebastian says, poking his head into Callan's room. "You all set?"

I nod and force a smile, even though every fiber of me wants to scream *don't go*. I hate that Sebastian—or any of the guys for that matter—are even playing in this game. But they made a good point when they said suspicions would be raised if they suddenly forfeited for no reason.

Sebastian crosses the room to me and checks the mic clipped under my shirt, then adjusts the charm on my necklace where the pinhole camera is hidden. I still have no idea how they got their hands on this gear, but at this point, I've stopped asking questions. I just go with it and trust the process.

"Everything's going to be fine," Sebastian says, pressing a soft kiss to my forehead. "Try not to worry too much. Klein is on standby as planned and if anything goes awry, he'll be there."

I nod, even though the knot in my stomach refuses to loosen.

Aidric had a meeting with Klein earlier this week and he told him just enough to get him on board. Now the detective's on standby with his badge off and his ego barely restrained. Aidric wasn't thrilled about involving him, but even he had to admit, we need every advantage we can get.

Sebastian lingers a second longer, his eyes scanning mine like he wants to say more but can't find the words. Then he finally says, "It's just one night. We'll play, crash at the hotel, and be back tomorrow afternoon. If anything changes, I'll text you the second it happens."

"You better," I mutter, my voice barely above a whisper.

His hand finds mine, fingers lacing tightly. "I don't like leaving you here like this."

"I'll be okay," I lie, forcing a smile. "Drake will be on me like a second shadow, and the plan is solid. Just go win your game."

He gives a reluctant nod, then gently lets go of my hand. "Be safe, Little Lamb. And call me if anything feels off."

"I will."

With one last look, he turns and walks down the hall. I watch him until he vanishes around the corner.

I stand there for a moment then finally suck in a deep breath and step out of Callan's room.

The silence hits me like a wall. The house feels gutted without the guys. Drake is around somewhere, ready to tail me wherever I go. It's a little unnerving, but at least I know I'm not alone.

As I step outside, I pull my hoodie around me tighter. The air is frigid, the kind that stings your cheeks and pricks your nostrils.

After a fifteen-minute drive, I make it to campus, park my car in the lot closest to the library, and pretend I'm just another stressed-out student.

Across the street, I spot an unmarked, black van sitting idling behind a row of student cars. Drake's behind the wheel with a couple freshmen. I can't see them, but I know they're in there, watching me like hawks, ready to pounce the second anything feels off.

I dare that fucker stalking us to strike. In fact, I sort of want him to because I'm done hiding. Whoever's behind all this has stolen our peace, our safety, and now a goddamn life. I hope he's tempted because I'm ready to fucking play.

My phone buzzes in my hand and I glance down at the screen.

B: Callan asked if you could come by. He said he wants to see you.

My heart kicks.

Me: Now?

> B: Whenever. He's having a really good day because he just found out he'll be going home very soon.

I don't hesitate. My fingers fly across the screen.

> Me: On my way.

My gaze lifts to the van, knowing they'll follow. I shoot off a quick group text to the guys still in town:

> Me: Heading to see Callan. Don't worry, Drake's watching.

I tuck the phone back in my hoodie pocket and start walking. The leaves crunch beneath my boots as I head toward the parking lot to my car.

So much for trying to catch up on schoolwork today. I'm not going to sweat it, though. Seeing Callan is far more important.

Chapter Thirty

AVERY

The rehab center smells eerily similar to a hospital lobby, like antiseptic and old coffee. I check in at the front desk and make my way down the long hallway. As I'm walking, I notice Evan's name on one of the plates outside of the room. I pause for a moment, then gently push the door open.

I haven't seen Evan since he was in the hospital when he squeezed my hand and started to wake up. Unfortunately, seeing him now, I'm not sure he ever did fully wake.

He's seated upright, head tilted back against the bed, eyes closed. Even when I step fully inside the room, he doesn't move.

From what I've heard, he's still in a catatonic state. He hasn't spoken, or even moved much at all. When he's awake, he just stares blankly ahead.

"Hey," I say softly, stepping closer. "It's Avery. I'm sorry I haven't been here to see you. Things have been...sort of chaotic."

I look around, noticing the flowers on the table beside him. They're wilted and gray at the edges, like they've been there for weeks and no one had the heart to throw them away. There's no color in the room, no sound except the low hum of the fluorescent light on the ceiling. It's almost like time forgot about this place—forgot about Evan.

"I should've come sooner," I add, guilt tightening my chest. "I just didn't know what to say."

The door opens behind me with a creak, and I turn to see Evan's brother. He's leaner than I remember, with a jaw that looks like it's used to being clenched.

He gives me a once-over and says flatly, "Didn't expect to see you."

"Yeah. I...just wanted to stop by."

"It's been, what, over a month now?"

"I know. Life's been—"

"Busy," he finishes for me. "Must be nice."

My eyebrows shoot up, taken aback. "I didn't come here to compare."

He shrugs, then glances at Evan. "Some of us don't get the luxury of disappearing."

There's a beat of silence before he adds, "I heard about Callan. Car crash, right?" His tone darkens. "Not exactly sorry after the shit he pulled. Karma's a bitch."

I knew Liam never liked Callan, or any of the Ice Lords, for that matter. Rumor has it he tried out for the team, didn't make the cut, and he's been bitter ever since. I'm sure he's even more pissed now that the video has gone viral of the guys pushing Evan around in the parking lot.

My spine straightens, heat rising to my cheeks. "You don't know what the hell you're talking about."

Liam scoffs. "Don't I? Looked like justice to me. That video's all over the internet now. You think people aren't watching? Detectives are working overtime because of it. Trust me, it's only a matter of time before all your little Lords fall."

I clench my jaw, the words digging deep, even though I know they're only half-right and fueled by hurt and anger.

"You can believe whatever you want," I say, keeping my tone low. "But don't pretend you know the whole story just because you only saw a few seconds of footage. Evan played a part in that, too."

Liam folds his arms, eyes narrowing. "I know what I saw, and I know Evan wouldn't be like this if it weren't for them."

I look back at Evan. He's still in the same position, still hauntingly quiet.

"I should go," I whisper, stepping back.

"Yeah," Liam mutters. "Probably for the best."

Without thinking, I go over to Evan's bed and squeeze his hand, just once. Just to say goodbye. He was good to me once, even if things didn't work out between us. He deserves dignity and compassion, and I want to give that to him because I know he would do the same for me.

Liam huffs as if me touching Evan annoys him, but I take my time, looking at his face and remembering the boy who made me smile when I didn't think that was possible. He was someone who helped me forget about my life outside of school for just a little bit, and for that, I'm forever grateful to him.

With a final breath, I leave the room, and the walk feels longer than it actually is. By the time I reach Callan's door, my heart's still racing. When I push it open, I see that he's up. *Actually up.*

He's moving across the room with a walker, each step slow but steady. He looks so damn sexy right now—shirtless with his tattoos on display and his wicked scars worn like battle wounds. He's wearing just a pair of gym shorts. As I'm drinking him in, his eyes meet mine and he grins.

"Look who's mobile." I smile through the tightness in my throat.

"Shocking, I know," he teases. "Still can't do backflips, though."

"Progress," I tell him, chuckling under my breath because there is no way he could do backflips before.

He moves to a small loveseat near the window and lowers himself down, patting the space beside him. I sit, and our knees brush just enough to make my heart stutter.

"How've you been?" he asks.

I shrug, forcing a lightness I don't feel. I could tell him

about my run-in with Liam, but there's no sense in bringing down the vibe. Callan seems happy and I want to keep it that way.

"Pretty busy," I tell him. "I competed in an archery tournament last weekend and took second."

"That's amazing."

"Not really. It would've been better if I took first, but I guess I can't complain." I wave a hand. "Doesn't matter. I'll win in the spring."

There's a beat of silence before Callan says, "Crazy shit last weekend, huh? Not every day a dead body drops at your own benefit."

"Crazy is an understatement," I scoff. "I still can't believe someone killed Julian."

"Heard it was an arrow straight through the heart."

My gut twists, eyes downcast as I fidget with a loose string on my crossbody purse. "So messed up."

What I don't say is that it was likely my arrow. That right now, the guys are playing in a game they were threatened not to, and there's a van outside with people ready to attack if anyone so much as blinks at me wrong.

"At least Julian's blood isn't on my hands like I thought it was," Callan says, throwing me off.

My head snaps up. "Wait. You remember?"

His lips press into a thin line, like he's already regretting saying it. It's clear he doesn't remember telling me before.

Before I continue, I tuck the necklace I'm wearing under my collar to hide the camera. Then, I turn slightly, reach under my shirt and pluck the mic, squeezing it tightly in my hand.

Drake and the guys have no business hearing this conversation.

"You told me about him once," I say, hoping to jog his memory." You said the Lords wanted you to..." I drop my voice to a whisper, "finish him off, but you couldn't do it. Do you remember that?"

Callan's face darkens as the memory claws its way forward. "I remember the act, but I don't remember telling you."

"You said you cut out his tongue," I whisper even lower.

"I did do that." His tongue clicks on the roof of his mouth, eyes searching me. "We must've really been close."

A faint smile touches my lips. "You have no idea. But hopefully you will, eventually."

We sit there talking, and before I know it, two hours have passed. At some point, I slipped off to the bathroom just long enough to whisper into the mic that I'm fine and going dark for a bit. The last thing I need is Drake storming in and making a scene.

Honestly, it's surreal how much being with Callan feels like old times. Our conversations are so effortless and comfortable, like nothing ever broke between us.

Callan tells me he's been having little memories of being with me and that after I kissed him last week, he knew he had to explore whatever it was we had.

Since those words left his mouth, my heart hasn't stopped fluttering.

Callan leans back, an eyebrow arched. "Can I ask you something?"

"Of course," I reply, the flutter in my chest still lingering.

"Why are you so concerned about me while you're fucking my best friend in my bed?"

My jaw drops, stunned into silence as heat floods my cheeks. "Callan. I..."

His voice stays eerily even. "It's not an accusation, Avery. I'm not mad. I don't really have a right to be." He shrugs. "I don't even remember what we had, but I saw what you have with him."

My lips part, breath caught. "Saw what?"

He shrugs, casual as ever like we're discussing the weather. "There's a camera in my room. I set it up after the incident with Julian. I actually forgot all about it until I logged into the feed a couple nights ago, hoping something in my room might trigger a memory."

Tears sting the corners of my eyes, shame and panic flooding my chest. "I didn't know. I swear, I didn't know."

He nods once, still frustratingly composed. "I believe you, and like I said, I'm not mad. Just confused." He glances down at his hands, then back at me. "Truthfully? I'm a little jealous. Because even though I can't remember us, watching you this last week has reminded me that there was something real there. But now I'm left wondering if this means you're moving on and leaving whatever we were behind?"

"No." The word flies out before I can think. "God, Callan, no. I don't know what's going on with Sebastian. I really don't. It just...happened. And I'm so sorry. I never meant for any of this to be messy, or to hurt you. I just...I didn't know what to do with all the pain."

"I gotta say, If there was any guy to step in for me while I was away, I'd want it to be Sebastian. But," he adds, "I need to know where that leaves us."

Silence stretches between us as I struggle to find the words I know I need to say.

"I watched you cry yourself to sleep, Avery. I saw you hugging my pillow, pacing the floor like your whole world was falling apart. I might not remember everything, but I feel how much you care about me."

His fingers reach out and brush down my arm and all of the guilt comes flooding in like a torrent.

I cover my face with both hands, the tears finally spilling. "I never stopped," I whisper. "Not for a single second."

Callan rests his hand over mine. "Hey," he says softly. "Don't cry. We'll figure this out."

I lower my hands from my face and look him in the eye, hoping he believes every word I say. "You mean everything to me, Callan. You always have, and I would never throw away what we had for anyone—not even for Sebastian."

He listens quietly, watching me with those eyes that used to know every inch of me.

"But..." I swallow hard, forcing the words out. "I also don't know if I can let go of what's happening with Sebastian either. I didn't expect it, didn't even want it. But it's there, and it's real in a way that scares the shit out of me."

Callan leans back against the cushions, processing what I just said. Then he nods slowly, eyes on his lap. "Okay."

"Okay?" I echo, almost in disbelief.

"Yeah," he says, voice still calm. "I meant it when I said I'm not mad. You don't owe me a perfect version of yourself, Avery. You've been living in this storm while I've been piecing my mind back together in this place. You don't have to have all the answers right now."

I blink, throat tightening. "But what if I never figure it out? What if I hurt you?"

He reaches for my hand. "Then I'll deal with it. I'm still figuring my own shit out, too. I don't remember everything, and maybe when I do, things will be clearer. Or, who knows, maybe they'll be messier. I don't know. But I'm not going to pressure you into choosing right now."

I nod, squeezing his hand. "You're a better man than I deserve."

Callan gives me a crooked smile. "I don't know about that. But I know I don't want to lose this, no matter what version of us we end up with."

A quiet sense of peace and understanding settles between us and for a second, we just watch each other. Me, wondering if he's remembering, and him, likely trying to.

He shifts slightly, a small smile tugging at his mouth. "Tell me something."

"Hmm." I tap my chin, grinning. "The sky is blue."

He laughs. "No shit, Sherlock. I meant, tell me something I might not remember. Something about us."

"Oh." I smirk. "So that's what you meant." I tilt my head, eyes scanning the ceiling as I dig through my memories, searching for my favorite one.

"Got it," I tell him. "I woke up to you grinning like a maniac, shoving donuts and coffee into my hands. You told me to eat and get dressed because you had somewhere you wanted to take me. I had no clue where we were going, but you just kept telling me to trust you, so I did."

A slow smile stretches across my face as the memory plays in my mind like a movie. "We hit the road, and I spent the entire fifteen-minute ride trying to guess, but you wouldn't give me a single hint. And then, just when I was about to give up, I saw the sign—"

"North Ridge University's Archery Range," he cuts in, his eyes bright. "You made me shoot...and I fucking sucked."

My hand flies to my mouth, stifling a gasp as tears prick at the corners of my eyes. "You remember?"

"How can I not? I was a terrible shot."

"Yeah." I laugh through the tears. "Yeah, you were."

He looks at me in a way he hasn't looked at me in a long time, and my heart swells.

"I remember thinking to myself," he says quietly, "how was I so blinded by hatred that I didn't see how much I really cared about you all those years?"

"Callan," I whisper.

"And I remember thinking, right then and there..." He leans in until our noses brush. "I never want to lose this girl."

My heart is pounding so fast I can barely breathe as I stare into his beautiful eyes.

The next thing I know, his familiar mouth is on mine. It's raw and passionate. It's a kiss that says...*I need you and I'm still in this.*

Memories of my own flood my mind. Late night talks, stolen glances, whispered promises, and I realize how much I've missed this—missed him. More importantly, I realize how much I don't want to lose him either.

Just then, my phone buzzes on the couch beside me and Callan pulls back slowly, his breath still mingling with mine. I wipe the back of my hand across my mouth and mumble, "Sorry about that," as I reach for the phone.

The second I see it's a text from Sebastian, my pulse spikes.

> Sebastian: We won, baby! We fucking crushed Westgate!

My heart jumps. "They won," I gasp, grinning as I throw my arms around Callan. "They beat Westgate!"

"Yes!" Callan beams, his arms wrapping tightly around me. "I knew my boys could do it."

For a second, everything feels like it's falling back into place. Maybe not perfectly and maybe not without chaos, but it's a start.

"Hey," Callan says, "I found something the other day. Figured it might make more sense to you than it does to me."

He leans forward, reaching for a black backpack near the loveseat, but it's just out of reach so I get up, grab it, and set it beside him.

"Thanks," he says, unzipping it and fishing out a folded piece of paper. He hands it to me and I unfold it, immediately laughing when I see the list.

1. ~~Benson~~
2. Liam
3. ~~Hayes~~
4. ~~Detective Klein~~
5. Julian

"No way." I grin, holding it up. "I remember this. We made this list in my dorm," I say, shaking my head with a smile. "We were trying to figure out who was stalking me. We argued about every single name. You were so convinced Hayes should stay on it, even though it made zero sense."

"Nah," he says with a smirk. "He's still a Devil and still dating my sister, so that's enough reason for me. Keep him on."

I laugh again. "Got a pen?"

He pulls one from the front pocket of his bag and hands it to me. I set the paper against my knee and start making edits. "Some changes need to be made."

I cross out one name and scribble in two new ones.

1. ~~Benson~~
2. Liam
3. ~~Hayes~~
4. ~~Detective Klein~~
5. ~~Julian~~
6. Jeremiah (he seems sketchy)
7. A scorned past member of the Ice Lords

I pass it back to him, and his brow furrows as he reads it. "Jeremiah Redmond?" He chuckles. "That guy doesn't have the balls to kill a fly."

"Maybe," I say, "but he's had balls he definitely wanted me to handle, so his name stays."

Callan's eyes widen. "Wait. He hit on you?"

"It was harmless," I say, brushing it off. "More annoying than anything."

We end up talking and laughing until I glance at the clock and realize it's nearly midnight.

"I should go," I say, though I really don't want to leave.

"Yeah," he says with a stretch. "I've got therapy bright and early so I should get some sleep."

I stand, smoothing my jeans. "I'll see you soon, right?"

"I hope so."

As I turn to go, he grabs my hand and I turn back around.

"I just want you to know..." His eyes soften. "I don't think I ever really hated you, Little Devil. Not when just one kiss can make me feel like this."

My breath catches. "Callan," I whisper. Then it hits me. "Wait...what did you just call me?"

He blinks. "Little Devil? So?"

"You didn't start calling me that until after I came into your locker room last month."

A slow smile tugs at his lips. "Guess we need to do this again soon. The more time I spend with you, the more I get my life, and you, back. Can I see you again tomorrow?"

"There's nowhere else I'd rather be." I lean in and kiss his cheek, my heart soaring as I leave.

As I walk to my car, there's a lightness in my chest that hasn't been there in a while. The visit with Callan went better than I could've hoped, and so far tonight, there have been no disasters.

For the first time in a long time, it feels like I've made it through a night untouched.

I climb into my car, exhale slowly, and start driving back toward the hockey house, my headlights cutting through the darkness.

I'm halfway there when I realize something isn't right.

Glancing back and forth from the rearview mirror to the road, I wait to see it behind me, but there's only darkness.

Where the hell is the van?

Something tugs at my gut, a feeling I've learned not to ignore.

I ease into a parking lot, roll to a stop, and fish the mic from my purse. Holding it close to my mouth, I say, "I'm heading back to the house. Are you guys coming?"

When there's still no sign of them, I turn the car around and retrace my route, scanning every corner like they might appear. The pit in my stomach deepens as I drive past the center again and spot the black van still parked in the exact same spot.

Drake didn't follow me.

My pulse spikes as I fumble for my phone and shoot a quick text to Sebastian.

Me: Where's Drake? He didn't follow me back.

His reply comes fast.

Sebastian: I've been trying to call him but I'm not getting any responses from him or the two other guys.

I sit there in the driver's seat, heart thrumming in my ears.

Me: What should I do?

There's a pause, and then another text comes through.

Sebastian: Already on it. I texted Brogan and Hayes. They're on their way to stay with you tonight.

Another...

Sebastian: And you better appreciate me because I just invited a Devil into my house. That's love, baby.

A laugh slips out before I can stop it. Even through panic, he always finds a way to make me laugh.

The next thing I know, my phone lights up with Sebastian's name.

I answer instantly, "Hey."

"Talk to me while you drive home," he says, voice calm.

I grip the wheel tighter, heart hammering. "Please tell me you don't think something happened to them."

"I'm sure they're fine," he says. "Probably got shitfaced and passed out. Or maybe they ditched the van thinking you were spending the night with Callan."

I chew my lip. "I don't like this."

"I know," he says, then his voice softens. "How was your visit with Callan?"

"It was nice," I admit. "I told him something I only just admitted to myself...that I have feelings for both of you."

"Well, shit." He exhales faintly. "I think I caught the fucking feeling bug, too."

I smile. "Really?"

"Can't you tell?"

"I can. It's just nice to hear you say it out loud."

"So what now?" he asks. "The ball's in your court, Little Lamb. But no matter what, I'm on your side."

I could cry hearing those words. Relief like I've never known fills me and I exhale, letting out a breath I didn't realize I was holding. "So you're not mad about Callan?"

"Hell no. That's my boy. Besides, I think we just have really good taste in women."

I laugh and some of the worry that's been weighing me down begins to fade. Callan and Sebastian are both being so understanding about this situation; it makes the guilt almost nonexistent.

"I'm here," I tell Sebastian as I pull into the driveway. "Please keep me in the loop about Drake. I have a really bad feeling about all this."

"I will, baby. You just worry about yourself tonight. I'll deal with everything else."

"Can't wait to see you tomorrow," I say, a rush of butterflies tightening in my chest.

"Same."

I end the call and shift the car into park in front of the house. Brogan and Hayes are already waiting on the front step. Hayes has a big ass scowl on his face and a pizza box in his hands.

Brogan sees me and rushes forward, throwing her arms around me.

"You scared the hell out of me," she says, squeezing me tight as I close my car door.

"I'm okay," I assure her.

She pulls back and nods toward the house. "Come on. Let's get inside and make Hayes comfortable in the Lords' house while we watch our favorite movie."

I poke her shoulder. "You better not fall asleep on me this time."

Brogan laughs. "Can't make any promises. But I can promise Hayes won't sleep a wink. He'll be too busy making sure his girl and his girl's best friend are safe."

My phone dings with a text and I steal a quick look.

Sebastian: Sweet dreams, Little Lamb.

I smile at his message, take a deep breath, and walk into the house, still uncertain, but no longer alone.

CHAPTER THIRTY-ONE

CALLAN

I'm staring out the window of my rehab room, watching a chipmunk drag a half-eaten granola bar across the courtyard, when I hear a soft knock on the door.

"Come in," I call out.

The door creaks open and the corners of my mouth pull into a smile. Avery steps inside, her hair twisted into a messy bun, her face bare, but beautiful as ever. She looks tired, like sleep didn't come easy last night. I can understand why.

Sebastian called me late and said Drake still hadn't checked in. If they didn't hear from him by morning, they'll be organizing a search. He filled me in on a few things happening and I am finally starting to piece together what it truly means to be part of the Ice Lords. I miss it, and the guys, and I can't wait to get the fuck out of here.

"Morning," Avery says, holding up two coffees like peace offerings.

I shift upright, swinging my legs over the side of the bed. "You trying to seduce me with caffeine?"

A laugh slips from her lips. "If that's all it takes, you're way too easy."

"Guilty." I grin, reaching for the cup. "But only if it has extra creamer."

She hands it over and I take a sip. My lip curls. "Mmm. Tastes like you're getting lucky."

Avery laughs, giving my shoulder a playful slap, as she sits down beside me. Her knee bumps mine, and for a second, the tension in my chest eases.

Even with everything hanging over our heads, Avery has this way of making it all feel almost normal. I still can't remember everything, but I remember how I felt and it's enough to know I'm not giving up on this.

"How are you holding up?" I ask gently.

She shrugs, holding her cup an inch from her face as she blows on it. "Honestly, nothing even fazes me anymore. I hope to God Drake is safe, but I think I've gone numb to chaos at this point."

I reach over, resting my hand on her thigh, my thumb grazing the fabric of her legging in a slow, grounding motion. "I get it. It's a lot."

"Too much," she says quietly as she takes a small sip.

Reaching out, I cup her cheek in my hand and for a second our eyes lock, then I slowly lean in, pressing my mouth to hers.

She melts into the kiss and I'd be lying if I said I didn't miss this—her, *us.*

When we part, she's smiling, and fuck if that doesn't do things to me. I shift in my shorts, feeling my want for her threatening to bust through the fabric. It's been so damn long and I'm starving for the day we can be together again.

"You look good," she says, swiping a piece of hair from my forehead. "You look stronger."

"Tomorrow," I say, tapping my fingers against her thigh, "I'm getting the hell outta this place."

Her eyes widen. "Seriously?"

"Yep. My doc signed off on it this morning. Of course, I'll still have physical therapy, follow-up appointments, and restrictions, but I get to go home."

"That's amazing, Callan. I'm thrilled for you."

It's hard to miss the shift in her body language and I can tell something's eating at her. Pictures of her in my bed come to mind and I suddenly realize what she is thinking.

"I guess that means I should probably vacate your room and go back to my dorm."

There it is.

I grab her hand, lacing our fingers. "Don't go."

She blinks. "Don't go?"

"I'm taking one of the downstairs bedrooms for a while anyways. There is no way I'm fucking with stairs right now. So my room is yours as long as you need it. Besides, I sort of like the idea of you being nearby."

Her shoulders roll, features twisted. "I don't know, Callan. It's your room and I'm sure you're ready to have it back. Besides, this situation with Sebastian—"

"You feel safer there, right?"

Sebastian told me she does and so did Brogan. Despite my stepsister not wanting to talk about Avery because I had one bad reaction, she found a way to bring her up without setting me off. She's the one who helped me remember her at some of my games when they were cheering for me.

Avery nods slowly. "Yeah. I do."

"Then don't leave yet. And as far as this thing with Sebastian, we'll figure out. There's no rush. And if we're being honest," I add. "I just got you back. I'm not ready to let go of you just yet."

"Okay," she says quietly. "I'll stay a little longer."

And just like that, something in my chest clicks back in place. Not a memory, at least, I don't think that's what it is. It's more like a recognition. Having her near is just the beginning of everything I want back. I always wanted her, even if I tried to deny it in the past. Now I have a chance to really be with her, and I'm not letting it go.

Avery's phone buzzes in her purse, shattering the quiet ease between us. She reaches into the front pocket and pulls it out, her face tightening as she looks at the screen.

"It's Sebastian," she says. "The team just got back to the house and they're organizing a search party for Drake."

Avery stands up fast, her coffee sloshing all over her hand. "Sebastian just said the camera footage from the businesses near the van's location has been wiped clean."

My stomach knots. "Shit."

"I need to go help," she says, panicked.

The instinct to jump in—to do anything—kicks in and I go to stand, but my legs aren't strong enough to hold my full weight just yet.

Avery is quick to come to my side. "We've got this," she assures me.

"I just wish there was something I could do."

She reaches in and puts both hands on my cheeks before kissing me. It's not rushed, or casual—it's just enough to anchor me. "Just take care of yourself and get better," she says firmly. "That's all you need to worry about right now."

I pull her in for one last kiss and she reciprocates, leaning into me until we break apart and our foreheads press together. "I'll be at the house when you get home."

She presses her lips to my cheek, burning need filling me. Need for her, for my life to get back to normal. But when she steps away, I know I can't have any of that until I can get my body to listen to me.

With that, she turns and she's out the door.

Fuck. I sit there, staring at the empty space she just left, feeling helpless. I glance down at my uncooperative legs and all I feel is rage. I don't have the luxury of time. I can't just lie here while the walls close in on everyone I care about.

I reach for my walker and grip it hard, then I push to my feet, jaw tight as I step into the hallway.

If I can't fight whatever's out there yet, at least I can start getting stronger. I walk, then I walk some more.

By the time I finally stop to catch my breath, I've done six full laps around the wing. Sweat clings to my back and my legs are trembling, but I've never felt more determined.

I lean against a wall, steadying myself when someone catches my eye at the end of the hall.

It's Liam, Evan's brother. I don't like that guy, but it's hard not to feel for him with what he's going through.

I've heard a little about Evan's accident. Apparently, he fell off Black Peak a little over a month ago. But from what I've also heard, no one knows how or why yet. And I have a bad feeling that after that video and the way my boys have been panicking, I played a part in whatever took place.

I watch Liam, noticing how he walks with purpose, his eyes fixed ahead and his shoulders squared. Something about his energy doesn't sit right.

He disappears into Evan's room, and curiosity gets the best of me. With nothing better to do, I push off the wall and follow.

When I reach the corner, I pause and peek around it just in time to see Liam place something on Evan's bedside table. Then, without a word, he walks out.

I duck back and wait for him to pass before moving to Evan's door. It's open a crack, so I peer through the gap.

When I look inside, I notice Evan sitting upright, wide-eyed and alert.

What the fuck!

That's not right. Evan's mind is supposed to be paralyzed or some shit, but from what I'm seeing, he's fully there.

I watch as he picks up the folded paper Liam left behind. He stares at it for a second before unfolding it. His expression darkens then he crumples it, and with a sharp flick of his wrist, he hurls it across the room.

"Fuck," he growls.

My pulse spikes and my brain can't keep up with what I'm seeing. Has he been pretending this entire time?

The air gets sucked out of my lungs, and suddenly, I'm hit with a jolt, like an old memory is colliding with reality.

A flash rips through my head.

I see Evan near the ledge of a cliff, his foot slips and someone reaches for him, but it's too late—he falls.

I clutch the walker tighter, trying to make sense of what I just remembered.

What the hell was that?

More importantly, now I know I was there the night Evan fell.

⚔

After I went back to my room, all I could think about was Evan being awake and aware. If only I could remember more then maybe I'd be able to make sense of this.

I still haven't told the guys. They've been tied up with the search for Drake, and this definitely isn't a conversation that can be had over the phone. If Evan's fall is tied to the Ice Lords, we can't risk anyone overhearing.

Now, it's just past two a.m. and sleep isn't in the cards. So here I am, restless and pacing the halls again. I stop in front of Evan's room, the door latched shut this time. But curiosity eats at me.

That note must have said something important to piss him off the way it did.

I grip the handle and twist it slowly, careful not to make a sound. I ease the door open an inch at a time and look inside, noticing the room is still. If I didn't know better, I'd think Evan was in a coma again.

Stepping inside, my heart pounds as I look around for the crumpled paper. With the only source of light being the moon shining through the curtains, it's slightly difficult.

I search his bedside table, scan the floor, and even look in the trash bin, but it's not here.

I move closer to the bed, looking around the space near Evan.

Everything looks normal at first glance, but then I notice a towel sticking out slightly from the corner of the blanket.

Carefully, I lift the edge of the blanket and peel it back a tad. My gut tightens as I pull back more and more, and as it falls away completely, realization hits.

Evan's not in the bed. It's nothing but a bunch of rolled-up towels.

I rip the rest of the blanket off in one angry motion. "That sneaky son of a bitch."

He clearly wanted everyone to believe he was in here sleeping. But I'm onto him now.

For a second, I think about leaving him a note of my own—something to let him know the jig is up. But then we'd lose the upper hand.

No. Evan can't know I know. At least, not yet. If he's out there wreaking havoc on the lives of my friends, the only shot we have at stopping him is to corner him. But first, the guys need to know, and this can't wait until I see them in person.

I rush back to my room, adrenaline surging as I grab my phone off the nightstand. My fingers fly across the screen as I type out a group text to Aidric, Sebastian, and Avery:

> Me: Evan Sanders is a fraud! Not only is he awake and aware, he snuck out of his bed tonight. Keep an eye on things. He might be lurking.

I hit send and stare at the screen, fully aware that I might not get a response until morning, but I had to try. If Evan is the one behind my accident, Julian's death, and Drake's disappearance, we might not have much time left to stop him before he claims his next victim.

CHAPTER THIRTY-TWO

SEBASTIAN

Twelve goddamn hours of searching last night and still nothing.

No tracks or clues. Absolutely no sign of Drake or the two guys who were with him. We ended the night with the same suffocating silence that's been haunting us since they vanished.

Drake didn't just wander off. Someone made him disappear and I don't doubt for a second it's the same masked psycho who's been flipping our world inside out.

What's worse is how clean it all was. There was no commotion or mess. Every security camera in that parking lot was erased like the night never fucking happened. We're up against someone either tech-savvy as hell or with deep connections that make people erase things for them.

Next to me, Avery stretches and lets out a slow yawn. I watch her for a second, grateful that she's safe.

Just as I'm about to push myself up, my door bursts open and Aidric storms in like a fucking hurricane. "Get your asses up," he barks. "Did you see Callan's text?"

I sit up fast. "What text?"

"He's awake," Aidric says, nearly breathless. "Evan. That

motherfucker's been faking it. Callan went to check on him and he was gone."

I wave a hand through the air, letting out a sharp breath. "He was probably just doing therapy or some shit."

"At two in the fucking morning?" Aidric snaps.

He's right. That is odd. I grab my phone, scrolling fast until I see it.

> Callan: Evan Sanders is a fraud. Not only is he awake and aware, he snuck out of his bed tonight. Keep an eye on things. He might be lurking.

Jesus Christ.

Adrenaline floods my veins. I sit on the edge of the bed, trying to piece it all together, but my head is spinning.

Avery sits up behind me. "Wait...what did you say?"

I look over my shoulder, jaw tight as I hand her my phone with the open text.

Her face pales as she reads it. "You're kidding."

"Wish I was."

Fuck. Evan is out there, and if he's been pretending this whole time, what the hell else has he been doing?

Snatching a T-shirt from my open drawer, I tug it over my head. "We need to get downstairs and let the others know what's going on."

Aidric nods and heads out while Avery cleans up quickly in the bathroom. When she's done, I do the same.

By the time we hit the bottom step, the front door opens and voices echo through the hallway. We round the corner just in time to see Callan coming in.

He's upright, walking with a cane now, but there's tension in his jaw and a fire behind his eyes that tells me something's coming. He spots us and gives the slightest shake of his head and I know he's raging after what he recently learned about Evan—we all are.

Callan's parents and Brogan follow him in, and we keep our distance while his stepmom fluffs the couch pillows like it's the stage for a damn photo shoot. His dad stands stiff, like he doesn't know what to say or where to put his hands. Brogan stays close to Callan, her arm lightly brushing his as if she's reminding him he's not doing this alone.

"You need anything at all," his stepmom says, cupping his cheek, "you call. We're so proud of how hard you've worked, sweetheart."

Callan nods. "Thanks."

His dad claps him gently on the shoulder and leans in for a hug. "Seriously, don't hesitate."

Then his stepmom turns to Avery before pulling her into a tight hug. "Take care of him for us, sweetie. He's lucky to have you."

Avery smiles softly. "I will."

Once the door closes behind them, the entire vibe shifts. Callan lets out a breath, then turns to face us. "Seems we've got a problem on our fucking hands."

Aidric doesn't miss a beat. "And that problem has a name—Evan fucking Sanders."

We circle around the couch where Callan takes a seat, anxious to hear the whole story. I sit down and pull Avery onto my lap, hoping it won't be awkward, but Callan doesn't even blink. He reaches out and takes her hand in his, giving it a gentle squeeze.

"You doing okay?" he asks her.

She nods. "For the most part."

Still holding her hand, he looks at each of us. "So, Evan's been awake, faking everything this whole damn time."

My jaw tightens and I wrap my arms around Avery, holding her closer. Her scent brings me a sense of calm I desperately need right now.

"I saw Liam go into his room," Callan explains. "He left something on the table, a note, I assume. Evan picked it up, read it, got pissed, and threw it. That's when I knew something was off."

I shift Avery slightly so I can get a better look at Callan beside us. "You sure it wasn't just a fluke? Like he just jolted awake momentarily?"

"No," he says firmly. "Last night, I went back and the bed looked full, like he was sleeping. But when I pulled the blanket back, it was just a bunch of rolled towels."

I can almost hear the crack of Aidric's tooth he's gritting so hard.

Callan leans forward. "This morning, I went again. And there he was, back in bed, same blank expression, playing the same game. He's been conning everyone."

"And Liam?" I ask. "You think he's involved?"

"I haven't quite figured that out," Callan says. "I wish I could have found that damn paper. Why would Liam leave something for his brother to read unless he knew he was capable of reading it?"

Aidric clicks his tongue. "Unless he knew."

I snap my fingers. "Exactly."

We all exchange grim glances because it's not just a theory anymore; the mask is off and Evan Sanders is the snake in the grass.

The air hangs heavy for a beat before Aidric crosses his arms and speaks again. "What's next with the search for Drake?"

My jaw flexes. "If we can corner Evan, we might be able to get him to talk. He's slippery, yeah, but not invincible. There's a good chance he knows where Drake is if he's behind all of this."

"And once we get Drake back safely," I add, "we can push for the rest and make him confess to everything else—Julian, the footage, the mask and the threats, all of it."

Callan leans back on the couch. "That's a big *if*. He's been pretending for months—manipulating people, lying to his family, to doctors. If he's that good, how the hell are we supposed to trap him?"

Aidric turns his gaze on Avery. "We use the one thing that might still matter to him."

Avery's brow furrows. "What do you mean?"

"You," Aidric says bluntly. "You're the only one he ever showed real emotion toward before the fall. If there's even a shred of feeling left, we need to use it to lure him out."

Avery lets out a short, humorless laugh. "You think he still has feelings for me after everything? The photo, the threats, the mind games, the fucking arrow in my bed that was used to murder someone?"

"He might," I say quietly, hating that I'm in agreement here. "Maybe it's not about love, maybe it's obsession.'

Avery crosses her arms, her posture stiff. "That's insane. When he and I broke up, we agreed it wasn't going anywhere between us and things were good. We were friends."

Callan rubs a thumb over her hand. "When I woke up, I was so angry with you I couldn't see straight. Maybe something happened to him in that fall. Maybe he sees you differently now."

Avery stiffens, those memories of Callan likely forming at the front of her mind. I press my lips to her shoulder and she breathes out a sigh. "So I'm the bait again, assuming he's our guy?"

"You've done it before," Aidric says. "And we'll keep you safe. You won't be alone for a second. He *is* our guy, I know it."

"Yeah," Avery mumbles. "Look how that worked out for me last time. The guys safeguarding me are missing." Her eyes flick to each of us, and I see the fight in her as she lifts her chin. "Fine. If it means getting Drake back, I'll do it. But I'm telling you, Evan has no reason to hate me so I think we need to keep our options open."

"Hate and obsession can go hand in hand," Callan says. "Either way, he'll come for you if we're right."

"Whatever," Avery scoffs. "Let's just burn this asshole once and for all."

"It's settled then," Aidric says. "Avery will go to his room tonight and if he's not there, she'll waits. He'll see she knows he's up and walking, and just like that, we flip the table back in our favor."

"I'm going too," I bite out, my hand sliding along Avery's leg. "I'll be outside the door the entire time."

"Same," Callan adds. "I'll wait in the damn car if I have to, but I wanna be there."

Aidric huffs and waves his hand through the air. "You two worry too damn much."

He walks over and claps a hand on Callan's shoulder. "By the way, Noah got your room ready down here. He moved some of your shit in already."

Callan nods gratefully. "Appreciate it."

"I'll help you get settled," Avery offers quickly, already standing. She glances at me briefly, and I give her a small nod in return as I get up off the couch. Oddly, I don't feel threatened by her love of Callan anymore. I want them both happy and Callan has no issue with me making Avery happy too.

She turns back to Callan. "Come on, I'll help you to your temporary room." She reaches for his arm as he leans into his cane. The two of them disappear down the hall, their voices fading when the door clicks closed.

I stand there, hands in my pockets, staring at the empty hallway for a second too long.

There's a softness in Avery when she's with Callan. It's always been there, but now it's more defined. She knows exactly how to help him without making him feel weak, and by the way he lets her, it's clear they have something deep.

What surprises me the most isn't the ache of jealousy, it's the absence of it. Instead, there's this strange sense of calm. Like I already knew Avery always held onto a piece of Callan. I guess some part of me also knew she'd never be only mine.

When I look at her, I see someone who loves fully and fiercely without asking for anything back, and damn if that doesn't make me respect her more. Avery always carries so much but still shows up for all of us. For once, I'm not afraid of sharing that with someone else. Not if it means she's protected—not if it means we all come out of this alive.

I exhale deeply and head for the kitchen to find Aidric who disappeared the minute Avery walked away with Callan. If we're gonna set this plan in motion, we're gonna need backup, brains, and a hell of a lot more caffeine.

Aidric comes into the kitchen, cracking open a bottle of water. Leaning against the counter, he pins me with that smug expression he's perfected over the years.

"So," he starts, cocking a brow, "you had to know this thing with Avery was gonna come crashing down eventually."

"It's not crashing," I say, grabbing a protein bar from the counter. "In fact, we're still going strong."

Aidric lets out a dry laugh. "Right. Enjoy fucking Callan's girl while it lasts."

I peel the wrapper halfway, then glance up at him. "Maybe Callan should enjoy fucking *my* girl. Or hell, maybe me and my boy can share."

That shuts him up for a second. He scoffs, shaking his head like I've lost my damn mind. "Good luck with that."

I just smirk and take a bite of the bar, chewing slowly.

She's worth it. That much I know for sure. If the two of us can make her happy then why the hell not?

Everyone else can keep their rules, but they can also keep their fucking mouths shut while we break ours.

Chapter Thirty-Three

AVERY

"I hope you realize I'm not giving up on us," Sebastian says, his knuckles brushing lightly across my cheek. He was waiting out in the hall when I finished up helping Callan adjust the room a bit. When I stepped through the door, his strong arms pulled me close and I went willingly.

I lean into the warmth of his hand, a small smile tugging at my lips. "Good. Because I don't want you to."

My chest tightens as I lift my gaze to his, nerves crawling up my throat. "But you should know something..." I pause for a beat. "I don't think I can give up on Callan either."

Sebastian just shrugs, cool and confident. "Then don't."

His words take me by surprise. The same words Callan said to me when I told him I can't walk away from Sebastian. "You don't want me to?"

"That's right," he tells me. "It's obvious to anyone with eyes that you and Callan have something special. I'd never ask you to walk away from that or force you to choose. Maybe it makes me selfish, but I'd rather share you than lose you completely."

My breath hitches, emotion catching in my throat. I thread my fingers through his hair, gently tugging him closer. "Oh, Sebastian. You wouldn't lose me."

I press my lips to his, holding them there longer than necessary. Every time I kiss Sebastian, it's electric. Not just sparks, but a full-body experience that settles inside me.

It's the same feeling I get with Callan...yet different. With Callan, it's warmth and gravity. With Sebastian, it's fire and motion. It's like my heart is split clean down the middle, and each of them owns a piece. What I feel for them is its own kind of wonderful.

A loud growl erupts from my stomach, cutting through the moment. I groan, dropping my forehead to Sebastian's chest.

He chuckles, his fingers tracing a pattern down my back. "Guess we should feed you before your stomach starts making louder threats."

I glance up at him, sniffing the air. "What's that I smell?"

"Aidric's famous tacos," he says, already leading me to the kitchen. "He's on dinner duty before the team heads to practice."

I follow, my stomach grumbling again. "Well, as long as they're edible, I'm in."

The scent of taco meat fills the kitchen, and Aidric stands at the stove, flipping tortillas like he's trying to keep himself from flipping someone else. It's funny watching him cook like it's a revenge mission.

I lean against the island beside Sebastian, and Callan joins on the other side of me a minute later.

"How's the new room?" I ask Callan.

He shrugs, settling his weight on one of the stools. He's still so much taller than me, even half sitting. "Not as good as the original, but it'll do for now. Unless you want me up there with you. Just say the word and I'm there."

"Hey," I say teasingly. "I wouldn't complain."

"I see how it is," Sebastian chimes in. "What am I now, the third wheel?"

"Nah," Callan says. "We can make an Avery sandwich." He jokes as he wraps his arms around me and at the same time, so does Sebastian. I can see them grinning at each other as if there was a secret between them and it makes me feel whole.

I laugh and when they let me go, I reach over to steal a handful of shredded cheese from the bowl on the counter.

Sebastian swats my hand away. "Woah Woah Woah. Tacos aren't ready yet."

Callan grabs the bowl and holds it out for me, grinning. His fingers brush mine and the charge between us sparks like it always does.

Sebastian notices, but instead of looking pissed, he just nudges my hip with his. "If Aidric bites her head off, it's on you."

Callan shrugs. "Worth it. Besides, I bite back."

"Jesus Christ," Aidric snaps, slamming the spatula onto the counter. "So this is how it's going to be now? You're gonna stand there and flirt with both of them and destroy their friendship in the process?"

The room stills and the laughter fades. My teeth clamp together because I don't know what to say to that.

Sebastian straightens his back, open palms pressed firmly to the counter. "Chill the fuck out, man."

"She's not doing anything wrong," Callan adds.

But I raise a hand, stepping forward. "I don't need either of you to defend me."

Aidric scoffs. "Oh, I forgot. You're the queen of chaos now. You think you can hold it all together with your quick wit and sarcasm."

I close the distance between us, staring up at him. "What happens between me and them is none of your damn business. So unless you're planning to join the triangle, back the fuck off."

His eyes narrow, and for a second, I think he might actually listen. Instead, he grabs a measuring cup full of water from the counter and throws it right at my chest.

The cold hits me like a slap. My white shirt clings instantly to my skin, and my nipples press through the fabric. Aidric's smug smile says it was exactly what he was aiming for.

A slow, venomous smirk curls on his lips. "You might want to cover up," he sneers. "Or is parading around like a slut part of the plan now? Lure one in with your tears and the other with your tits, then watch them destroy each other for the honor of fucking you?"

My blood turns molten. Before I process it, my palm lands across Aidric's face with a deafening smack. The room goes silent as I stare in his eyes, but I refuse to back down. He wants to play; I'll be a worthy opponent.

Aidric steps forward, fists clenched as a red mark begins to bloom across his face. When his lips purse, he does the last thing I expect. He spits on me.

My hand goes to the saliva on my cheek and neck, shock filling me along with this awful feeling of hurt and betrayal. My body tenses readying for a fight, but Callan's hand takes mine, distracting me.

At the same time, Sebastian's already slamming a hand into Aidric's chest and shoving him back a full step. "You ever do that again, and I'll make damn sure you don't have legs to skate on."

Aidric chuckles darkly. "Careful, Banks. Don't forget who built your throne in the first place."

Callan grabs a towel for me. "You okay?" he asks, his voice calmer than I expected.

I take the towel and press it against my soaked chest, my pulse thumping in my ears. "Yeah," I bite out. "But I'm done playing nice."

I take a step toward Aidric and stab a finger into his chest. "You wanna throw shit at me, spit on me like I'm beneath you, go right ahead. Just know the next thing coming for you won't be petty games for little boys. You might push around a lot of people in this house, Aidric, but I refuse to be one of them."

"Then fucking go," Aidric snarls, jabbing a finger toward the door. "Pack your shit and get out before you destroy something else. We were all fine until you showed up. So do us all a favor and get the fuck out."

That one hits deeper than I want to admit, but I don't cave.

My lips press into a hard line as I nod slowly. "Go fuck yourself, Aidric. I'm not going anywhere."

Without another word, he slams the plate of fried tortillas down on the counter so hard the dish cracks.

Glaring at the guys, he sneers, "Eat up, boys. You'll need the stamina to keep up with this whore."

A sharp gasp tears out of me, stunned silent for a split second. No one has ever spoken to me like that. My body shakes in equal parts rage and hurt as Aidric storms off, muttering about seeing them after practice.

Callan moves in slowly, taking his time with his legs being so weak. His hands close around mine. "Don't listen to him," he says. "He's a damn idiot who speaks before he thinks. He didn't mean any of it."

I let out a bitter laugh. "Oh, he meant every last fucking word." I glance at Sebastian and toss the damp towel onto the counter. "What did he mean, 'see you guys after practice?' Aren't you going?"

"Nah," Sebastian shakes his head. "Taking the night off. There's too much shit going on, and with Callan still recovering, I didn't wanna leave you two alone."

I want to ask if that's the only reason, but I don't because, deep down, I already know it is. He's not jealous. Neither of them are. And it's strange how natural that feels.

Now if only everything else in my life would fall into place as easily.

Once the voices outside the kitchen fade and the front door slams shut, I exhale the breath I didn't realize I'd been holding. I tug at the hem of my shirt, trying to fluff it dry. "After all this, I could really use a distraction," I murmur.

"I've got a distraction for you that should do the trick," Callan says, and as he steps closer, seemingly steady on his feet now, my gaze immediately falls to the growing bulge in his joggers and I'm forced to clench my thighs.

I grin as he slinks up to me, his fingers teetering with my waistband and a smirk growing on his lips.

"Is that so," I say, biting the corner of my lip. "Let's see what you've got then."

I shove my hand down the front of his pants. My fingers wrap around his cock, stroking in slow motions.

From across the kitchen, Sebastian watches, a lazy smirk tugging at his lips. "Callan's really out here getting all the fun, huh?" he muses, striding over until he's standing behind me with his hands on my waist.

Slowly, and deliberately, he grinds against me, showing me just how ready he is. My breath catches as I slide my hand back, fingertips tracing the waistband of his pants. A growl rumbles low in his throat.

His palms slip beneath my shirt, warm against my cold skin. I arch into his touch with a soft moan, my head falling back onto his shoulder.

Sebastian's mouth brushes my ear. "How about we double up on that distraction." His hands roam under my shirt, rough palms teasing the swell of my breasts. His thumbs circle my pebbled nipples, each stroke sending heat straight to my core. I melt into him, arching my back further as Callan shifts in front of me, his eyes dark and ravenous.

Callan's hand replaces mine, curling around his length. He strokes himself slowly, his gaze locked on the way Sebastian's hands play with my tits like I belong to them both.

"You like putting on a show, Little Devil?" Callan grumbles, voice husky. "You gonna let us make you forget everything but this?"

I nod, breath shaky. "Please."

Sebastian groans behind me, sliding one hand down my back and slipping beneath my leggings. His fingers dip lower, brushing over my slick heat.

"Goddamn," he mutters. "You're drenched."

My cheeks flush with heat, but I welcome it. "I'm ready for you guys."

Callan drops to his knees, tugging my leggings down with slow precision. He helps me step out of them, tossing them to the side before he presses a kiss to the inside of my thigh. "Then let us take our time."

His tongue traces upward and I gasp as Sebastian's fingers sink into me from behind, finding a rhythm that has me panting. My legs shake, caught between the pressure of Sebastian's teasing and Callan's mouth as he licks me like he's starved.

"Holy shit," I whimper, one hand in Callan's hair, the other gripping the edge of the kitchen counter for balance.

Sebastian's mouth moves to my neck, lips dragging across my skin, his teeth grazing my pulse. "You're gonna come like this," he growls, "with both of us wrecking you."

Callan groans against me, the vibrations pushing me to the edge. His fingers dig into my thighs, holding me open as he devours me. Sebastian's fingers speed up, and my whole body starts to shake.

"Come for us," Sebastian commands, his breath hot against me. "Let go."

And I do. My orgasm rips through me, my knees buckling as I cry out their names. It's a euphoria I didn't know was possible, the feeling of them both here making me feel this way is a dream, one I never want to wake up from.

My eyes open as Callan stands, wiping his mouth with a smug grin, and Sebastian's arms wrap around me, holding me steady.

But we're not done—not even close.

I spin to face Sebastian. "Your turn," I say, dragging my fingers over the waistband of his pants.

Callan steps behind her, pulling his shirt off, his chest heaving. "Think she can handle both of us?"

"She's ours," Sebastian answers. "And tonight, I think we need to make sure she never forgets it."

I get the feeling they've done this before, but I don't press. In my mind, I'm their first together. I don't want to hear about anyone else because if they want to keep their pretty dicks, I'll be their last first.

"She said she needed a distraction," Callan murmurs against my lips. "I plan on delivering."

Sebastian chuckles low and rough, his hands gliding beneath my shirt again. "Then we do it right. No half-measures tonight."

I suck in a breath as Sebastian's thumb brushes along the undersides of my breasts teasingly while Callan nips gently at my jaw, dragging me forward against him. I feel every taut muscle, every bit of heat radiating from his skin.

My legs nearly buckle when Sebastian's mouth finds the back of my neck, his lips trailing fire down to my shoulder.

In the next breath, Callan is completely naked in front of me. My eyes trained on his hard cock, desperate to feel it inside me—somewhere, anywhere.

Callan tugs my top off over my head, exposing me to the chill in the air. "Jesus," he breathes, stepping back just a fraction to take me in. "You really don't know what you do to us, do you?"

I stand there as I'm stripped down, my head in the clouds as I anxiously await what comes next. I'm at their mercy and fuck, it's the best place to be.

My body arches between them, lost in sensation. Sebastian holds my face in his hands, brushing his thumb across my lips. "You still want a distraction, baby?"

"Yes," I breathe, voice trembling. "Please."

Without another word, their mouths are everywhere—lips and tongues tracing every inch of skin, tasting me, claiming me.

Callan presses his forehead to mine as Sebastian's fingers slide between my legs

"Then let us give it to you," Callan says, voice thick with desire. "Let us show you what it means to be ours."

The next thing I know, I'm being bent over the center island. Callan reaches around me and grabs my hand, laying it over his cock. "You feel what you do to me, Little Devil?"

Then, without warning, he drops my hand and pushes inside my pussy, thrusting a gasp out of my mouth.

Sebastian moves in one quick motion until he's crouching on the counter in front of me. His fingers hook beneath my chin, tilting my face toward him. "Eyes on me," he says, his voice thick and raspy. "I wanna see your face while my best friend fucks you."

Callan drives into me with a force I didn't know he was capable of in his state. It's delicious and punishing. I watch Sebastian as he strokes himself in front of me and the mixed sensations are so hot, I'm close again already.

When he's at his full length, my mouth waters as he says, "Open wide, baby."

My lips part on instinct, breath shallow as the world narrows to nothing but the two of them and the way they're devouring me.

Reaching up, I wrap my fingers around the base of Sebastian's cock and stroke as I drag my tongue up and down his length.

Behind me, Callan grips my hips tighter, his rhythm deepening, dragging sounds from my throat I don't recognize as my own. I brace myself on the countertop as waves of pleasure crash through me, my hips digging into the granite with so much force I know I'll have bruises of this moment on my skin.

Sebastian's hand curls around the back of my neck. "You like this?" he whispers, his breath hot. "You like being between us?"

All I can do is nod. All I know is the electricity sizzling through me as our pleasures collide in perfect synchrony. It's like we were made for each other, the atoms of the universe erupting between us, heightening our lust.

I keep my gaze locked on Sebastian, watching him watch me. His mouth falls agape, eyes glassy. His hips thrust back and forth as he fucks my mouth like he owns it.

My breath catches as Callan's pace grows more deliberate, every thrust hitting deep, while Sebastian watches like I'm a miracle unraveling just for them. The pressure and the way their bodies cage mine awakens every nerve in my body.

Sebastian leans in, dragging a finger around my lips as I keep sucking him off. "You're incredible like this," he whispers.

Callan growls behind me, one hand gliding up my spine, then fisting gently in my hair as he draws my back into an arch. "She's perfect," he rasps. "Look at her fall apart."

I tremble, lost in the way they move with me, how they seem to know exactly what I need. There's no hesitation between them, only rhythm and control.

A soft moan slips through my lips, humming around Sebastian's cock.

Callan shifts, angling deeper, brushing against that spot that makes my vision blur.

My body tightens again, heat spiraling, threatening to snap. I reach back, clutching Callan's wrist as if holding on could delay the inevitable, but it's too late.

My body clenches around the intensity and I come undone, not with a scream, but with a gasp so raw, it burns my throat. Everything inside me unravels into pleasure so intense it borders on holy.

The next thing I know, warm liquid is coating my tongue and I keep sucking, milking Sebastian of every last drop because he is *mine*.

My knees buckle, and Callan supports me before I fold completely. "I've got you," he whispers, kissing my back. A second later, he pulses inside me and my walls clench around him as he grunts through his orgasm.

Callan's hands smooth down my sides, grounding me. Sebastian runs his fingers through my hair then over my lips, bending down to press a kiss to them like he doesn't care in the slightest that his cum is still on my tongue.

My heart races, not just from the intensity, but from how full I feel—physically and emotionally. They don't just take from me, they give and that's how I know this is going to work. These are my guys now, and I'm their girl.

Sebastian eases around the counter and, without a word, he

scoops me into his arms. He cradles me against his chest like I weigh nothing, carrying me to Callan's new room with a tenderness that makes my chest ache. I feel like a queen in his arms—the Ice Lords' queen.

Callan follows with his cane, a smile on his face that matches mine. After we're cleaned up, we regroup in the kitchen where we finally dig into the tacos Aidric so ungraciously prepared. I hate to admit it, but these are damn good.

I help tidy up, loading the dishwasher and packing away the leftovers for the rest of the team when they get home from practice.

Then I crash hard. The second my head hits the pillow in Callan's temporary room, sleep drags me under. Sebastian is at my back, Callan at my front, and for the first time that I can recall, I feel safe, whole, and like the world around us isn't falling into a million pieces.

CHAPTER THIRTY-FOUR

AVERY

"Wake up, Little Devil," Callan says, shaking me gently.

My eyes flutter open to find both him and Sebastian hovering over me like twin shadows.

"It's two a.m.," Callan says. "Which means it's go time. This is when Evan snuck out last night and if he does it again, we need to be there."

My brain scrambles to catch up. "Huh?"

Sebastian taps his wrist like he's wearing a watch. "We're going to Evan's room. Come on, baby. I'll help you to the car."

Still foggy, I sit up and rub my eyes. The next thing I know, I'm in the passenger seat with Callan shoving a coffee into my hands.

"Drink up," he says. "This might take all night."

I sip the lukewarm caffeine, and slowly the fog lifts.

We're going to bust Evan. Holy shit. This is happening.

Between my run-in with Aidric in the kitchen, getting double teamed by Sebastian and Callan, and crashing early, I didn't even have time to mentally prepare.

I chug half the cup and set it in the center console before

finally checking my phone for the first time since I crashed at eight.

My heart skips when I see I have a message from Uncle Dave. With a shaky finger, I open it.

> Uncle Dave: No match on the prints but we found a small trace of blood and ran it through the system. Came back positive for an Evan Sanders. Does this name mean anything to you?

A sharp gasp escapes me and I toss my phone out in front of me without thinking.

"What is it?" Sebastian asks from the seat behind me.

"Holy shit," I cover my mouth, still in shock.

Once I've pulled myself together, I bend down, pick my phone off the floorboard, and hold it up to show him. "We were right," I breathe, the words catching in my throat. "I didn't tell you guys because I didn't want to get your hopes up, but I went rogue and had the puck we found analyzed for prints."

Aidric turns, eyes narrowing. "You what?"

"There were no prints," I say, voice trembling. "But they found blood. My uncle ran it and it came back a match for Evan fucking Sanders."

Aidric slams his palm against the steering wheel so hard the entire car jolts. "Son of a bitch."

"Then that's it," Sebastian says. "We've fucking got him."

Callan exhales like he's been holding his breath for days. "Time to end this shit."

Just like that, the night shifts. For the first time in weeks, instead of spiraling, we're celebrating.

"We were fucking right," I say again, still breathless from the rush of it. "All this time, we were chasing shadows, and now we've got proof it was Evan."

Sebastian leans forward between the seats and grabs my hand, giving it a firm squeeze. "You did good, Little Lamb. You just helped break this wide open."

Aidric lets out a wild laugh. "I can't fucking believe it. Evan Sanders of all people. That sneaky, little bastard."

"And the blood on the puck," Callan adds. "He left it behind like some calling card that just got his ass busted."

"Or maybe it was a mistake," Sebastian says. "Either way, he screwed himself."

"Finally," Aidric grits, slamming the steering wheel again. "We've got the bastard by the throat."

We all sit in our thoughts for a few minutes, letting the magnitude of what this means settle over us. This wasn't just mind games and sabotage; this was a murder. Julian didn't collapse at the area from natural causes, he was taken out. And now we know who the hell did it.

"So what do we do now?" I ask, breaking the silence.

Callan leans forward between the front seats. "I say we stick with the plan, but we boost backup. If Evan's capable of killing, we're not taking any chances. There's no way you're going into that room alone."

Aidric gives a tight nod. "We make a few tweaks. I'll go in the room with her and hide in the closet, or behind a curtain. Doesn't matter to me. When Evan walks in, I take him down."

I watch in the rearview mirror as Callan leans into the back seat. "Throw a sack over his head if we have to then let's haul his ass back to The Chamber."

Aidric nods. "That's where this ends."

I suck in a long breath, trying to control the fire in my chest. "You're really going to kidnap him?"

"We're sure as hell not calling the cops," Aidric replies flatly. "If we want them involved then we better lawyer up."

"We could do it that way," Callan tries.

"No," Aidric snaps. "We're handling this the Ice Lords' way. The same way Julian was supposed to be handled so we didn't get bit in the ass."

I roll my eyes, biting back the urge to tell Aidric where he can shove his holier-than-thou tone. "Then I guess we better make sure we don't screw this up, huh?"

He looks over, glowering at me, but I just put on the biggest, fakest smile I can muster.

A few minutes later, we pull into the rehabilitation center parking lot and Aidric kills the engine, but no one moves right away. Whatever rush we felt earlier has been replaced by the reminder that the dangerous part starts now.

When Aidric finally pops the door, the three of us step out. I move around to the back seat where Callan's sitting, his hands resting on his knees.

I grab his face and kiss him hard. "Be safe out here."

I start to pull away, but he grabs my hand and yanks me back in, pressing his forehead to mine before stealing another kiss. "You be safe *in there*."

"Always," I whisper, then shut the door before I can change my mind.

I keep my head down, eyes scanning the rows of cars. Two of them match the one we came in, both loaded with Ice Lords ready to jump if anything goes sideways.

Aidric made the call to leave Klein out of this one. He said Evan's downfall was ours to claim, not his. For once, I agreed with him. We've made it this far on our own, might as well see it through.

We slip around the side of the building, ducking beneath a busted security camera Sebastian swears hasn't worked in weeks. How he knows that is beyond me, but I trust him.

The front door isn't even locked, which shows just how little this place cares about the safety of their residence. No wonder Evan was able to get in and out so easily.

Aidric eases it open, and we slide inside without a sound.

The hallways glow with the kind of fluorescent light that makes it feel like we're in a haunted asylum instead of a treatment facility.

At the front desk, the night nurse is half-asleep, slouched in her chair, her head bobbing behind a computer screen. She doesn't even look up as we pass.

Every step makes my pulse thud harder in my chest. We don't speak, or stop, until we're at the fourth door on the right—Evan's room.

Aidric's hand hovers over the handle. "Ready?" he whispers.

I want to say no. I want to turn around, climb back into the car, and go back to bed with one of my guys.

Instead, I nod once.

"I'll be right around the corner," Sebastian says, eyes locked on mine.

With that, Aidric pushes the door open slowly. I step inside, gripping the handle until it slips from my fingers, the door clicking shut behind us.

My shoes barely make a sound but my heartbeat is deafening. Aidric is behind me, trailing me like a shadow.

I inch closer to the bed, hoping like hell it's just rolled towels under the blanket, but when I lift the corner a sharp gasp rips out of me.

A choked sob follows. My legs threaten to give out and I fall backward into Aidric's chest. He catches me fast, arms locking around me like a shield.

Evan lies there, pale with an open, blank stare. His body is twisted like he moved at the last second, but it wasn't fast enough.

Then I see his throat—sliced clean open.

My body goes numb and Aidric holds me tighter as the horror sinks in.

Blood pours in a thick, syrupy trail down the side of the mattress, dripping onto the floor, the puddle still growing.

I stare—I can't breathe, can't scream. This just happened. How did this just happen?

"It's okay," Aidric whispers. "I've got you...I've got you."

But it's not okay. Evan is dead!

Bile burns the back of my throat, the room spinning as it closes in. Aidric grips me tighter, saying something I can't hear over the sound of my own ragged breathing.

"Come on," he says urgently. "We have to get out of here."

He pulls me out of the room and into the hall where the lights seem brighter now.

Sebastian is there in an instant. I hear him say something, but the words are scrambled and distant.

As soon as we're outside, I break away from Aidric and collapse into Sebastian's arms. His hands find my back, holding me like he's anchoring me to the floor.

"I...I can't..." I try to speak, but nothing comes out.

"I know," Sebastian says gently, stroking my hair. "I know."

Evan is dead. Drake and the others are still missing, and the chances of them being found alive is not likely at this point. Everything is falling apart.

As we approach the car, I glance back once, and I swear I can still hear the sound of blood hitting the floor.

Drip. drip. drip.

We pile into the car quickly. Sebastian slides in beside me, and Callan's already there, his arm reaching for me the second the door shuts. I collapse between them, still shaking and still seeing Evan's lifeless eyes every time I blink.

Callan pulls me into his chest and Sebastian takes my hand. Neither of them speaks, but they don't have to because their touch says enough. Even if I am spiraling, they're doing what they can to keep me here in the present and not stuck back in that room.

Aidric gets behind the wheel and slams the door shut without a word. The only sound is the dull hum of the engine and tires crunching over gravel as we pull out of the lot.

I rest my forehead against Callan's shoulder and try to breathe when my phone buzzes from my coat pocket; at the same time, everyone else's goes off, too.

Aidric curses under his breath and grabs his phone from the

console. Sebastian checks his next to me with his jaw clenched while Callan just holds me closer, like he already knows whatever's waiting is bad.

My fingers tremble as I swipe open the text message.

Unknown Number: Every game has its casualties. Evan was one of them.

My grip tightens until my knuckles scream, the shake in my hands spreading through the rest of my body.

Aidric's voice slices through the silence. "What the fuck is this?"

No one answers because we already know. Evan wasn't the predator; he was the pawn.

But if he wasn't the one pulling the strings, then who the hell is?

Epilogue

AIDRIC

The sky is darker up here. Not just night-dark but deeper than that. Like the stars know better than to shine on the shit we're about to do.

Evan's been sniffing around for weeks, getting bold. He thinks he can catch us with our masks off and stash some dirt for leverage. Maybe he wants to blackmail us, or maybe he's doing it for clout. Either way, he crossed a line.

Initiation night is sacred. It's a night for fire, blood oaths, and secrets, and he fucking ruined it.

Him thinking he had something on us was his first mistake. So we did what we had to do and we lured him to Black Peak Mountain.

The dumbass followed—of course he did.

"Teach him a lesson," I say to my fellow Ice Lords. "Scare the shit out of him. Rough him up if you have to."

With our masks on, we spread out like wolves circling their prey. Some of us laugh while others toss out threats like knives.

Sebastian hangs back, his eyes cold and watching. He doesn't like when things get messy, never has.

Callan hesitates too, always trying to be the moral compass of the family.

But I push forward because one of us has to.

Evan runs fast, his breath sharp, and even when his sweatshirt snags on a branch, he keeps going. The ground up here is slick from last week's rain, so I move cautiously, following behind my brothers with little restraint. I'd love nothing more than to tear Evan Sanders to shreds, but then everyone would see what a monster I truly am.

We reach the cliff, and Evan skids to a stop just feet from the edge.

"Who's the fucking tough guy now, Sanders," I growl, stalking toward him with my mask still in place. "Let this night be a lesson. No one fucks with us and gets away with it."

The next thing I know, headlights are cutting through the darkness. Evan lifts his hands to shield his eyes and his feet nearly slip, but he catches himself.

I whip around just in time to see Noah's Jeep flying toward us with the top down and the music blasting. Jeremiah's standing through the roof bars like a damn lunatic, hooting and hollering like this is all a game.

Noah comes rolling up fast—too fast. "Slow the fuck down," I shout as panic rips through my chest.

He keeps coming, forcing me to jump out of the way, and then in the blink of an eye, Evan takes one step back. Just one, and he's fucking gone.

Silence swallows us as we listen to his scream fade away. Then, a thunderous smack echoes off the mountain.

"What the fuck?" I snap, turning on Noah and Jeremiah as they stumble toward us like drunken idiots. "Do you see what the hell you just did?"

"It was an accident!" Noah shouts, his mask pushed up onto his head, face pale. "I didn't mean to—"

"Well, you fucking did," I seethe. "And now you better make damn sure none of us are connected to this mess."

Callan sprints to the cliff's edge, looking over with shaking hands. "Shit," he breathes. "I can't see him."

I step beside him, glance down, and scan the area. It's dark, but when my eyes catch on something, it isn't what I expected.

His mouth is moving, terror in his eyes as blood begins to coat his body. "Too late" he whispers over and over again as his body seems to grow closer, levitating in the air as if he were a ghost coming to haunt me.

"You were too late! Now who will keep her safe?"

⚜

I shoot awake, my entire body slick with sweat and my chest heaving.

The edge where Evan fell is still etched in my skull. No matter how many nights pass, I still see his body slipping and the flash of panic in his eyes.

Now, those eyes are like stone when I see them. His body paralyzed, blood dripping from his corpse.

Ever since we found Evan murdered in his bed two nights ago, it's all I see.

It's all I fucking see.

I shove the blanket off and swing my legs over the side of the bed, cursing under my breath. Sleep is a luxury I haven't earned lately. The terrors that we embrace to become Ice Lords have haunted me for years. They still haunt my father. But the price for power is high, and I am willing to pay it.

I head downstairs, moving through the dim-lit hallway toward the kitchen.

The house is quiet. It's the punishment I deserve—being stuck in my own fucking thoughts. The only thing worse than nightmares is being awake with them crawling around in your head.

I throw open the fridge and pull out some leftover pasta, sitting to eat it straight from the container because fuck it, it's 3 a.m.

The floor creaks, and when I turn my head, I see Avery

moving like a ghost in Sebastian's t-shirt. Actually, it's my t-shirt that Sebastian must've stolen. Her hair is messy, eyes puffy with sleep. She doesn't even look at me as she opens the fridge.

This girl loves ignoring me, and I love getting under her skin any chance I get.

I jab a finger at the bottom hem of her shirt and flick it upward.

"Nice choice," I mutter. "Tell Banks I want my shirt back."

She turns just enough to shoot me a glare. "Fuck off, Aidric. It's been a harsh couple days. Just lay off for once."

I smirk around a mouthful of cold pasta. "Fine. Don't tell him. How about if you just give it back to me right now."

"You want your shirt back?" she seethes, gripping the hem. But I know better. She's bold, but she's not that bold.

Nevertheless, I taunt her. "Fuck yeah, I do. At the very least, I don't want you wearing it."

In the next breath, she's peeling it over her head. My mouth drops open in shock. I watch as her breasts spring free and my cock twitches at the sight. *Down boy. We don't want that one.*

Or do we? *Fuck.* If my boys can share her, I should be able to partake, too. Right?

She tosses the shirt at me and I catch it against my chest, watching as she resumes filling her glass halfway with milk and slamming the door shut.

I lean against the counter, arms crossed over my chest. "Don't spill that milk on yourself, Little Devil. It'd be a shame if I had to clean you up."

"In your fucking dreams," she scoffs, turning just enough to cup her tits, giving them a taunting little jiggle that makes my mouth ache for a taste. "You're just jealous your best friends can suck on these and you can't."

I lick my lips, eyes locked on what she claims I'll never have. That was her first mistake.

My boys refuse to let her go and if she won't surrender to the leaders of the Ice Lords fully, I'll make her. She belongs to all three of us. Her body, her mind, every trembling breath.

"Keep telling yourself, that," I mutter as she turns and walks off, tits bouncing like an invitation.

She flips me off over her shoulder without glancing back.

I watch as her shadow retreats. Every step she takes away from me feels like a dare, a challenge meant to draw me into deep dark waters. But I've never been afraid of drowning.

I lift the shirt to my face, inhaling deeply as I breathe in her scent.

Avery Castle thinks she's untouchable, but she has no idea what's coming. I plan to strip our Little Devil down to the bone until there's nothing left but the pieces I choose to keep. I've always had a soft spot for broken things, especially the ones I break myself.

When she finally begs, it won't be for mercy...It'll be for more.

The End.

I hope you enjoyed reading Bend The Pucking Rules. More is coming soon and questions will finally be answered. Preorder the third, and final book in the Ice Lords series, Shoot Your Pucking Shot and get ready to hear from Aidric!

Shoot Your Pucking Shot

http://mybook.to/syps

ALSO BY RACHEL LEIGH

Ice Lords

Book One: Break Your Pucking Heart

Book Two: Bend The Pucking Rules

Book Three: Shoot Your Pucking Shot

Bastards of Boulder Cove

Book One: Savage Games

Book Two: Vicious Lies

Book Three: Twisted Secrets

Wicked Boys of BCU (Coming March 2023)

Book One: We Will Reign

Book Two: You Will Bow

Book Three: They Will Fall

Misfits

Heartless Monster

Wicked Scandal

Beautiful Devil

Redwood Rebels Series

Book One: Striker

Book Two: Heathen

Book Three: Vandal

Book Four: Reaper

Redwood High Series

Book One: Like Gravity

Book Two: Like You

Book Three: <u>Like Hate</u>

Fallen Kingdom Duet

<u>His Hollow Heart</u> & <u>Her Broken Pieces</u>

Black Heart Duet

<u>Four</u> & <u>Five</u>

Standalones

<u>Forget Me Not</u>

<u>Ruthless Rookie</u>

<u>Devil Heir</u>

<u>All The Little Things</u>

<u>Claim your FREE copy of Her Undoing!</u>

Acknowledgments

Thank you so much for reading Bend The Pucking Rules. Get ready for the third and final book, coming this winter!

A special thanks to my wonderful team for all the hard work you put into helping me create this book: My dedicated PA, Carolina Leon. All my girls for your support, friendship, and advice. My Rebel Readers VIP team for your help in getting the word out.

A an extra special thanks to...

My amazing alpha reader, Taylor you're a rockstar and I can't imagine putting these stories out there without your help! Love you, girl!

Tease Designs for the stunning covers and graphics!

Fairest Reviews Editing Service & Inked In With Tay for the beautiful

Valentine PR for spectacular PR Services.

XOXO Rachel

ABOUT THE AUTHOR

Rachel Leigh is a USA Today and International bestselling author of new adult and contemporary romances. She loves to write—and read—flawed bad-boys and strong heroines. You can expect dark elements, a dash of suspense, and a lot of steam.

Her goal is to take readers on an adventure with her words, while showing them that even on the darkest days, love conquers all.

Rachel lives in Michigan with her husband, three little monsters (who aren't so little anymore) and a couple fur babies. When she's not writing or reading, she's likely lounging in leggings, with coffee in her hand, while binge watching her favorite reality tv shows.

Join My Reader's Group: Rachel's Ramblers

facebook.com/rachelleighauthor

instagram.com/rachelleighauthor

bookbub.com/profile/rachel-leigh

goodreads.com/rachelleigh

amazon.com/author/rachelleighauthor

pinterest.com/rachelleighauthor